Push
COMES TO
SHOVE

Dear Reader:

Thanks for picking up a copy of *Push Comes to Shove*, a novel that I am confident that you will enjoy. Oasis has once again done a phenomenal job of creating relatable characters and an unforgettable storyline. Life can be hard, especially in today's recession, and many people become desperate to make ends meet. *Push Comes to Shove* examines the parallel lives of two men struggling to survive: GP and Miles.

GP and Kitchie have two children and a field of dreams. GP is a talented artist peddling his "soon-to-be-famous" cartoon character on T-shirts until his big break comes along. Unfortunately, that doesn't quite cut it when it comes to paying bills so he walks a thin line between legal and illegal activities. Then a single incident sets off a butterfly effect that ends up leaving him and his wife homeless, childless, and hopeless.

Miles has an entirely different money problem that leaves him owing a lot of cash to the wrong person. Idle threats of physical harm are followed up with real tragedy once Miles fails to come up with the cash. Miles decides that he has nothing else to live for…except revenge.

Two men from the same world, yet perfect strangers, end up crossing paths in the ultimate train wreck in life. You will not believe what happens when both of them are shoved a little too far.

As always, thanks for supporting Oasis and the other authors that I publish under Strebor Books International. We try our best to bring you the future in publishing today with cutting-edge, risk-taking titles that spark thought, conversation, and controversy.

If you would like to join my email list, please send a blank email to eroticanoir-subscribe@topica.com. You can also find me on Facebook, on Twitter at "PlanetZane" or join my online social network at www. PlanetZane.org. My personal email is Endeavors@aol.com and my personal web site is www.eroticanoir.com.

Blessings,

Zane

Zane
Publisher
Strebor Books International
www.simonandschuster.com/streborbooks

ALSO BY OASIS
Duplicity

Push
COMES TO
SHOVE

OASIS

SBI

STREBOR BOOKS

NEW YORK LONDON TORONTO SYDNEY

Strebor Books
P.O. Box 6505
Largo, MD 20792
http://www.streborbooks.com

ISBN 978-1-59309-299-3
ISBN 978-1-4391-8402-8 (ebook)
LCCN 2010940494

First Strebor Books trade paperback edition March 2011

Cover design: www.mariondesigns.com
Cover photograph: © Keith Saunders/Marion Designs
Edited by Docuversion

10 9 8 7 6 5 4 3 2 1

Manufactured in the United States of America

For information regarding special discounts for bulk purchases,
please contact Simon & Schuster Special Sales at 1-866-506-1949
or business@simonandschuster.com

The Simon & Schuster Speakers Bureau can bring authors to your live event.
For more information or to book an event, contact the Simon & Schuster Speakers
Bureau at 1-866-248-3049 or visit our website at www.simonspeakers.com.

For JaVenna...
Because of you, I'm the luckiest guy on the planet.

PROLOGUE

Greg Patterson hung in the nude from a vaulted ceiling by his young wrists. His 110-pound body was no match against the leather restraints. He wriggled and rocked himself past the brink of exhaustion. There was nothing else he could do now but wait.

He'd lost track of time, hanging there in the cold dark. He wanted to relieve himself, but pissing on Mr. Reynolds's floor wasn't an option. It would only make matters worse.

Footsteps fell in the hall right outside of the door. Greg hated this part with passion, but at least…at least it was almost over.

The tarnished doorknob spun left.

He braced himself.

The group home's disciplinarian, Mr. Reynolds, stood in the entrance with a bucket of sudsy water in one hand. His wide-spread body covered the majority of the doorjamb. "You refuse to learn your lesson."

"I won't steal again. This time I…I promise." He gestured *no* with worry.

"Foolhardy boy, you've made that meaningless promise since you learned how to talk." He dowsed the frail boy with the sudsy water. "A little incentive will keep you focused. You should really keep your hands off things that don't belong to you." He wrapped the ends of a heavy-duty extension cord around his bone-colored hand. "You'll learn one way or the other."

"Mr. Reynolds, please don't beat me this time." Greg clamped his burning eyes shut, hoping the soap would stay out. "I needed the art supplies for school. Untie me and...and I'll take them back right now."

"After I give you an ass cutting for being a habitual rule violator." He hiked his gravy-stained sleeves past his pudgy elbows and stood behind the boy.

Greg tensed, anticipating the first blow.

Mr. Reynolds raised his arm and swung the cord with a batter's determination. "If I could beat the color off of you, I would."

The cord sounded like thunder when it cracked against Greg's brown skin.

"Aargh...no more! I'm sorry, Mr. Reynolds." Greg stiffened all over. "Please, no more. I won't do it again. I'm sorry."

"You *are* sorry, aren't you?"

The cord slapped him once more, this time breaking the skin on his back.

"You're a piece of stinky shit, and that's all you'll ever be is shit."

Thunder struck again.

Greg yelled out so loud, he threatened to short out his vocal box.

"You're a bum, Greg." He switched hands and swung from a different approach. "That's all you'll ever be. Why do you think you've been here all these years? Nobody wants a bum; not even your mother."

Mr. Reynolds had lashed Greg until his arm was tired. He went into the hall and looked at his aged yes-man. "Untie him. Lock the thieving bastard up until his wounds heal. And get rid of those drawings he's always wasting time on."

"Right away, Mr. Reynolds."

CHAPTER 1

GP decided that tonight his family would eat good for a change. He eased the Renault Alliance to the order box; it stuttered and backfired every inch of the way.

"Welcome to Wendy's. May I take your order?"

He shut the car off so that he could hear. "Excuse me...uh, could you run that by me again?" He could hear the cashier suck her teeth through the speaker, as if she was annoyed.

"Good evening, how may I help you?"

"Gimme six number sevens with large fries...and extra cheese. Make the sodas orange, no ice." He thought about how Kitchie loved Dave's chicken. "Uh, let me get two spicy chicken sandwiches and four baked potatoes with cheese. I guess that'll be cool."

"Would you like to try our apple turnovers this evening?"

Fuck it. "Yeah, why not? Gimme six and six large chocolate Frosties." He waited a few seconds for her response.

"That'll be forty-eight twenty-three at the pickup window. Thank you for choosing Wendy's."

GP tried to start the Renault. "Come on, baby, crank up for Daddy." The engine strained but wouldn't catch. He pumped the gas and rubbed the dashboard. "Come on, girl. I need you now more than ever."

He turned the key again. The engine backfired, then came to life. With three vehicles in front of GP, his order would be ready in a matter of minutes.

His car sounded like a Harley Davidson outside of the pickup window. An attractive cashier rolled her cat-like eyes and shook her head. *Derelict.* She turned her lip up with attitude as she passed him three large bags and two drink-holder trays.

"That's forty-eight twenty-three." She smirked and stared at GP.

GP secured the drinks on the front passenger seat, then stomped the gas pedal. The Renault backfired.

The cashier all but jumped out of her skin.

With the power-steering pump broken, it was a difficult task for GP to make the sharp left turn. He jerked and tugged the rebellious steering wheel until he yanked the car onto Euclid Avenue.

He stuck a fry in his mouth and smiled. GP knew that, on this April Fool's Day, he would be the cause of three beautiful smiles.

Four city blocks away from his home, the Renault had had enough. The engine light came on right before the car stalled.

"Come on, baby, I thought you loved me." He coasted to the curb. He tried to restart the engine but it refused; it only made a clicking sound.

If he started his journey on foot now, he would make it home long before the food was cold. With a bag between his teeth and two in his hand, he reached for the door handle but hesitated when he saw a Cleveland police car pull up behind him.

"Fuck me!" he mumbled, then lowered the window with a pair of vise grips. *Damn cashier could've let me slide. Ignorant chickenhead didn't have to call the cops.*

§ § §

Miles dropped his skateboard on the sidewalk, then stepped on it with an Air Force 1 sneaker.

A fragile image appeared in a screen door behind him. "Miles... Miles, baby, you hear me?"

He removed the headphones from his ears as his broken arm remained at rest in a sling.

"Miles, baby?"

"Huh?" He turned toward the house as his mother walked out onto the porch.

"See if you can find your brother. It's dark. I'm starting to worry; this isn't like him." She adjusted the belt of her housecoat and folded her arms.

"Jap is probably somewhere standing next to a tree, testing his camouflage gear. Better yet, he might be with one of his weird friends on some type of mock-military scavenger hunt."

"I'm serious. Don't tell me what you think; do like you were told. We have to get a fitting on him in the morning for his graduation gown and cap, and I want him home."

"Okay, Ma. I'll check a few places on my way to work." He started off on the skateboard.

"Miles, baby ..."

He stopped and faced her again. "If you don't let me go, I won't have enough time to check on Jap and make it to work on time."

She removed a prescription slip from her housecoat. "Drop this off at the drugstore, and I'll pick it up in the morning. I'm getting low on my heart pills."

He hurried up the steps, took the slip, and kissed her cheek. "See you later, Ma."

She grabbed a hold of his cast. "Why don't you get yourself a car? You can't afford to get too many broken arms on that thing."

He followed her gaze. "I love my board, Ma. I'm gonna ride until I'm an old man."

"You're still a baby to me; you ain't considered young no more."

The officer surveyed the car and shined his flashlight toward the back seat. "What seems to be the problem tonight, sir?"

GP had replaced the large order on the front passenger seat. "Damn thing conked out on me. Four cylinders are supposed to run forever."

The officer looked at the beat-up car from front to rear. "What year is this?"

"It's an eighty-five." GP was starting to feel comfortable.

"Twenty years old *is* forever for a car." He pointed at the Wendy's bags. "Looks like you're going to be late for dinner."

"Yeah, I'm pushing it."

"Well, you can't leave it here overnight." He shined his beam on a *No Parking* sign. "It'll be towed by morning…which is probably the best thing for it."

"This is all I got."

"Come on; let me help you push your headache to that lot." He pointed.

The officer wiped his dusty hands on a hanky after they had rolled the car onto the lot. "Wendy's doesn't sound like a bad idea."

"Not at all. Thank you, officer." GP pointed his feet in the direction of home.

§ § §

Kitchie Marie Patterson glared at GP through a set of powerful brown eyes. "Let's talk…in the bedroom." She led the way.

GP shut the door behind himself. "Before you start, Mami, I only wanted to do something nice for you and the kids."

"There's at least fifty dollars' worth of food in there, GP. You stole it, didn't you?" She shook her head with disappointment.

"You and the kids deserve the world." He stroked her almond cheek; she turned her face away. "I can't give it to you right now, but one day I will. Until then it frustrates me to want y'all to have things that are beyond my reach."

"Then get a job—a real job. You don't have to quit your hustle but get a job, GP. How far do you think we can get on your hopes and dreams alone? This is the real world we're living in; not some animated world like them cartoon characters you're banking our future on." She thought for a few seconds. "Now you're to the point of stealing again. Yeah, you made the kids happy tonight and saved me the humiliation of throwing some bullshit together, but what's gonna happen to their happiness—" She pointed toward the living room. "—when you get yourself in some trouble?"

"You act like I steal for the sport of it, Kitchie. I steal for one reason: because *we* really need something, and I have no other alternative of getting it. I felt like we *needed* to sit down tonight and share a decent meal with each other, like a regular family."

"A real nine-to-five will make that possible every night, Papi Chulo."

He heard something else in Spanish that he didn't quite understand, but understood she was trying to take this conversation to a place he wasn't willing to go.

"Listen…my work is honest; it's what I love to do. I don't want to go back and forth with you. This isn't what I intended. All I want to do is see your beautiful smile as much as I can." He lifted her chin with a finger. "Let's eat. The food is getting cold. I got your favorite."

She bit her bottom lip. "Chicken?"

"Dave's spicy chicken sandwich. Now let me suck on them Puerto Rican lips of yours."

She stood on her tiptoes to reach his six-foot height, then kissed him on the mouth. "I wish you would shave and get your hair braided; it looks like you gave up." She pulled back. "GP, you can't keep stealing whenever it's convenient for you. One day stealing is gonna get you in some trouble you're gonna catch hell getting out of."

"Or get me out of some trouble I'm already catching hell with."

§ § §

Greg Jr. took a bite from the double classic. His seven-year-old teeth barely plugged the cheeseburger. "Daddy, I need my own bike. Secret's bike is hot pink with that stupid, flowered basket on the handlebars. Everybody makes fun of me when I ride it."

Secret was trying her damnedest to suck the Frosty through a straw. She gave her jaws a break. "Stay off my bike, then, since it's stupid and pink, punk. I don't like sharing it with you anyway, you little—"

"Hey, kill the name-calling." Kitchie stopped chewing and frowned at Secret.

"Little man." GP squeezed Greg Jr.'s shoulder. "Bear with me; I'm gonna get you the best bike in the neighbor—"

"Don't be doing that, GP. It ain't right." Kitchie swallowed her food. "Okay, fine, tell him you're gonna get him a bike. But don't be making these fantastic promises that you can't deliver. You're doing terrible in the delivery department. Don't do him like that."

"How many times do I gotta ask you not to challenge me in front of the kids?" He wiped the corners of his mouth with a napkin. "When you feel like I said something that should be corrected, talk to me behind closed doors."

"We can still hear y'all in the bedroom arguing." Secret kicked Greg Jr.'s shin.

"Ouch." He tried to kick back but his legs were too short to reach her under the table. "Ma, tell her—"

"Stop, Secret, and quit being so damn grown." Kitchie focused on GP again. "I apologize, Papi...I'm a little frustrated; that's all. I still don't want you to get Junior's hopes up only to let him down. That'll hurt him more than getting made fun of."

GP finished the last of his burger. "There's nothing wrong with hoping, having faith in something; especially when I know that I can make it happen." He looked at his family one by one. "Let's get this out in the open so we all know. Secret, what do you want? What does my baby's heart desire?"

"Hmmm...I can say anything I want?"

"As long as it's appropriate coming from a nine-year-old." Kitchie sipped her soda between bites.

Secret's expression was thoughtful. "Daddy, I want my own room." She rolled her eyes at Junior. "Lots of new clothes like my friends would be nice, too. Oh yeah! I want a puppy, and I hope you give me my piggy bank money back that you borrowed last month."

GP stroked the top of Junior's head. "And what about you?"

"All I want is a bike, but I'd take a PlayStation if what we're saying is real."

"What about you, Mami Chula?" GP blew Kitchie a kiss. "Tell me what you dream of when you close your eyes."

"This is pointless. I'm not getting involved with this...stuff." She started on her apple turnover.

"Aw, Ma." Secret sucked her teeth. "Tell us; we wanna know."

"Yeah, it's only a game." Junior dropped a French fry in his lap. "We're playing pretend."

Five seconds passed and GP leaned forward. "We're all waiting." He was unsettled by his son's comment.

"This is foolish, GP, and you know it. If it must be known, what I want more than anything in this world is for my marriage to defy time." She began to blush, then the reality of their current situation hit her. "I want us to have a bigger house—bought and paid for. I'm not big on having a lot of money, but I wish we could at least be comfortable and able to send you guys to college when it's time."

"Your turn, Daddy." Junior balanced his chair on two legs.

"The first thing I want is to be in a position to give y'all everything you want. And I want to always be able to protect y'all from danger. Comfortable might be cool for your mother, but I need our bank account to be sitting on at least a million. Of course, I want the Street Prophet to get recognition on a national level, a Saturday morning cartoon or something."

"Take the French fry out your nose, boy, before it gets stuck." The look Kitchie cast across the table put Junior right in line.

Someone knocked at the door.

"I'll get it." Secret pushed away from the table.

Kitchie grabbed her by the pants. "Make sure you know who—"

"It is before I open the door." Secret finished Kitchie's sentence. Secret stood in front of the door. "Who is it?"

"Publishers Clearing House Sweepstakes," came from the other side of the oak.

Secret pulled the door open as far as the chain lock would allow. She studied both white men in their jeans and button-down shirts.

One had a clipboard with a large envelope fastened to it.

"Where's the microphones and TV cameras?"

The bigger of the two men laughed. "That's only for our grand prize winners. Third place doesn't get that type of publicity. Is Kitchie Patterson in?"

"Yes, would you hold on a minute?" She freed the chain lock and ran into the kitchen. "Mom, Dad, you're never gonna believe who's at the door. The Publishers Clearing House people. Ma, you won."

Kitchie looked at the ceiling. "*Gracias Dios.*"

The Patterson family rushed into their living room.

The smaller, balding man was unplugging their TV from the wall outlet.

The other man thrust the envelope toward Kitchie. "Your Rent-A-Center bill is overdue. You've been ducking us for over a month now. We're here to collect or repossess." He turned to his coworker. "Set that down and go around the corner and get the van."

"Don't you people have an ounce of feelings?" GP stepped between Kitchie and the envelope.

"Sometimes it's an ugly job, but it pays my bills. If you would tighten up on your payments, I wouldn't even be here." He slid the envelope under GP's armpit. "Straighten out this five-hundred twenty-three dollar bill and I'm out of here."

GP sighed. "I don't have it right now." He heard Mr. Reynolds's antagonizing voice in his head loud and clear. *You're a bum, Greg. That's all you'll ever be.*

"Then I'll start with the kitchen set and work my way through here." He pointed to the furnishings.

⊛ ⊛ ⊛

The Patterson family watched through a window as the two men loaded the last of their furniture into the van. Kitchie fought to hold back the tears.

The bigger man came back inside with sweat beads on his temples.

"Mrs., I'm sorry. Would you please sign here?" He passed her the clipboard and put his finger on the spot where he wanted her signature. "Would it be possible for me to trouble you for a glass of water?"

GP stared at the man as if he had asked for blood.

"Junior, get the man something to drink." She scribbled her name on the form.

Moments later, Junior returned with a tall glass of water.

The man drained the glass. "Ahh, now that was good and cold." He turned and left.

Kitchie surveyed their bare living room. Secret was sitting on the radiator, finishing her meal. So much for having a decent meal like a normal family. She went and stood beside GP at the window. "Publishers *fucking* Clearing House. They cleared us out all right." She and GP watched the Rent-A-Center van drive away. "Papi, this ain't an April Fool's joke. You need to do something. This is only a prelude to what's next."

GP dropped his head and heard Mr. Reynolds shouting at him for what had to be the millionth time. *You're a worthless piece of shit. Your mother should have swallowed you.*

Kitchie walked away. "Maybe a glass of cold water will calm my nerves." She turned on the faucet to fill her glass. The water was lukewarm. She checked the refrigerator. No water jug. No ice. "Junior!" She put her hands on her round hips. "Where did you get the cold water from?"

He looked at Secret and they laughed. "Promise you won't get mad, Ma."

She returned to the empty living room, hands still on her hips. "Boy, what did you do?"

"Everybody knows the coldest water in the house is in the toilet."

CHAPTER 2

The morning sun cast its strong rays through the living room. Secret sat in the middle of the floor with her lip poked out and arms crossed. "Why can't I stay home and go to work with you and Ma?"

GP tied his worn-down boots. "Because school is important. You don't take days off just because." He yelled upstairs. "Kitchie, you and Junior get it together. If we're not out this door in the next five minutes, the kids will miss the school bus, and we'll miss our bus, too." He went and sat down beside Secret on the floor. "The only time you don't want to go to school is when you have to ride the bus. Is someone bullying you?"

"Yeah, right! You should be asking if I'm bullying somebody. How soon before you get the car fixed this time?"

"I'm not sure if it can stand another fixing." He straightened her collar. "Secret, when did you start keeping secrets from me? If you don't talk to me, I can't help you."

She sighed. "It's these two girls—sisters—Tameka and Kesha Stevens. Everything is about money with them. They be bragging and showing off because they was in Bow Wow's video. I only see them at the bus stop and that's when they shine on me. They think they're so special because their father is a bank president. National City this, National City Bank that. They be having the hottest stuff, and I gotta go to school in this." She ran a hand over her skirt. "I got this last year, and I got this shirt on my seventh birthday. They don't forget nothing; they make sure everybody else remembers, too." She sucked her teeth and lowered her head. "When you drop us off at school, I never see them because our grades are different."

"Secret, some people are blessed more than others."

"Does that mean they have to be mean and embarrass me because they are?"

"No. Some people are ignorant and don't know it." He put his arm around her neck. "What do you be doing while they're... broadcasting their ignorance?"

"Shoot, I be getting smart right back."

"But you're the one with bruised feelings in the end."

She looked down at the floor. "Seems that way."

"Being made to feel small or embarrassed isn't fun. People shine on me, too, when they can. I don't like it at all, but I learned something."

She looked at him with wonder.

"I found out that people will keep running their mouths as long as you fuel them with a response. Your mother and I are raising you to be tough, right?"

"What does tough have to do with it? I can beat them both, if they don't jump me."

"Tough goes beyond being physical, Secret. If you're tough enough to ignore them, they'll leave you alone and find someone else to bother. Someone they can get a response from."

Kitchie sauntered into the room with calculated grace, holding Junior's hand. "Let's go."

GP helped Secret up. "Would you ignore them for me today?"

"I guess." She threw her backpack over a shoulder. "Try and get the car fixed fast."

"I'll try. Promise that you'll be tough until I do."

"I promise."

"Daddy, there they go right there." Secret rolled her hazel eyes. "The two with the Cartier shades and Gucci sneakers."

GP did a quick examination of the two little girls across the street. He had to admit that the sisters looked like a million bucks. He kissed Secret's forehead. "Don't sweat it. Remember what I told you." He gave Junior a high-five and whispered in his ear. "Hold your sister down."

The children kissed their mother, then headed across the street.

"Secret, hold your brother's hand." Kitchie thought about how much things had changed from the time her children were toddlers.

The folding hydraulic door hissed open as the Rapid Transit Authority bus halted in front of GP and Kitchie. They gathered their belongings and climbed onto the bus.

"Good morning." Kitchie flashed a bus pass and gasped. "Did you see that?" She pointed a manicured finger toward something outside the window.

The driver followed the direction of her index finger. With a sleight of hand, she slipped GP the bus pass.

"See what, lady?" The driver turned back.

"That man over there almost got hit by a car." She went and took a seat.

GP climbed the last step, flashed the pass, then sat beside Kitchie.

By noon the hustle and bustle of downtown Cleveland was in full swing. Vendors of all varieties had their booths lining the sidewalk between East Fourth and East Eleventh Street off Euclid Avenue.

Kitchie's part of the hustle was powered by two sources: undue beauty and charm. She was a people magnet. No man could resist the urge to regard her almond hue stretched with precision over a five-foot, four-inch frame accessorized with a tiny waistline, firm breasts, and a thirty-four-inch curve that stuffed the backside of her jeans. Whenever she tossed her nut-brown hair and smiled, Kitchie would reel them in every time.

"Do you have this for a toddler?" Suzette Sanders held up a Street Prophet sweatshirt.

"We don't stock that particular item in children's sizes. But my husband can custom-make you one." Kitchie noticed a man standing near the costume shop's display window, and his blue eyes were undressing her. "If you give me your child's size and a way to reach you, I'll have it ready for you in a week."

"That'll be fine." Suzette dug a business card and pen from her purse. "The choice is yours. I'm a volunteer at the mission two blocks over."

"I know the place."

"I'm there every day until around this time." She finished writing on the back of the card. "You can stop by there or call me, and I'll come by and pick it up."

Kitchie took in the information on the card. "Real estate."

"In my spare time. The majority of my time is spent trying to leave the world better than I found it."

"I'll give you a call. I can remember this number by heart, prefix all fives." Kitchie shoved the card in her back pocket as Suzette strolled away.

Blue Eyes was still watching.

Kitchie rested both hands on her hips. "You can't get a proper look from over there." She flashed her admirer a smile. "Come closer so you can really see what I'm working with."

Blue Eyes stepped away from the costume shop positioned in front of her booth. "If I knew it was that easy, I would've come over here twenty minutes ago."

"Well, now that you realize it wasn't as difficult as you thought, let me help you make up your mind on what you should buy from me." She tossed her hair away from her face. "Now you wanna be the first to get this, because when the Street Prophet goes global, you wanna be able to say you were down with the Prophet from day one." She held a T-shirt up to Blue Eyes and saw GP approaching with a struck-out look etched on his face. "You look like an extra large. T-shirts are ten a pop, but for you… I'll give you two for fifteen." She tossed her hair again and tucked a lock behind her ear. "And I'll throw in some Street Prophet stickers for the kids." She looked at GP in his Street Prophet shirt and air-brushed jeans. "There goes a loyal supporter of the Prophet."

Blue Eyes glanced at GP with contempt, then focused on Kitchie again. "I'm not interested in any of your Street Prophet merchandise. What *does* interest me is your number and a dinner date to discuss my e-zine endeavor."

"Forgive me, but it's a rule of mine not to give out my number on the first purchase. So what'll it be, two for fifteen?"

He laughed. "Sexiness and persistence. I like." He peeled off a twenty-dollar bill. "Where is that adorable girl I've seen around here a few times?"

"My daughter? Why?"

"I thought we could discuss this over dinner. I'm in the process of launching an internet magazine, and I'd love to use your daughter as a model in an issue or two. She's beautiful; you two look just alike."

"Thank you. When you're ready, come back and my husband and I will see what you have and consider it."

"Keep the change." Blue Eyes took the shirts and blended into the sidewalk traffic.

Kitchie stuffed the money in her pocket and rose up on her toes to kiss GP. "What did they say?"

He began setting up the airbrushing equipment. "We can't get another extension. The bank's attorney said if I come up with the principal, penalty charges, and his fees, he'll stop the foreclosure proceedings. Other than that, foreclosure is final and we have five days to be out."

Kitchie pulled the bill from her pocket. "I've been standing out here all morning and this is what I made." She waved the money. "Papi, you tried but this ain't panning out." She motioned to the Street Prophet items around the booth. "I know your dream is to give this character a life; I've supported you in everything. It's time to give it up because these twenty dollars can't pay our bills. We're past the point of do-or-die." She scrutinized the money closer. "*Vete pal carajo!*" She turned in the direction that she'd last seen Blue Eyes.

"What's the matter, Mami?"

"That bastard burned me." She passed GP a dollar bill with the corners of twenties glued over the numeral one.

A Korean woman hung the pay phone up next to GP's booth and it soon began ringing. She went to answer it.

"Excuse me, ma'am; that's for me." GP stepped away from the tables, unconsciously glanced at the street sign, then lifted the phone from its cradle. "Ninth Street Artwork, home of the Street Prophet. How may I help you today?"

"May I speak with Greg Patterson?"

"He's in the art room with a customer. Can I tell him who's calling?"

"Tracy Morgan. I'm an acquisitions editor for the *Plain Dealer*."

"Hold on a minute, I'll get him." GP covered the phone and gave Kitchie a thumbs-up.

A local bum strolled up with a cup in hand. "Spare some change, GP?"

He shoved Blue Eye's pseudo-twenty into the cup, then placed the phone on his ear. "Greg speaking."

"Good afternoon, Mr. Patterson. I'm Tracy Morgan with the *Plain Dealer*. You filled out an application with us some time ago. Sorry I'm just getting back with you."

"It's cool. What's up?"

"Your sample work has impressed quite a few people in my department. If you're still interested, I'd like to interview you. I have a comic column available that I believe you'll do great in."

GP wanted to say hell yeah; instead he chose to keep things professional. "I'm interested. When would you like to meet?"

§ § §

Kitchie had worked pedestrians moseying the sidewalk; GP had solicited various motorists who had been delayed by a stoplight near the booth's curb. At the end of the day, they had earned a little over ninety dollars, which barely covered the booth's weekly rental fee.

Due tomorrow.

"I sure hope they give you that column. It'll help out a lot; plus it'll get your foot in the door." Kitchie cleared a table, stuffing merchandise inside a duffle bag.

"Keep your fingers crossed." He packed the airbrushing guns.

A 2005 Chrysler 300C with mirror-tinted windows stopped at the red light near the booth. The car wasn't moving, but the chrome rims appeared to continue spinning.

The window was lowered.

"The starving artist who thinks he's gonna draw his way to financial freedom." Squeeze looked past GP and studied Kitchie's round ass. "Long time no see."

GP squatted some and leaned on the passenger door of the Chrysler. A gorgeous woman sat there, snuggled with a dozen roses. GP nodded at the woman, then addressed Squeeze. "It's been a while. What's up with it, Squeeze?" He admired the man's diamond-studded pinky ring. "I see you stepped it up a few notches from knocking over candy stores. What is it, you poison people for a living now?"

Kitchie was now standing beside GP, caressing his shoulder.

"I'll be the first to tell you that crime pays the bills. Candy stores were just a stepping stone, though. I'm the neighborhood loan officer now. Got fucked-up credit but need some cash? Holler at your boy." He stared at Kitchie's crotch, pulled her pants down with his eyes, and had his way with her. When he was done, he turned his attention back to GP. "I see you still holding on to all that woman. I never could figure out why she chose you. I must not have been square enough."

"Don't act like I'm not sitting here," the woman holding the roses said.

Squeeze hit her with a backhand across the mouth. "Stay in your place."

A car horn sounded off. Squeeze ignored it and pulled out a business card. "Don't be bashful; if you ever need a loan, I'm sure I can work it out for an old friend." He gave GP the card, then took a long-stem rose from his date's bundle. "Give this to Kitchie. I'm sure you haven't bought her any in a while." He winked at Kitchie.

The window was raised and Squeeze sped away.

"God, I can't stand him." Kitchie took the rose from GP and dropped it in the curbside drain.

ⓢ ⓢ ⓢ

"What are you gonna tell Mom and Dad?" Junior squashed a caterpillar that was crawling on the porch steps.

"Shoot, that I had to kick her butt. She put her hands on me first." Secret watched her brother scrape the bug from the bottom of his shoe. "You think Daddy will ever get us all that stuff we named last night?"

Junior ran the question through his head, then shrugged his shoulders. "I don't know…Nah, not all of it."

"Go in the house and get us something to drink."

"I ain't; you go."

Secret nudged him. "Scaredy-cat, you're too old to be afraid of the dark."

"I'm not thirsty. Go get your own drink."

"Chicken."

"You must be scared yourself."

She smirked. "No, I'm not."

"Go get something to drink, then, with your ugly—"

Kitchie pointed to the light pole while coming up the driveway. "What did I tell y'all hardheaded butts about being outside when them street lights are on?"

"It's lighter out here than it is in there." Secret aimed a thumb toward the house.

Junior skipped to Kitchie. "Something's wrong with the lights. They broke, Ma."

Kitchie sat the duffle bag down, looked at the dark interior of their home, and began to cry.

§ § §

GP climbed a steep hill that led to Cliffview Apartments. He never understood why they were called apartments when they ranked as no more than drug-infested projects.

He went into the building and held his breath to avoid inhaling the thick cocaine smoke as he passed a group of addicts smoking crack on the stairwell. He reached the third floor and pound on his best friend's door.

"Don't be banging on my shit unless you're in a hurry to get fucked up." The metal door squealed as Jewels yanked it open. "Oh, what's up, homeboy? I thought you were somebody coming to borrow some shit. A motherfucker asked me to borrow my dustpan yesterday."

Their fists touched in a greeting manner.

"I did come bumming."

Jewels turned away from the door. "You don't count."

She wore brush waves and dressed better than any man GP had ever known. Beneath today's expensive urban wear was an average-looking woman. She was built like Serena Williams but much stronger.

She lay back on the weight bench and pumped 225 pounds effortlessly. "I didn't hear that raggedy-ass car of yours pull in the lot doing the beat box." She racked the iron after ten reps.

"You got jokes. It broke down yesterday. I went to check on it before I came here, but it was gone." GP plopped down on the designer couch in front of a McFadden and Whitehead album cover littered with marijuana.

Jewels sat up and stuffed a rolling paper with marijuana while looking at him from the corner of her gray eyes.

He shrugged. "I had to leave it in Chang's Chinese Food parking lot. Ignorant-ass Chang said it sat there too long, called my bucket an eyesore. Fake chink could've left my ride alone, you know?"

Jewels nodded and put a flame to the joint.

GP kicked a foot up on the coffee table. "He had it towed. Damn thing ain't worth more than it'll cost to get it out the impound and fixed."

"That's fucked up. Anything is better than footing it...unless you enjoy a good walk." She passed GP the joint. "Chang do got more Black in him than me and you, fronting like he grew up in China."

"Rent-A-Center stuck me up yesterday. I got five days to pay the bank or the foreclosure is final." He choked on the smoke, then released it. "And the list goes on. Junior wants a bike— which he deserves. Secret needs, and wants, new clothes to keep up with the Joneses. She's a good kid, too."

"You need some money, homeboy. It's cool to have big dreams and shit." She tugged at his Street Prophet shirt. "But you got a good wife and kids, too. They don't deserve to get dragged through a mud puddle while you chase your rainbow." She averted her gaze to her kickboxing trophies lining the top of the entertainment center. "It's not about you no more, GP. You need to come up or do something to start contributing to your social security. Do your cartoons on the side. Fool, you ain't young no more; you got real responsibilities."

"Twenty-seven ain't old."

"It's too old to be dead broke." She pointed the remote at the flat screen. "You lucky I ain't never been on dick. If I had been the one to give you some pussy, for real, I'd do something vicious to you if you didn't take care of me and mine right." Jewels pulled out a nice-size bank roll. "How much you need?"

"I didn't come over here for money. I'll ask if I need it."

"You the one who said you came bumming. What your foolish ass want, then?"

"I have an interview tomorrow at the *Plain Dealer*. I need to borrow something to wear."

"Get out of here." She made a huge fist and tapped his chin. "Greg Patterson, Senior, a job interview? Hell must be below zero. Not only can you borrow something, you don't ever have to bring it back." Jewels led him to her immaculate bedroom.

GP fell back on the oversized bed. "As nice as you put this place together, why don't you move somewhere…more fitting, like Cleveland Heights or Shaker?"

"This stolen shit ain't nothing." She motioned toward her elaborate furnishings. "Wait till I come off with this account fraud. I'm strictly hood, though. Ain't no place like it. Damn suburbs are too quiet. I'll be forced to fuck up the noise ordinance." She slid the closet open and selected a garment bag. "This should fit you nice." She laid a tan Christian Lacroix suit beside him. "It hasn't been altered yet."

"You're really a jewel. I promise you, one day I'm gonna buy you a big diamond because I appreciate you."

She picked up a newspaper from her nightstand. "Check this out. Technology is a beast."

GP took a moment to examine the article. "FamilyGewels? Who the hell thought of some shit like this? Turn dead people into diamonds; come on."

"All they need is your ashes. I wouldn't mind coming back as a phat-ass diamond ring. But you don't have vision; the cemetery is full of dead motherfuckers. That ain't nothing but money."

"Forget about it." He tossed the paper on the nightstand. "We're not stealing dead people."

"Cremated pets work, too."

"No, Jewels."

"Buy yourself some shoes." She counted out a hundred dollars and put it in the suit pocket. "Listen, GP, if for some reason this interview doesn't work out, I'll set you up with a few ounces to get your pockets right."

"I'm not selling crack no matter how bad it gets. I can't believe you just tried me. Every time I see somebody on it, or hear about something happening because of it, I think—"

"About how your mother was a pipehead. How she gave birth to you in prison. You forgot that I know all about you and I'm tired of hearing it." She browsed through the clothes on hangers. "When are you gonna stop feeling sorry for yourself and get over it? Anybody that had to go through what you have should be as strong as a gorilla. Sorry I tried to help." She took out a collarless dress shirt matching the cream stitching of the suit. "On everything, if I come up with this money I need for this account hustle, I'm gonna do something real proper for you so you can handle your business."

"You stay in something." He pictured himself in the suit.

"What can I say but I'm a hustler. I'm thinking about changing my name to Dividends. All I need is one hundred grand, and it will yield me six hundred grand in a month's time—guaranteed. Why wouldn't I play at them odds?"

§ § §

As GP neared his home, he slowed his pace and frowned upon the unusual sight. He scrutinized the other homes on his block and ruled out a power outage. *Maybe Kitchie put the kids to bed early*. Then, he noticed that the porch light was out.

That light never goes out.

He burst through the front door. "Kitchie!"

"We're upstairs."

He flicked the light switch at the bottom of the stairs.

Nothing happened.

He climbed the stairs and stood in the entrance of his bedroom. His family was bunched together on the bed. Two candles had burned down to their base, casting small flames from both night-stands.

GP dashed out of the back door and into the garage. He dumped his tool box onto the concrete. *Why is the world caving in on me all at once?* He grabbed a monkey wrench, then went to the light meter that was fastened to the aluminum siding. With rage and frustration driving him, it only took four determined tugs to break the meter's lock.

"What are you doing?" Kitchie's brown eyes were plagued with concern.

He snatched the meter out. "What does it look like?"

He removed the plastic breakers obstructing the electrical current. He shoved the meter back in place.

The house illuminated.

"There's no way in hell we're gonna sit in the dark looking crazy at each other. I'm doing the best with what I got to work with, and I'm not willing to let the little bit of food that we have in the fridge go bad."

Kitchie folded her arms and turned to go inside but paused long enough to see her meddlesome neighbor watching them from his kitchen window. *Nosy old bastard.* "Come in the house, GP, and talk to your daughter." She trudged up the back stairs; GP followed.

He placed the wrench on the Formica countertop. "Who scratched you like that?" He leaned in closer, examining Secret's bruised face.

"I tried to ignore her like you said, Daddy. But she pushed the back of my head like this." She reenacted by pushing the back of her own head.

Kitchie brushed the hair away from her face. "Now this child is suspended off the school bus for a week."

"I'm glad the lights are fixed." Junior came in the kitchen carrying a sneaker with a hole in its sole and waving a piece of cardboard. "Ma, would you fix my shoe now?"

CHAPTER 3

S queeze looked inside the deep trunk of a Mercedes at a frightened youngster dressed in army fatigues. "All of this is your brother's fault. It's a shame that you're caught in the crossfire, but some people have to learn the hard way." He closed the trunk and faced Hector Gonzales. "Take him to the country and lay low. If Miles don't cash in by tomorrow night, have fun with the kid and clean up your mess."

Hector chomped on a wad of chewing gum. "You should let me kill Miles and get it over with."

"Then who's gonna pay me?"

When Jap felt the car begin to move, he hit the *Mark Home* button on his watch.

§ § §

"Good afternoon, Mr. Patterson." Tracy Morgan stepped from behind her desk to shake GP's hand. She had no idea that GP was so handsome—braids hanging below his shoulders, a perfectly groomed goatee just the way she liked them. To have him in her department from time to time would suit her fine. She took in his tan suit with detail. It hung on to his muscular frame with style. She gazed at his scuffed work boots and the melody in her head came to an abrupt stop. She pulled her hand away from his. "Please have a seat."

"Thanks for considering me for this column." GP eased onto a cozy chair facing her desk.

"Your artwork is captivating. May I have a look at your portfolio?"

GP handed her a soft leather folder that was resting on his lap. "You'll find the first series of an underground comic book in there that I put out last year." He watched her facial expressions as she flipped through the drawings.

"This is great stuff. I'm in love with this Street Prophet character."

"I've been developing him since I was a kid. He's like an urban version of the *Tales of the Crypt* character, but he's more upbeat. A character that identifies with the Hip-Hop culture." He wiped the sweat off his palms onto his slacks. "The Street Prophet tells stories through the eyes of an all-wise black man of morals and integrity. Stories that the reader can draw a positive experience from."

"I like the concept." She closed the portfolio. "I—"

"Ms. Morgan, I apologize for interrupting, but if you give me this column I'll be an asset to the *Plain Dealer*. I have at least three years of material ready to go. I'm a fast learner and I don't have an editing complex."

"The comic page could use a new black face. It's a two-year contract that pays close to fifty thousand in six equal payments over the term of the contract."

GP smiled.

"Your strip will be syndicated. When we run the Street Prophet, he'll receive national exposure. But there are some minor changes that will need to be made."

"Cool. What kind of changes are we talking?"

She leaned forward and rested her forearms on the polished desktop. "Morals and integrity doesn't sell newspapers. The public wants the dirt, violence, and political corruption. I need you to portray the Street Prophet as challenging, outrageous, politically opinionated, offensive to the point of being censored. I need him to play the race card. I want most of the truth in this paper…" She pointed to a newspaper that was encased in glass and mounted on the wall. "…to come from the Street Prophet's comic strip. He needs to be the voice that screams at the injustices designed by the government." She took a deep breath and smiled. "You pull this off and I promise you that this type of controversy will draw you more media attention than Aaron McGruder's *Boondocks*." She produced a contract from her desk drawer and pushed it toward GP. "All rights to the Street Prophet must be signed over to the *Plain Dealer*. You'll retain the artistic rights."

"I can create you a character to fit your requirements, Ms. Morgan. I'm sorry, but the Street Prophet is not your man."

$$\textbf{\textit{S S S}}$$

"We're in no position for you to be turning down jobs, GP." Kitchie stuffed a T-shirt and some Street Prophet stickers in a bag, then thrust it at a customer.

"I apologize for that." GP collected the money from the man.

"I don't believe you would do something so stupid and irresponsible."

"Get the hottest Street Prophet gear right here." Secret walked back and forth in the front of the booth, holding up a T-shirt. "Special on customized airbrushing until one o'clock. Get your issue while it's hot. Don't be unhip and go home empty-handed." She had heard her parents solicit the crowd a thousand times.

"That child is s'posed to have her tail in school." An older woman lugging a Gap bag nudged a heavyset woman wobbling beside her.

GP stuck his finger through Kitchie's belt loop and pulled her to him. "I'm not gonna argue with you in public. Period. They wanted me to sign over all the rights to the Street Prophet. I'm not about to give my life's work away like that."

"But it's okay for us to be out on the street? And don't forget that forty-seven hundred dollars is a lot of money to come with in the next few days. GP, we don't have but a couple hundred to our name."

He took out a hundred dollars from his breast pocket. "Jewels gave me this to buy some dress shoes."

The pay phone rang.

"Get that, Secret." Kitchie leaned against the table.

"Ninth Street Artwork, home of the Street Prophet. Secret speaking, how can I help you?"

"Secret, baby, what's the deal?"

"Hey, Aunty Jewels. When you coming to get me?"

"We'll go catch a flick or something when I come back from New York."

"Ooh, bring me something back."

"You already know I am. Did your crusty father get the job?"

Secret glanced at her parents and saw Kitchie talking with her hands. "I don't think so. Him and Mommy trying to pretend like they not arguing, while I'm hustling."

"Why you ain't in school?" Jewels tied her wave cap on.

"Had to kick some butt. I put that move you taught me on this bigmouth girl named Kesha. I got suspended off the bus, and I didn't have a ride today."

"She knows what time it is now, right?"

"Yeah."

"You don't sound too sure. Let me hear you say *you motherfuck-ing right, she know.*"

Secret put a hand over the mouthpiece. "You motherfucking right, she knows what time it is."

"Give me that." Kitchie scowled at Secret, then snatched the phone. "Jewels, I asked you not to influence my child to cuss. She's too grown for her own good as it is."

"How you know it was me?"

"I'm on to y'all. This stubborn husband of mine turned down a decent job today. He act like he doesn't understand we're having bread-and-butter nightmares."

"You got to be fucking joking. I talked to that knucklehead yesterday about taking care of his business. Put him on so I can bite his head off."

Kitchie let the receiver hang. "Jewels wants to talk to you." She rolled her eyes at GP, then walked over to Secret and popped her on the lips. "Watch what the hell you let come out your mouth, girl. Cuss again and you're gonna get your ass whipped."

A white man with solid gray hair, wearing a business suit, came to the booth. He studied the various Street Prophet merchandise. He shifted his head as though intrigued by the Prophet's appeal. "Who's the artist behind the character?"

Kitchie pointed at GP. "Can I bag that up for you?"

"Yes, yes. I'll take one of everything."

"What size shirt and pants would you like?"

Secret passed Kitchie a bag.

"Any size; it doesn't make a difference. I like this guy. I want some friends of mine to see him—"

"Mr. Lee, we must be going or we'll be late," another man in a suit and tie said.

"Just a moment, Hartford. You can wait for me in the car. I'll be along in a moment." Mr. Lee paid for his purchase.

GP watched the exchange from the pay phone. "Come on, Jewels, you know it ain't even like that. That broad had me confused. I created the Prophet. He's supposed to work for me; not the other way around."

"You even talk like that damn drawing is real. Man, you bugging."

"He's real to me."

"I gotta let this conversation go before you piss me the fuck off."

"You do that, then." GP waved at the owner of the costume shop.

"I'm taking Ndia on a boosting spree in the morning. Use your spare key if you need my ride. We're taking the bus."

"Where are you going?"

"The Big Apple. I called to see if you needed anything before I left. I'll be gone for about a week, but if it's good to me, I'll be longer."

"I'm good. Bring the kids something." GP stared at his battered boots. "I might need you to loan me the balance of whatever I don't come up with on this mortgage."

"How much is it?"

"Forty-seven hundred."

"What you got on it so far?"

"Including the hundred I got from you…about three hundred. And whatever we make today."

"You already owe me your life, but I got your back. Hit me on my cell; I'll wire it if I have to."

"I'm gonna pay you back one day, Jewels, I swear. I'm gonna buy you that diamond, too."

"I know. I'll carve your black ass up if you don't."

§ § §

Trouble nudged his partner when he saw Jewels sauntering down the avenue with a sexy woman on her arm. "How a butch snag a fine broad like that?"

Dirty took a gulp of beer from a forty-ounce bottle. "I don't know. Jewels did her thing. She got the finest bitch in the hood. If I had her, I'd be out here flossing with her, too." They both watched Jewels and her beautiful companion close the distance.

Jewels slid her arm around Ndia's neck and pulled her closer. "Listen here, baby. I'm gonna let you do what you do when we touch down in New York. I can't afford for the order to get messed up like the last move did." She caressed the small of Ndia's back. "When I get this money together, we'll be batting in the major league. These chump-change licks will be history."

"Jewels, I'm gonna do my thing and give it my all." She looked at Jewels with devotion. Ndia was a tall woman with boney extremities—model extremities. She wouldn't have made it on a catwalk, though, because her buttocks and thighs were much too big. Just as Jewels liked them.

Jewels squeezed Ndia's back pocket and kissed her cheek. "That's what I wanted to hear."

"We should have drove. This is going to be a long walk."

"Don't start complaining. I can't stand that shit. I enjoy a good walk every now and then. Besides, you already know I don't drive unless I absolutely have to. So what's the point in bringing it up?"

"I don't know why you even bought a car. Nine—"

"What is a pretty woman like you doing with that Amazon?" Trouble stepped out of the foyer of a building. "Come spend a few hours with me and let me show you what a real man's dick feel like. I know you're tired of the rubber she's packing."

Dirty stepped outside, laughing, as Jewels's face hardened.

Jewels turned her apple cap to the back. "I'm not with no disrespectful bullshit. These motherfuckers about to make me hurt something."

"Forget them clowns…let's go." Ndia pulled on Jewels's wrist but failed to move the solid muscle.

Trouble leaned against the building and put a foot on the wall. "Ugly bitch, you ain't tough. Don't act like it ain't a pussy in them jeans." He touched fists with Dirty.

Jewels snatched away from Ndia. "They got me fucked up." She was swift as she closed the gap between her provokers. She staggered Trouble with a head-butt across the bridge of his nose.

Dirty had a change of mind when she yanked a nickel-plated .45 from beneath a throwback jersey and pointed it at him.

She spat a razor from her mouth, caught it with her free hand, and held it to Trouble's throat. "What you say to me? I don't think I quite heard you right." She pushed the razor just enough to draw blood. "Go on, tough punk, fix your mouth and say it again."

"Jewels, baby, let's get out of here. They were just talking shit."

Jewels refused to take her eyes off of Trouble. "Check these lames for pistols."

"Jewels, come on."

"Do what the fuck I said!"

Trouble pressed his head against the brick building as hard as he could in an attempt to ease the blade's pressure on his Adam's Apple.

Ndia found a Saturday Night Special on Dirty and a Beretta .22 in Trouble's back pocket.

"Now what I want you lames to do is apologize to my lady for being disrespectful."

Dirty was moving too much for Jewels's comfort. She pulled the trigger and blasted a chunk of brick inches away from his ear.

"I'm sorry." Trouble was as still as paralysis.

"That you are." Jewels pushed the blade. "Sorry for what?"

"Being disrespectful."

Jewels stroked the handle of the .45 with a thumb and averted her piercing gaze to Dirty. "Something wrong with your noise-maker?"

"I apologize for disrespecting your woman."

"Now if you poor-excuses-for-men will excuse us, we'll keep minding our business." She considered something else. "On second thought, you look like you're gonna need a constant reminder of how you should address ladies." With one motion, she had left behind a cut across Trouble's cheek.

Dirty's heartbeat quickened. The bones beneath his hips trembled. His eyes bulged. "Goddamn, Jewels. What…Why did you have to cut him?" He spoke over his ringing ears.

After hearing the word *cut*, the left side of Trouble's rugged face began to burn. He covered the burning sensation with a hand. "You cut my face! On everything I love, you started some shit that I ain't never gon' let go."

"Shut the fuck up before I slice your bitch ass again," she spoke through clenched teeth with a scowl on her face. "Pussy, you don't stand a chance in hell fucking with me. Your soft ass better recognize." Jewels backed away and collected their guns from Ndia.

Trouble and Dirty watched as Jewels threw the first gun up on the roof of a nearby vacant building. When she launched Trouble's .22, her cell phone popped from her waistband and fell between two bags of garbage. She put her arm around Ndia and continued down the avenue.

Blood oozed between Trouble's fingers. "I'll be damned if I let that bitch get away with carrying me like I'm some chump. On my dead mama, Jewels is gonna feel me. That's my word." He tapped Dirty. "Go see what she dropped."

"You're gonna need a gang of stitches." He stalked off toward the garbage bags. *I'm glad it was his ass and not mine.*

§ § §

Bright and early the next morning, a taxicab driver leaned on his horn outside of Jewels's apartment.

She lifted the window and stepped out onto the fire escape. "I'm coming, dammit! Chill with the noise-maker." She pulled herself back inside. "Ndia, let's go before this impatient punk leaves."

Ndia came out of the bedroom carrying a pillow.

"What are you doing?"

"It's a long ride. Them Greyhound seats get uncomfortable after you sit on them awhile."

They headed to the door. Jewels hesitated. "I still can't figure out where I lost my phone."

The horn blew.

"Fuck it, come on. I don't need no one keeping tabs on me anyway." She patted Ndia's ass, then picked up their luggage. "Let's ride."

§ § §

Trouble sat behind the steering wheel of an old Buick, picking at the stitches in his face. He frowned as he watched Jewels and Ndia get chauffeured away by Yellow Cab. After a few moments of thinking, he picked up the cell phone from his lap and pressed redial.

The phone rang twice.

"Ninth Street Artwork, home of the Street Prophet. Kitchie speaking, how may I help you?"

Trouble terminated the call, climbed out of the car, and made his way over to a man who was constantly peeping out of a stairwell door. "Slow out here this morning, huh?"

The frail man nodded his unkempt head. "Yeah, I ain't got high since last night. It'll pick up soon, though. The banks just opened and welfare checks is circulating." He checked out Trouble's urban attire and assumed that he was a go-getter. "Don't you hustle at the bottom of Cliffview? I've seen you before."

"You know the butch that just left?"

"Jewels? Sure, I know her. Who's asking?"

Trouble dug in his crotch and pulled out a sack of crack rocks. The man's eyes widened.

Trouble took out a tiny rock. "How would you like to be my main man and make one of these every day?"

"What I gotta do?" He held out his hand.

CHAPTER 4

Miles removed the headphones from his ears. He stood in front of Squeeze's mahogany desk, a fiberglass cast covering most of his boney arm. "I need a few more days. I'll have it all put together for you by then."

"I see a broken arm don't mean a damn thing to you." Squeeze zoomed in on Miles with a set of cold eyes. He had the face of innocence and the grin of corruption. "You turned a forty-thousand-dollar loan into a ninety-thousand-dollar calamity."

"Ease up on me some. I just need a few more days."

"I won't ease up on my mama when it comes to my cash."

Miles sighed. "I bumped into an unexpected situation, but everything is together now. Five more days; that's my word."

"Your word don't mean a motherfucking thing to me." Squeeze rested his square chin on a fist. "You fucked that up when you reneged on our agreement. I gave you until tonight to have my cash, but I guess you're gonna need some more motivation."

Miles held up his good limb. "You gonna break this one, too? I can't conduct my business—"

"That's exactly why I don't have my cash now; you're selfish. You only think about yourself. My cash is much bigger than you. How's your family? Your brother? Is everybody in good health?"

Miles felt weak. He leaned on the desk. "You know where Jap is? Don't hurt him; my mother is worried sick about him."

Squeeze threw his hands up. "I don't know what you're talking about. I just asked if your people are all right."

"I'm gonna get your money."

"I know. The problem is that I need that little bit by tonight."

§ § §

"Ninth Street Artwork, home of the Street Prophet. Kitchie speaking. How may I help you?"

The caller hung up.

She went back to the booth and sat in a folding chair beside Secret. "It's too hot out here."

GP stopped airbrushing a jean outfit and turned to Junior. "Do you understand what I'm saying?"

"Nope. All I know is that you have money in your pocket right now." He touched GP's front pocket. "This one. You even said I deserve a new bike when you get the money. So why don't you buy me one with the money you got?"

"Let me see how I can explain this to you, little man." GP set the airbrush gun on the ground. "Just because you see me or Mommy with money doesn't mean we have any money to spend on things like bikes and remote control cars. Maybe you can understand me better this way." He pulled the money out, separated a portion of it, then stuffed the rest back in his pocket.

Secret rested her head on Kitchie's arm as they focused on GP's demonstration.

"This is fifty dollars. Pretend this is all we had. You with me?"

Junior nodded. "I'm good at pretending."

"Okay… For us to have a place to live, it'll take, let's say, twenty of this." He gave Junior a twenty. "Hold on to that. Now we need another twenty for food." He handed Junior two tens. "Then, we need twenty for lights so you don't have to be in the dark like last night."

Junior grabbed the remaining money. "But this is only ten dollars."

"That's right, and I haven't gotten to gas, transportation, your bike, or Secret's new—"

"Maricon." Kitchie sat straight up.

"What?" GP faced her. "Who's the faggot?"

"Over there." She pointed to the book vendor two booths away. "That's the guy who ripped me off." She was on her feet headed in Blue Eyes's direction with a club that GP called the *act-right stick*.

"Park it; don't either one of you move." GP shifted his eyes from Secret to Junior. He hurried after Kitchie.

Blue Eyes picked up a copy of *White Heat*. He studied the woman on the alluring book jacket. *She's sexy.* He held the book to the merchant. "What's this about?"

"You bastard, where's my money!" Kitchie grabbed his arm.

White Heat fell to the sidewalk, revealing the author's name— Oasis.

"Lady, I don't know you." He snatched his arm free. "And I don't owe you shit."

Kitchie clobbered him with the act-right stick, then jumped on his back. "Puto, you're gonna give me my money."

He started to spin in an effort to shake Kitchie.

Dammit. Kitchie! GP screamed in his mind. He put Blue Eyes in a tight headlock so Kitchie wouldn't fall and get hurt.

Junior put his holey sneakers to work on Blue Eyes' shins. Secret clamped her teeth on to Blue Eyes's forearm.

GP put enough pressure on the man's neck to obstruct his breathing. "Man, give us our money."

"Kiss...my ass. Take it as a loss."

Onlookers formed a complete circle around the brawl.

"You black fucker, stop kicking me." He tried to kick Junior back.

Kitchie's first thought was to bite him as hard as she could, but she opted to pound the top of his head with a closed fist when she saw that Secret had beaten her to the punch. "I want my money."

Junior kept kicking; GP wrestled Blue Eyes to the ground.

Secret pulled his blond hair. "Get in his ass, Mommy."

Kitchie dug inside Blue Eyes's pocket and removed his wallet while GP pinned him to the ground. "One way or the other, I'm gonna get mine."

Whistles were blown loud enough for some onlookers to turn toward the direction of the sound. The Pattersons never heard the whistles.

Two officers dismounted their buckskin colts. The slim officer broke through the dense crowd.

The taller one pressed the button of his walkie-talkie. "This is downtown Horse Patrol Fourteen. I need some assistance; I have an assault in progress at Euclid and Ninth Street."

§ § §

Secret and GP sat in the backseat of one squad car; Kitchie and Junior were seated in another.

Kitchie glared at Blue Eyes through the window.

He held an ice pack to his head. "I swear, I was just walking down the street when she—" He jerked his head toward Kitchie. "—came from nowhere and attacked me with a pipe. She demanded my wallet and threatened to kill me if I didn't give it to her. Then the rest of them jumped on me and kept punching me. And that GP guy took all my cash. They're really crazy. It's because of black people like them, public streets aren't safe anymore."

The slim officer jotted a few more notes, then closed his note-pad. "After you get that bruise taken care of, we'll need you to come down to the city jail and file a formal complaint if you wish to press charges."

"As soon as I leave the hospital, I'll be there." He was assisted into an ambulance by a paramedic.

§ § §

"Warrant?" GP was unsettled by the implication. "Are you sure you have the right Greg and Kitchie Patterson?"

"I don't steal." Kitchie massaged the bruises that had been left behind by the cuffs. "We haven't stolen anything."

"That's what they all say. Convince the magistrate. You're wasting your breath with me." The desk officer glanced at them over his round spectacles.

"I want to see my children."

"They're fine, Mrs. Patterson. You'll be arraigned within seventy-two hours, and your bonds will be set shortly after that. My advice to you is have someone come for your kids." He adjusted his eyeglasses. "In a few hours, they'll be turned over to the Department of Social Services. They're too young to be released on their own."

GP sighed with grief and kneaded his temples. He couldn't believe that the Man upstairs would let life single him out to be treated so terribly. "Can we make a call?"

The officer led them to side-by-side cages with phones mounted to the walls. "Dial nine, then your numbers." He locked them in and paused in front of Kitchie's cage. "You have about five minutes before they come to process you on the women's side."

Tears trickled down her face as she punched in a telephone extension. "Mama."

§ § §

GP held his jeans up. He had been stripped of his belt and shoe laces. He dialed a number of his own. As the phone rang, he watched Kitchie's depressing expressions.

And rang.

"Hello." Trouble turned the car stereo down.

"Thank God, Jewels—"

"She's away for a minute. I'm supposed to take a message."

"Who is this?"

§ § §

"...but, Mama—" Kitchie wiped her tears away. "—this doesn't have anything to do with it."

"There is nothing I can do, Kitchie. I begged you to not marry GP; you wouldn't listen to me. He's a loser. New York is entirely too far away for me to do something, even if I wanted to help." Mrs. Garcia took a pan of homemade cornbread from the oven. "You told me you were grown when you left home. I'm sure you're grown enough to work this out."

§ § §

"All that ain't important." Trouble eased away from a traffic light. "Me and Jewels is taking care of some business together, and I'm working the phone. You leaving her a message or what?"

"Did she leave to go out of town yet?" GP prayed that the answer would be no.

Trouble flashed back to when Jewels had tossed a suitcase into the taxi's trunk, and he remembered when her pretty woman had tossed her hips across the parking lot clutching a pillow. "Yeah. Who's asking all the questions?"

"GP. When is the next time you're gonna talk to her?"

"Tonight. Why, what's up?" Trouble parked in Dirty's driveway and honked the horn.

"Tell her that me and Kitchie is in jail, downtown on some bullshit. I need her to come get the kids; they're down here, too. These people is threatening to turn them over to DSS if someone doesn't come for them."

Too damn bad. "That's fucked up."

"Is there some way you can get in touch with her before later? This is important." GP stared at Kitchie through the wire mesh and watched her eyeliner run.

"Nah, dawg. I gotta wait until she hits me. I'll let her know, though. Keep your head up in there." He hung up, then touched fists with Dirty when he climbed in the car. "The butch went on a little vacation. I say we stop by her apartment tonight."

"I'm with that."

$$S \quad S \quad S$$

GP placed the receiver on its cradle.

Kitchie stuck her fingers through the wire. "My mother is impossible."

GP faced her and laced his fingers with hers. "Jewels is gone. I don't know who else to call. I'll figure something out."

"We can't let the kids stay, not even one night, in some custody crap." She wept. "Junior is afraid of the dark...and Secret has to sleep—"

"Time's up." The officer stuck a key in the first cage's lock. "Mrs. Patterson, your escort is here to take you to the women's lock-up."

"Kitchie, listen to me." GP penetrated her with his eyes. "I'll do something."

Kitchie turned to the officer. "Please. Let me see my babies first."

§ § §

"Uno!" Secret threw a card onto the table.

Junior sat on his knees to boost himself in the chair. "Uh-uh, you draw four."

The conference room door swung open. Nancy Pittman strolled in wearing a tacky business suit. "Hello, Secret, Greg Jr. How are you guys doing this evening?" She set her briefcase on the table and tucked a lock of blonde hair behind her ear.

Secret's face tightened. "We're fine. Can we go home now?"

"I'm here to speak with you about that. I'm Ms. Pittman. I'm with the Department of Social Services."

Junior laid his cards on the table. "Where's my mom?"

Ms. Pittman squatted beside him. "I'm afraid that she and your father will have to stay in jail; at least overnight. Are you hungry?"

"I said, we're fine." Secret sucked her teeth.

Junior looked at Ms. Pittman. "That real fat police lady gave us McDonald's."

"Secret, do you have any relatives that can come for you and your brother?"

"We already called my Aunt Jewels and left a message. She'll come when she checks the answering machine."

"Does your Aunt Jewels have a cell phone? Do you think she's at work?"

"Aunty Jewels says she's allergic to work; it breaks her out with the hives." Junior scratched a mosquito bite. "Secret doesn't know the cell phone number."

"Would you shut up!"

"I ain't got to."

Ms. Pittman pulled out a third chair and seated herself. "Where are your grandparents?"

Secret looked at the ceiling and exhaled. "Are you always this nosy? They live in New York."

"Yes, I am. I'm concerned about your well-being. I'm not your enemy; I'm here to help."

"Then let my mom and dad out so we can go home." Secret curled her lips up out of frustration.

"Yeah, they're not bad people." Junior stared.

"I have no say in the matter, and I'm sure your parents aren't bad people. Do you know your grandparents' phone number?"

Secret showed Ms. Pittman her ID bracelet. "All of my important information and telephone numbers are on here."

"Can I see it?" Ms. Pittman noticed the same bracelet on Junior's wrist.

Secret gave it to her. "The first number is Aunt Jewels's; the next is my *abuela*."

"I don't understand what you mean."

"It's Spanish for grandma." Junior stacked the cards.

"And whose number is this?" Ms. Pittman pointed to a third set of digits.

Secret rolled her eyes. "It's to a pay phone downtown."

"Excuse me a minute. I'll bring this right back." She took the bracelet and left the room.

Ms. Pittman seated herself in the hall and tried the first number from a cell phone.

It only took Squeeze forty minutes to travel from the inner city to the country. He guided the Chrysler up a quarter-of-a-mile gravel driveway. Squeeze loved his ranch-style home because there wasn't a neighbor's house in sight.

He went inside and found Hector standing over a fish bowl. He felt an unpleasant vibe seeping from Hector. "What's wrong with you?"

Hector turned around with watery eyes. "I went to feed Pablo and he was floating in his bowl. He won't wake up."

Squeeze never understood Hector's attachment to the goldfish. Had he been the one to find the dead fish first, he would have had it replaced just as he had all the other times.

Hector stuck a fresh piece of gum into his mouth. "Pablo and me been partners for five years now." He thought for a moment. "What are you doing here? Miles must've come clean."

"No." Squeeze's eyes communicated all that needed to be said.

Hector pushed the door open and entered a large bathroom. He didn't bother to wipe his tears. "It's your fault Pablo is dead."

Jap was gagged and duct taped to a chair sitting inside a round tub in the center of the room. His eyes widened with alarm. "Hmmh, umm hmmh." He wiggled as Hector approached with a .357 aimed at his face.

"All your fault." He pulled the trigger.

Blood and brain matter splattered inside the tub as the bullet passed through Jap's face and created a crater in the back of his head.

"Feel better now?" Squeeze leaned on the doorjamb.

"Uh..." He pulled the trigger two more times. "...a little."

§ § §

Mrs. Garcia was putting dinner dishes away when the phone rang. She wiped her hands then answered. "Garcia residence."

"Yes, Mrs. Garcia, I'm Nancy Pittman, a social worker for the Department of Social Services here in Cleveland. Forgive me for disturbing you this evening, but I'm here with your grandchildren."

"I've spoken with my daughter earlier."

"Then you're familiar with the situation."

"Yes, I'm aware."

"I'm putting forth my best efforts not to put your grandchildren in the care of the state. To be truthful, I'm running out of options."

"Kitchie had you call me, didn't she?"

"No, ma'am. I actually got your number from Secret. She's quite a lady. Is there some way that I can turn the children over to you until their parents handle their legal affairs?"

"Miss, I'm more than nine hours away. I don't have transport-ation."

Ms. Pittman crossed her legs. "If you would take them, we'll make the arrangements to get the children there safely."

Mrs. Garcia sat down to rest her aching feet. "Miss, I'm up in my age. My husband and I live in a one-bedroom apartment on a fixed income. We're not capable of handling them children. Where will they sleep? I can't give them the attention they need. I already raised my children. I'm sorry."

"So am I. Thank you for your time, Mrs. Garcia. You have a good evening."

"Do the same." Mrs. Garcia ended the call.

Ms. Pittman stared at the door for a minute before she went in. "Secret, Greg Jr., gather your things. We're leaving."

Junior stood and stretched. "Where are we going?"

Even after nine years of being a social worker, this was the part of the job that she still hated to perform. "To a place where you guys can play with other children your ages."

$ $ $

Trouble kept a close eye on the stairwell as Dirty jimmied Jewels's door.

Two years ago, Dirty could have walked up to a door with a crowbar and opened it like he had the keys. Tonight, he'd been trying to gain access for over five minutes.

"Would you hurry up! Goddamn!" Trouble talked over a shoulder.

"Chill, I almost..." He pushed with everything he had. "...got it."

The door burst open with a sharp sound.

"About time." Trouble closed the door behind them. "Who said you have to play a number to hit the lottery?"

Dirty was amazed by the living room. "She got this rinky-dink apartment looking like something you'd find in a *Florida Design* mag. Look at this shit." The more he took in, the more he was impressed by Jewels's living arrangement.

"Stop fronting; you can't read."

"I count good as hell, though." Dirty stood at the entertainment center. "These eight kickboxing trophies right here explain that big-ass speed knot on your head, and that constant reminder she left on your face."

"Fuck you. Let's toss the place; see what we come off with." A blinking number stole Trouble's attention as he rubbed the lump on his forehead. He seated himself at the computer and pressed play on an answering machine beside the monitor.

"Aunty Jewels...Mommy and Daddy—" He skipped to the next message.

"Aunty, if you're there, pick up the—" Another skip.

"Jewels, you're not going to believe this shit. I'm in jail—" Skip.

"Yo, Jewels, I plugged you in. I got you the—" Skip.

"Yes, I'm with the Department of Social—"

Dirty had a handful of jewelry. "Man, you got to see the bathroom. Play that last message again. Swear that sound like that old-school hustler, Sticky Fingers."

"Sticky wouldn't fuck with Jewels. She's out of his league."

"Don't be so sure; look around you." Dirty motioned toward the plasma flat-panel television and the designer glass and cashmere theme throughout the apartment. "Play it back."

Trouble mashed the button.

"Yes, I'm with—"

"The one before that one." He began adding up the total weight of the iron on the bench press. 200...225.

"Yo, Jewels, I plugged you in. I got you the sweetest deal I could on those corporate numbers. Ten stacks a piece. If you cop ten, my connect will throw in all the equipment you need to work your magic. The equipment alone will run you fifty stacks. The only thing dividing you from petty hustling and real wealth is you linking with us next Saturday at the Improv with your paper. Holler at your boy, Sticky Fingers."

"Told you I knew that voice." Dirty laid a Patek Philippe watch against his wrist. "They say he's nasty with a gun and don't have no problem getting his man in broad daylight."

"That was in his heyday. It's official street thugs like me now." Trouble glanced at the jewelry Dirty gathered and began wiping his prints off of the phone. "Put all that back, and clean up behind yourself."

"You got me fucked up. I didn't pull a B and E for the fun of it. This here is me."

Trouble's voice hardened. "Don't get hurt! I'm not about to go through this bullshit with you. Use your head sometimes and stop being greedy. Sticky Fingers is calling this bitch personally. Didn't you hear what he said?"

"What you know about corporate numbers? I don't know shit about them."

"I don't need to know about 'em." Trouble smiled, displaying his chipped tooth. "What I do know is how much it takes to buy them, when Jewels is supposed to buy them, and where she's going to buy them."

"I doubt she has that type of cash stacked. And if she does, it's stashed in here—" He pointed to the carpet. "—right now."

"All right." Trouble stroked his goatee. "Put that petty shit back, and let's find the money. If we don't, we lay on her like bandits and intercept the ball next Saturday."

Dirty hunched his shoulders and stalked toward the bedroom.

Less than three minutes into their search, someone banged on the door.

Trouble froze; his eyes widened. Dirty tipped into the living room with a .40 caliber pointed at the door. His heart thumped in his chest.

More door banging.

"Ms. Jewels Madison, this is maintenance. We had a tub overflow in the apartment above yours. We hate to bother you, but I'm afraid we're gonna need to get in to check for water damage." An old salt-and-pepper-haired man nodded at his balding co-worker.

Baldy unclamped a large key ring from his waist and began his search for the key that would unlock Apartment 302.

Trouble slid the couch back in place and pointed to the fire escape. The sound of keys entering the mechanical lock registered in their ears. Dirty stuffed the big gun in his waist, then lifted the window.

The door was pushed open without turning the key. Baldy examined the doorjamb. "While we're here, might as well fix this thing, too. Anybody can get in here."

The old man picked up his tool bucket. "The more overtime, the more Viagra I can buy." He pushed past Baldy.

Trouble eased the window shut and followed Dirty down the fire escape.

CHAPTER 5

Bacon and scrambled eggs scented the air this morning, a once-a-week occurrence in the Reynolds's Eastside Group Home. Secret sat in the gloomy cafeteria, holding Junior's hand under the table. "Go on; eat your food."

"I wanna go home with Mommy and Daddy."

She squeezed his hand to reassure him. "They're coming for us."

"Hi, I'm Samone." A high-yellow girl with two long cornrows placed her tray on the table and sat beside Secret. "Has anybody told you yet?"

"Told me what?" Now Secret's legs began to shake underneath the table.

"Nah, you don't know shit." Samone bit a strip of bacon. "I'll give it to you raw. Mr. Reynolds is evil. He hates everybody. Stay out of his way and away from his 'off-limits' room."

"What's that?" Secret posed the question, but she and Junior looked at Samone and waited for the response.

Samone forked some eggs and washed them down with milk. "Actually, it's not a room. It's a door that leads to the loading dock. He stores his caskets there."

"Caskets, as in dead people caskets?" Secret blocked out the collective chatter from the other children in the cafeteria.

"Yeah, it's his side hustle. He owns the shop next door; sells headstones, too." She stopped eating and looked at Secret and Junior as if to say *I'm serious*. "But the most important thing is to do your chores, stay out of his way, and don't break his rules."

Junior leaned forward and looked past Secret. "What's the rules?"

"Who knows? He makes them up as he goes. I'm always getting in trouble...well, breaking the rules by being out of bed some nights. You gonna eat that?"

Secret slid the tray, allowing Samone to get the bacon. "Then, why don't you stay in bed if you know you're gonna get in trouble?"

"It's not like I want to break the stinking rules, but I sleepwalk sometimes."

Denise, a rough-looking girl, sat down across from Secret. Two other girls stood behind her. Denise looked at Samone. "Go scrub a toilet or something."

Secret watched Samone walk away without saying a word.

Denise snapped her fingers. "Hey, I'm over here. What you in for?"

"Huh?" Secret noticed that the rest of the children scattered throughout the cafeteria were watching them now.

"Y'all runaways, your parents abandon you, they died in a freak accident, y'all just fuck-ups or what?"

"No." Secret rolled her eyes and popped her head with intended sassiness. "We won't be here long."

Denise laughed and her entourage followed suit. "One of *those*. Hate to burst your bubble; everyone is here long. You smoke?"

"No, I'm only nine."

"You do now." Denise put a pack of Newports in the empty slot that was soiled with bacon grease.

Junior's chest rose and fell with anger. "Leave us alone."

"Wooo, little brother to the rescue." Denise's rough features turned fiercer as she narrowed her focus. "You fucking punk! Say something else and you'll be wearing black eyes to lunch."

"Nobody's gonna do shit to—"

"Shut up." Denise leaned forward. "This is how it works around here. I'm running shit. Either you can be down with me and be cool like us…" She motioned to the girls behind her. "…or you and the tough guy can be our personal punching bags like the rest of these sissies."

"How am I supposed to hang out with somebody whose name I don't know?" Secret still held on to Junior's hand.

Denise smiled. "Nise, that's what my girls call me. What you go by?"

"Nise, I'm not scared of you. You might kick my butt, but you're gonna know you've been in a fight if you mess with us. All we wanna do is go home."

Mr. Reynolds walked in, his hard-bottom shoes thudding against the floor. The cafeteria fell silent.

The two girls, who had stood behind Denise, were now rushing to find seats.

Denise stared at Secret and lip-synced the words, *I'm gonna fuck you up*. "Promise."

Secret sucked her teeth and shrugged.

The children did not dare make direct eye contact with the heavy man as he walked the aisles between the tables. At fifty-seven years old, he had earned his respect amongst children by his actions.

The thudding hard bottoms came to a stop behind Secret. "There's a punishment for every rule broken under my roof."

Denise smiled.

Mr. Reynolds put his liver-spotted hands in his trouser pockets. "I don't believe in leniency, not even for new people, Secret Patterson."

"What did I do?" Secret looked at Mr. Reynolds over a shoulder with surprise.

"There is no smoking under my roof. Cigarettes are forbidden."

"These ain't mine." Secret glared at Denise.

Mr. Reynolds urged Secret from her seat when he grabbed her ear.

Junior didn't let go of her hand.

"Sit down, boy!" Mr. Reynolds put his wrinkled face in Junior's. "I'm sure you'll do something stupid and get your turn."

§ § §

"What is it?" Hector's Spanish accent boomed through the intercom.

"Buzz me in; it's Miles. I came to straighten my hand with Squeeze."

The glass door hissed. Miles put the skateboard under his broken arm, adjusted the backpack on his shoulder, and went inside. Once on the elevator, he turned the Walkman's volume up a few notches and rode the mechanical box to the penthouse.

Hector was blowing a bubble when the elevator opened. He waited for Miles to step off. "Put your hands on the wall." He frisked Miles and smiled when he saw the money inside the backpack.

Squeeze was lounging on the balcony, stimulated by the spectacular view of Lake Erie, when he heard Miles approaching.

Miles dropped the bag beside him. "Now tell me where my brother is. I know you know."

"It's a helluva morning to be in good health." He pulled in a breath of air as if it were a piece of heaven. "Is it all there?"

"Every penny." Miles took the headphones from his ears and let them rest around his long neck. "My mother is worried that something has happened to Jap. He's been missing going on a week now. Please tell me where he is."

"I would like to help you uncover your brother's whereabouts, but I don't have a clue. He's probably laid up somewhere. You know what I mean?"

Miles unconsciously fingered the cast and drifted back to the day Hector had broken his arm with a golf club. He could still hear Squeeze's menacing voice in his head. *This time it was an arm, next time I'll pluck a leaf from your family tree. Get my cash to me.*

The sun reflected off of the murky lake. Hector stood in the balcony's entrance smacking on fruity-flavored chewing gum.

Miles' shoulders sagged from the heavy tension. He wore a pained expression on his handsome face. "So you don't know where Jap is?"

Squeeze squinted in the direction of the sun. "Who knows? Maybe he'll pop up somewhere, you *dig*?" He turned to Miles. "It was a pleasure doing business with you. Get at me if you need another loan. Hector will see you to the door."

"I'm through gambling." He headed for the elevator.

Outside of the building, he jumped on top of his skateboard and rode it to an awaiting van three blocks away. He climbed inside the Astro van and tossed the cassette to Detective Crutchfield. "He knows where my brother is."

§ § §

Secret cried out each time the rawhide connected with her skin.

"Be still!" Mr. Reynolds jerked Secret's arm and whacked her again. "You little bastards need a good ass cutting to keep you in line." He whacked Secret for the last time. The strip of rawhide wrapped around most of her body. "While you're under my roof, you'll learn to follow rules. Do you understand?"

Secret fell to the bed and curled her partially nude body and cried.

Mr. Reynolds raised the rawhide over his head and brought it down on her fast. "Speak when you're spoken to."

She managed to push out a choppy, "Yes."

"Yes, what?"

"Yes, sir."

Mr. Reynolds threw the rawhide beside her. "I'll be back for that, next time you need a reality check. Get up and cover yourself. There are boys here. Be in my office in five minutes; it's time I assign your chores." He paused at the door. "Bring your brother."

Secret dressed herself while praying that her parents would soon come for them. They had never given her a beating that intense. She thought about Junior and ran toward the cafeteria.

§ § §

GP couldn't stand to look across the conference table to see Kitchie handcuffed. He lowered his head and sighed. Kitchie was an emotional wreck. He could tell that she had spent the majority of last night bawling and stressing. This was the longest time they had ever spent apart since Junior's birth. GP felt her eyes searching the small room for his, but he refused to make the connection. *You're worthless; you'll never amount to nothing.* Mr. Reynolds had invaded his thoughts.

"I'm Vivian Green. I've been appointed by the court to represent you."

Kitchie might as well have been completely broken because she talked as if she were. "Could you tell me where my kids are?"

"They're at the Eastside Group Home on Eddy Road."

GP slammed his fists against the table and sprang to his feet. "What?" A folding chair fell back. "This shit can't be happening!"

Mrs. Green jumped. Her heart began to sprint at the onset of GP's unexpected outburst.

An overworked, droopy-eyed correctional officer rushed into

the attorney-client room. "What's the problem? I don't like to work for free money. Sit yourself down, Patterson."

GP scowled at Droopy, wanting to throw his angry engine into Drive and run the man down.

"Boy, watch your eyes. You making me nervous." Droopy wagged the point of a finger on one hand. With the other, he rested a thumb on his radio's panic button. "Do what I tell you, sit yourself back down and relax some. I don't want to terminate this attorney visit."

"GP...Que te pasa, Papi?"

"That group home is what's wrong." GP made eye contact with Kitchie for the first time. A tear of anger formed as he sat the chair upright.

"Attorney Green." Droopy was relieved that GP had put his rage on standby. It saved him the task of filling out an incident report.

"We'll be fine." Attorney Green waved him off.

They all remained quiet until the door shut behind the officer.

GP sat at the edge of his chair. "Mrs. Green—"

"Call me Vivian. Mrs. Green makes me feel old." Which she was not.

"Vivian, you have to get my kids out of that place. They abuse children there."

Kitchie raised her head and arched a brow.

"I know you're concerned about your children's welfare, Mr. Patterson. If the situation at hand were reversed, I'd be just as concerned. But—"

"Look, goddamn...Vivian, I grew up in that place from an infant until my eighteenth birthday. I know what goes on under Mr. Reynolds's roof."

The Reynolds name sent a shock wave of fear through Kitchie that only a mother could feel. She remembered in great detail all the horrific stories GP had shared with her about his experiences under the supervision of Mr. Reynolds. She had been rubbing him down for years with cocoa butter and love in an effort to mend his wounds and emotional scars. Tears leaked from her eyes as she constantly shook her head. "Don't say that. Please move them somewhere else until we get out of here."

"There's other places they can go." GP lowered his head in defeat, matching Kitchie's voice.

"The Reynolds home no longer accommodates children over the age of twelve. The other facilities are either overcrowded or your son and daughter don't fit the age requirements." Vivian shuffled through papers in her briefcase. "I have a friend who works for DSS; I'll see what I can do. In the meantime, let's work on getting you both out of jail so you can take your children home yourselves."

Silence.

Vivian opened a manila folder. "We'll be in court for arraignment after lunch. You both have several charges. A criminal complaint was filed against you by the light company Saturday morning, so you're also being accused of destroying city property and theft. I've been advised that they're going to prosecute to the fullest extent of the law."

"I did that alone." GP interlocked his fingers. "My wife didn't have anything to do with it. She tried to stop me."

"If either of you expect professional and competent help, I need for you to be honest with me. I don't care what roles either of you played in the commission of these alleged crimes. I need the truth in order to best represent you on these allegations."

"That *was* the truth." Kitchie fiddled with her handcuffs. "We don't need to lie to you. Who the hell are you?"

"Fine, have it your way." Vivian opened the folder. "The light company has an eyewitness who will testify on their behalf. He claimed that he watched you both in the commission of the crime from his—"

"Mr. Irvington." Kitchie buried her face in her hands.

"Our neighbor?"

"No, our *cat*. I told you, you shouldn't have done that."

"Not right now, Kitchie."

"Whatever the case." Vivian pushed an ink pen behind her ear. "You're both being charged. Also, on the same day the warrants were issued on this charge, you were both arrested for aggravated assault, strong arm robbery, child endangerment, creating a public disturbance, and, Mrs. Patterson, you managed to add resisting arrest to your list."

"I'm responsible for those charges, too." GP couldn't stop tapping his foot.

Vivian wrote herself a note. "That is honorable of you, Mr. Patterson, to claim responsibility, but there is no way I can get these charges—" She eyed Kitchie. "—against you dropped, Mrs. Patterson. You were caught red-handed with the victim's wallet in your possession."

"It wasn't like that; he stole from us." Kitchie wiped her tears with the back of a hand. "Can you get us out of here or not?"

"Mr. Patterson, you have a history of theft. With these charges, the judge will probably set bail at...about eighty thousand. Mrs. Patterson, your ballpark figure should be somewhere around fifty thousand. Before we go into this courtroom, how about letting me in on what's going on?" She leaned back and crossed her arms.

$$ \text{\$ \$ \$} $$

Trouble swerved in and out of lanes, laughing at the "Star & Buc Wild" radio show. It wasn't all that funny to Dirty, though.

The cell phone rang.

"Hello." Trouble turned down the radio.

"Put Jewels on. Tell her it's Sticky Fingers."

"She went out of town to take care of something." Trouble tapped Dirty. "She said to let you know that it's all good for Saturday."

"Cool."

"All right, Player." Trouble hung up and tossed Jewels' cell phone out of the car window.

Dirty knew that Trouble was a little off his rocker, but now he was thoroughly convinced. "You gone. What did you tell him that for? We don't know if Jewels even has that type of money. We don't even know if she's gonna meet Sticky Fingers after she listens to her messages. And we don't have the slightest idea if she'll be back by Saturday."

"It don't make a difference." Trouble shrugged. "Somebody is getting robbed. Either Jewels for the loot or Sticky for the corporate numbers. If things go right, we'll have our cake and eat it, too. Feel me?"

"We can't do diddly with a set of fucking numbers."

"True, but Ms. Hobbs in the projects know all about them. She said if I come through with it, she'll get me top dollar."

$$ \ast \ast \ast $$

Junior and Secret observed a group of children playing kickball in a field from the sleeping quarters' window.

He shoved his ashy hands inside his pockets. "Why haven't they come for us yet? I don't...Maybe they can't find us."

"Good question. I think they're still in jail."

"Do you know the way home from here?"

"Think so. If I could find Euclid Avenue, I know the way from there."

Junior eyed Secret. "Let's find it. I got this." He flashed some money.

"Where did you get all that from?"

"It's only fifty. Daddy gave it to me, showing me why he couldn't buy me a bike, remember?"

"Give it to me." She stuffed the bills in her left sock. "We should find Aunty Jewels."

"If you find Euclid Street, can you take us to her house?"

"Yup." She watched a little boy running bases to reach home plate.

"Time's up." The heavy wooden door closed with a thud behind Nise and her two sidekicks. "You must've thought I was playing about fucking you up. And when I'm done tapping that ass, you gonna pay me for my smokes." She made sure her hand-me-down sneakers were tied tightly.

Secret pushed Junior aside, stepped in front of him, then balled her small fists and stood in a kickboxer's stance. "Nise, find someone else to beat up on. I don't want to fight you." Her heart was pounding a mile a minute. In the confines of her head, she heard Jewels's reassuring voice. *Calm down and relax. The bigger they are, the harder they fall. Let your opponent commit to the attack. Use their force to counteract.*

"I found who I wanna crush." Nise charged.

Secret squatted some, then sprang into action, meeting Nise's momentum with a snap-kick to the solar plexus.

"Oof!" Nise hugged the pit of her stomach.

Secret caught Nise with an openhanded power thrust to the nose, then pushed toward the ceiling. She jumped back into a fighter's stance and stared at the tall girl blocking the door. "My aunt taught me that."

First Nise's eyes watered, then she fell to the hardwood floor unconscious.

"Ooh, I'm telling. You gonna be in a world of hurt." The door blocker rushed out of the room. "Mr. Reynolds!"

The other girl tried to wake Nise from her forced sleep.

Secret held Junior's hand and stepped over Nise.

Junior gave Nise a good, swift kick. "Told you to leave us alone. That's what you get."

They made it to a flight of stairs before being confronted. The unqualified door-blocker and Mr. Reynolds were on the landing right below them.

"Right there, Mr. Reynolds." She pointed. "She did it; she jumped on Denise for no reason."

Mr. Reynolds cracked his knuckles. "I see that I have a habitual rule-breaker on my hands." He turned to the door-blocker. "Go get me an extension cord—a thin one." He started up the remaining steps.

CHAPTER 6

The detectives were keeping an area under surveillance from a parked car.

"Stop with the bullshit. It's not as complex as you make it, Thomas. You're doing too much fucking thinking as usual." Detective Crutchfield stretched and yawned. "It's simpler than that. I think the boy is dead. Hell, he's been MIA for, what is it, six days now? He doesn't have a history of being a troubled or wild kid; a little eccentric maybe. If I had to take an educated guess based on the information I have, Squeeze and Hector nabbed the kid and wasted him as a personal message to Miles. The arm job didn't get the damn point across."

Detective Thomas kept his eyes focused on the rearview mirror. "Could be, but you're a professional speculator. We need more to go on than this." He tossed the mini-cassette player onto Detective Crutchfield's lap. "You're talking murder without a body to support that claim. No murder weapon, no snitch, no eyewitness. Pure speculation. Jap could be laid up in a tender piece of ass somewhere. I've been after Squeeze for as long as you have."

"I'm the fool for even talking to a thick head. They really screwed up when you made detective. There's no standard anymore. Jap is dead and Squeeze knows about it." He looked at the cassette player. "This conversation isn't a coincidence. Squeeze was taunting in his sarcasm. This conversation is so broad, it asks more questions than it answers. If Jap isn't dead, what did Squeeze mean by 'uncover your brother's whereabouts?' Why did he place so much emphasis on 'maybe he'll pop up somewhere, you *dig*?'"

He told us everything we need to know, if you listen with those things mounted on the side of your head. Uncover the body's whereabouts and dig it up."

Detective Thomas started the car. "Our boy is on the move." He watched Hector open a car door for Squeeze. "You think you have all the answers."

"A man who knows he knows something knows that he knows nothing at all." Detective Crutchfield buckled his seatbelt as Thomas pulled into traffic, four cars behind Squeeze and Hector. "We'll get the other answers when we ask the right people the right questions."

❦ ❦ ❦

"How did it go?" GP's cellmate came in and lay across the bunk.

GP watched rush-hour traffic on Ontario Avenue from the window, ten stories above. "The judge had it out for me 'cause I've been in his courtroom before. Prejudiced bastard gave me a ninety-thousand-dollar bond. Hit my wife with sixty. He wouldn't even release my wife to her own recognizance so she can see after my kids."

"That's what these crackers do; make shit hard for us so we never forget our place. They get a kick out of reinforcing the Willie Lynch Syndrome."

"Can I use your three-way before we eat?"

"Yo, my brother, you're getting real heavy. I don't mind helping, but I can't carry you. The collect calls are stressing my queen, and she's venting on me. This gonna have to be the last time, at least until my queen come off her period. Feel me?"

GP nodded.

"Dinner'll be here in a few. You want to try now?"

GP nodded again.

§ § §

"Girl, you have to chill with all that crying. You'll get in touch with somebody. At least you know your next court date." A shapely woman sat down beside Kitchie. "Dinner wasn't bad today."

"I don't know many people; I don't socialize like that." Kitchie wiped her tears. "And the few people I do talk to have blocks on their phones. Court ain't until next month; I can't stay here that long."

Trish giggled and scratched her neck. "Well, when you use your key to open the door, take me with you. Until then, you're stuck like the rest of us." She flipped her hand at a large day room packed with women, then rested it on Kitchie's thigh. "Move in my cell with me; I could use a close friend." She rubbed. "I'm sure you can use someone you can open up to."

"Working on another one already, Trish?" A boney woman sat on the bench behind them. "Damn, your last bitch ain't been gone two days."

Kitchie removed Trish's hand.

"Mind your business, Logan. Don't you have something to do?"

"I'm doing it. Don't be around here putting the press game down on every bitch you want to lick."

Trish sighed. "Logan, I don't get in your shit; stay out of mine." She began scratching her arm raw.

"I'm not into none of that, anyway. Thanks for the lookout, Logan." Kitchie went to the opposite side of the day room and stood in line for the phone.

Trish held out a hand. "Come clean."

Logan gave her a pinch of heroin. "That pretty bitch is so green. I'm gonna enjoy it even more because she don't know better."

Trish shook her head. She took a peek at the heroin in her hand. *What I did isn't as bad as what Logan is gonna do.*

The first person Kitchie called didn't accept the charges. She held the lever down, breaking the connection.

Thinking.

A woman who looked as distraught as Kitchie, if not more, tapped her. "You done with that?"

"Uh." Kitchie stared at the keypad. "Let me try one more number." *I can remember this number by heart.* "Prefix all fives," she blurted and dialed the number.

The phone rang. Twice.

Kitchie crossed her fingers.

"Hello, Sanders' residence." Suzette set a shopping bag of Gerber's baby food on the kitchen counter.

"You have a call from a correctional institute. Caller, state your name after the tone."

Beep!

"Please don't hang up. I need help."

🅢 🅢 🅢

Junior sprang upright in bed. "Secret! Secret!"

"Shut up and go to sleep before you get us all in trouble," a biracial boy warned from one of the other beds jammed in the room.

"Secret!"

She came from the girls' sleeping quarters across the hall.

"What's the matter?" She squatted beside the bed.

"My stomach hurt. I gotta go to the bathroom."

"Then go."

He shook his head negatively. "It's too dark down the hall."

"Come on." She grabbed his hand.

He stepped in a pair of sneakers and pointed them in the direction of the bathroom.

§ § §

Suzette dabbed her eyes with a Kleenex. "Kitchie, no one should have to go through that. I have so much empathy for your family, it breaks my heart. I wouldn't have done one thing different, you hear me?"

The phone beeped, warning that they were about to be disconnected.

"These phone calls are so short." Suzette wound the phone cord around her finger. "Call me back one more time."

Kitchie stole a furtive look at the clock. "It's nine-thirty; we've been talking back to back for an hour now. Maybe you should check on Junior and Secret for me."

§ § §

"What are you two doing out of bed?" Mr. Reynolds cleared the stairs on his way to make hourly rounds on the second floor.

Secret faced him, still holding on to Junior's hand. "His stomach hurts."

"And what does that have to do with you being out of your room?"

"He's afraid of the dark so I'm taking him."

Junior hopped from one foot to the other as if he would piss himself any second.

Mr. Reynolds looked at him, then shifted his gaze back to Secret. "Hurry up and get back in the bed." He watched them walk into the bathroom and close the door. *Misbegotten bastards.*

Secret put her ear to the door. "What are you waiting on?"

Junior went into the cabinet under the sink and removed their clothes. He took his PJs off, dressed himself, then switched places with Secret while she dressed. When she took her PJs off, he could see the sore bruises scattered across her skin.

She eased the window up. "You first; I'm right behind you."

Junior hoisted himself through and landed on a porch roof. As promised, Secret was right behind him. She was thankful that the window was nowhere near as high as her bedroom window.

§ § §

"I'll call you back in the morning…and I promise to reimburse you for the calls." Kitchie blocked out the collective ruckus from the day room.

"Don't you worry about that." Suzette began to unpack the grocery bag. "Think it's too late to call there?"

"It's never too late to check on children, Suzette."

The phone beeped again. Five seconds until disconnection.

"I'll come visit you tomorrow and tell you personally how the children are."

"Thank you, Suzette. Tell them I love them and that their father and I will be for them soon." Kitchie began to sprout tears.

"I will. I sure—" The phone went dead. "Will." She cleared the line and dialed 4-1-1.

§ § §

Mr. Reynolds did his walk-through in the girls' room and was on his way to the boys' sleeping area when he was drawn to the light sneaking under the bathroom door. He started toward the light.

Junior jumped from the roof to a tree branch and climbed to the ground.

Mr. Reynolds grabbed the doorknob—

"Mr. Reynolds." A part-time employee approached. "You have a Mrs. Sanders, Suzette Sanders, on line two. She says it's urgent."

He released the knob. "I'll take it down the hall."

Secret lowered herself to the ground, looked up at the street light, and remembered how her mother felt about their being outside when the lights were on.

§ § §

"Yes, they're fine children. Under the circumstances, I'm honored to have Secret and Junior here. They're well-mannered and polite." Mr. Reynolds clamped the cordless phone to his ear as he headed for the children.

"Are they adjusting well?" Suzette was taking notes.

"Yes, yes, they are. There is no need to worry yourself. In fact, I spoke with them no more than ten minutes ago. Secret is such the big sister, she was escorting Junior to the restroom. He's a little bothered by the dark."

"Yes, I know. So you wouldn't mind if I spoke with them for a minute?"

"Not at all, since they're awake." He opened the boys' room and took note that Junior's bunk was empty. "Hold on, Mrs. Sanders. They're still in the restroom." He went to the bathroom and opened the door.

§ § §

The inner city's nocturnal life was operating at full throttle. Lurking in every dark alley, abandoned house, and ungodly corner was much more than Secret and Junior were ready for.

"Secret, are you sure you're going the right way?"

"Hope so." She watched a squad car roll to a stop sixty yards ahead of them. "If we don't get off this street, we're gonna get in trouble."

"We're lost, aren't we?"

"We were lost when we left."

The squad car made a left turn and was now moving in their direction at a snail's pace. Its driver scanned the drug-infested area for misconduct.

Secret tugged on Junior's hand and led him up a driveway. "We can't let the cops catch us." She was moving faster now.

"Cops are supposed to help us."

"Taking us back to that place isn't helping." She opened the door to a Lincoln Mark LT parked in the driveway, and she and Junior climbed into the back seat. "Daddy said when you must win, everyone is a contender."

"I didn't know what he meant when he said it, and I still don't know now that you said it."

"Everybody is our enemy right now; especially the police."

"Oh."

The officer brought the car to a halt. He flashed his searchlight at the driveway and the Mark LT. After seeing nothing out of the ordinary, he continued his patrol of the area.

When the bright light vanished, Secret was relieved.

"We better keep moving. Euclid has to be close."

The driver's door was opened.

Mayor Brandon Chambers climbed in, then reached over and pushed the front passenger door open.

Secret put a hand across Junior's mouth.

A woman settled inside.

Secret could smell her Escada perfume—Kitchie's preferred fragrance.

The mayor backed out of the drive.

"Let me have a blast now." The woman unwrapped a crack pipe from a wad of toilet paper.

"Dammit, Shea, you know the routine. Do we have to go through the same shit all the time? You suck my dick, you get a hit. I fuck, you get a hit."

Junior's eyes widened.

Secret scowled at him and put a finger to her lips.

Shea shoved a piece of coat hanger in the end of the pipe. "I need a little something to wake me up and put me in the mood."

"You take care of your business first, then we can get high together. You did this to yourself. I give you a hit now and I can forget about my blow job and some of that champion pussy."

"Brandon, baby, don't be like that." She scooted over, unzipped his pants, pulled his penis out, and stroked it. "Betcha your wife can't make you feel like this." She buried her head in his lap and flicked her tongue against him.

Mayor Brandon took his wedding band off and dropped it in his breast pocket. "I can't fool around all night. I have a meeting in the morning with the city council." He caressed the back of her head.

Junior felt the car pick up speed as highway signs began to blow by. He wished that they had stayed at Mr. Reynolds's.

Shea kept her head dunked in the mayor's lap until she felt him tense.

"Why did you stop?" He put on the right turn signal. "Keep sucking. I was almost there."

"Give me a blast." She took out a lighter.

He exited the highway on East 72nd and parked at the Cleveland Municipal Boat Dock. "Take your clothes off." He pulled his pants down to his ankles. "'Cause if I take a hit of this good shit first, I ain't gonna want no pussy."

She slipped her hand beneath the miniskirt, eased the thong off, and tossed it in the back.

Secret's nostrils flared when the underwear got snagged on her ponytail.

"Let me see them titties." The mayor put a piece of crack on her pipe.

Junior smiled as he imagined a pair of breasts.

Shea ignited the lighter. The mayor grabbed her hand. "Stop fucking around. Get naked. You know how I like it."

The skirt. The blouse. The bra. Everything found itself on the back seat. She stuck the flame to the pipe and sucked until the crack vanished.

Secret and Junior could hear something sizzle as a dim glow lit the interior.

Shea handed the mayor the pipe. She held the smoke and covered his penis with her mouth again. She filled his lap with smoke as the cocaine escaped her nose.

While she swallowed his stiff organ, he balanced a rock on the pipe and smoked it.

"Give me some." She pushed and pulled his organ with a gentle touch.

He put his lips on hers and blew the smoke into her mouth.

Shea choked. "This some good shit, Brandon."

"Tell me how good it is with your mouth. Kiss my dick." He

pushed a finger into the folds of her drenched vagina, then rubbed the moist finger on the glass pipe to cool it.

The mayor took another hit while Shea took him.

The car became filled with smoke.

Secret pinched her nose closed. Junior followed suit. This was the first time Secret wasn't angry with him for being a copycat.

"Let me hit this champion pussy while you hit this." He pulled her from his lap and gave her the pipe with a rock stuffed in it.

Shea smiled. She sat back and tried to recline the seat. Secret was too big to dodge the back seat in such a tight area. The seat began to smash her.

"Achoo! Achoo!" Junior couldn't hold it any longer. The cocaine smoke was too much.

"The hell? What's going on?" The mayor looked at Shea; they looked over the seat and saw the frightened faces of Secret and Junior. The mayor damn near brush-burned his ass, pulling his pants up so fast.

Shea didn't bother. She felt around for the lighter.

"Who are...What the hell are you doing in my car?" The mayor turned the interior light on.

Shea put the flame to the pipe.

The force behind the slap was somewhere between brutal and extreme. "What the fuck are you doing, stupid motherfucker?" The pipe shattered against the dashboard. He reached between Junior and Secret, plucked Shea's clothes from the seat, and shoved them at her. "Put your shit on, you dizzy bitch. As a matter of fucking fact, get out! You see these children."

"Brandon, I'm sorry, baby. You know how it is."

"Walk it off." He reached over, opened the door, then threw her clothes to the asphalt. "You'll be good and sober by the time you get where you're going. Out."

Shea picked up what she could salvage of the pipe and climbed out.

The mayor locked the door behind her.

He took out his cell phone. "What's your parents' number?" He looked at them through the rearview.

Nothing.

He turned around. "I'm not going to hurt you. You don't know who I am? No, you don't." He glanced at the heavens. "Thank you, God. What are you guys doing in my car?"

"My mom and dad ain't..." Secret felt bad for Shea, who was now standing beside the car in a thong. "We're lost. I'll give you ten dollars to take us home."

Junior didn't have to imagine much anymore as he stared out the window.

"I'll take you home." He started the car. "How about we call your parents? They must be worried." He checked his watch. Eleven-fourteen p.m. "They probably have the police out looking for you."

Police. Crack. Missing Children. The Mayor of Cleveland. He shifted a worried look between Junior and Secret. "Where's home?" He pulled next to Shea and rolled the window down.

Junior fiddled with his identification bracelet. "We live—"

Secret clamped a hand over his mouth. "You better not."

The mayor understood that Secret was hiding something. He figured his sure bet was to drop them off somewhere and never look back.

Shea looked into the car. "Brandon, why are you doing me like this?"

He thought about the police again. "Here." He handed her the bulk of his cocaine and drove away.

As the power window rose, he could hear Shea's voice fading. "Brandon, stop. I need the lighter..."

The mayor pulled the seat belt over his shoulder. "Okay, buckle up." He held Secret's gaze through the rearview. "Little lady, tell me where it is I'm going."

"Uh...take us to Indian Hills Apartment. You know where that is?"

"In the city of Euclid." He put on his turn signal.

Junior's seat belt made a dull sound when it locked in place. "Why not home, Secret?"

"I'm with him." The mayor drove up a highway ramp. "I'd rather take you home and make sure you're safe."

"I'll make sure we're safe. Indian Hills is fine." Secret heard GP's warning, *Everyone is a contender*, in her head. "We don't know you well enough to show you where we live."

CHAPTER 7

Suzette Sanders paced the Justice Center lobby, biting what was left of her nails.

A corrections officer emerged from an elevator and began to call visitors. His enthusiasm was zapped. He read from a list of names as if he'd much rather be parked in front of his wide screen with a cold beer. Halfway down the list, he called for Suzette Sanders.

She rubbed a hand over her brunette French twist, then went to the elevator where the other concerned and loved ones were gathered.

§ § §

She drummed her fingers against the table. This place was more relaxed than what the media had led her to believe. Prisoners filed in wearing orange outfits. They dispersed throughout the visiting room. Most hugged; some shared an intimate kiss; others shook hands with their visitors.

Kitchie spotted Suzette and smiled. They shook hands. "You don't know how much I appreciate you coming here." She felt Suzette's hand trembling in hers. "How are my babies? Did they seem...sad?"

Suzette lowered her gaze. A tear splashed onto the table.

"Is there something wrong?" Kitchie sank in the seat to get a visual on Suzette's face.

"They're missing." Her voice was lower than the hum of the collective chatter.

"Excuse me."

Suzette straightened her posture. She found strength with a deep breath. "Your children have been missing since last night. I'm sorry, Kitchie."

Kitchie felt dizzy. The visiting room spun as if it were a merry-go-round. "Ay Dios mio crucificado…porque?"

§ § §

GP approached a compact man who looked as if he had swallowed steroids for breakfast and had drunk dumbbells for dinner. "Are you gonna use that?" GP nodded toward the phone the man was propped against. The man made him think of Mighty Mouse.

"Waiting for a call; just paged somebody." He settled his massive back on the receiver and stared at a group of undesirables shooting dice for commissary.

"Man…why the hell you trying to play me? You can't beep nobody from these phones." GP was a smoldering bomb on the verge of detonation. "I'm not new to this. If you not about to use the phone, I am." He wrapped a hand around an ink pen in his pocket.

Mighty Mouse shoved GP, forcing him back several feet. "You calling me a liar, motherfucker? Huh, motherfucker, is that what you called me?"

"I didn't call you nothing." GP reclaimed the spot he had been pushed from. "I asked to use the phone." Before his eyes, he witnessed the man's muscles expand. He snatched the ink pen from his pocket, praying that this display of matched aggression would end the bullshit and gain him respect from everyone watching.

Mighty Mouse laughed. "Now you're gonna have to use that." He pulled off his T-shirt, wrapped an end around each hand, and stretched it as if it were a shield. "Come on, motherfucker, let's work. You better hope you know what you doing." He crouched some and called out for someone to watch for the police.

GP cursed himself over and over. Now he had to explore territory that he really wanted no parts of.

"Yo, Tiny, hold up, homie. Let me holler at you." A tall guy with a patch covering his eye stepped forward, followed by four other hustlers from the Cliffview area.

"In a minute." Tiny pulled the T-shirt tighter. "I got me one; it'll only take a minute."

Patch Eye ignored him and whispered in his ear.

Tiny shifted his focus from GP, stood straight, and looked at Patch Eye. "Jewels? Gangster-ass Jewels?"

Patch Eye nodded.

"I was about to catch a body in this bitch. Why ain't nobody been said something?" His attention returned to GP. "I have a lot of respect for Jewels. Use my phone anytime. If somebody call for me, tell 'em to hit me back." Tiny strolled away with Patch Eye and the fellows.

GP was relieved to put the ink pen back in his pocket. He stared at the phone for a moment, then exhaled. He picked up the receiver and punched in a number.

$$\$ \ \$ \ \$$

Killer grinned as he stuffed a skimpy nurse outfit and fishnet stockings into a bag. "Where's the costume party? Undecided on what to wear? Second time you've been in here this week."

The customer smiled but she did not respond.

The phone rang.

She studied the short man, absorbing his details from head to toe. She smiled. "Your accent shifts my tide. I love it. Can't place it, though."

"Rough Buff."

"And that is?"

"Buffalo." He leaned on the glass countertop. "Can I get an invite to the party? I would love to surf your tide."

"I'm afraid you can't surf the Marian Trench. You have to dive in the deepest spot known to man to appreciate it."

They laughed.

"Invite me to the party. I'll bring my wet suit."

"Sorry." She licked her lips. The cherry lipstick remained. "Don't do parties. I'm into role-playing."

The phone refused to stop ringing.

He glanced at the phone, then back at the gorgeous woman. "Can I get a role in your play?"

She leaned across the countertop and traced the contour of his lips with a finger. "You're short but cute. Any good at acting?"

"Didn't you see my cameo in *How to Be a Player*?"

The look she gave him was intense. She smiled. "There's a part I'd like to see you star in when the time comes. I know where to find you." She touched his lips once more, grabbed her bag, and sashayed to the door. Before she went out into the busy street, she paused. "Answer your phone."

He danced his way to the phone. "Killer Cal's Costumes and Accessories, Killer speaking?"

"You have a collect call from a correctional—"

He pressed five, assuming that it was one of his partners, Tutu or Fruit. "What's good, son?"

"Killer, this GP. What up?"

"That was wild as shit. Man, you and Kitchie was bugging. I can't believe y'all touched that kid like that in public. Think it's a game, if you want. They still breaking black folks off crazy for mishandling whites. What's the deal with that?"

"It's a long story. I need a loan. Bail me out. No, I need you to bail Kitchie out."

"GP, I don't know about that. Every time I loan you something you get selective amnesia and act like you don't owe me. You still owe me eight hundred from last year."

"I thought I paid that back."

"I bet you did. That's what I'm talking about. You haven't given me one dime on that tab. How much is Kitchie's bond?"

"Sixty thousand, ten percent."

"Oh, hell no! You my mans, but that's too rich for Killer Cal's blood. I ain't gonna be able to do it."

"Come on, Killer. Is it that you can't do it or won't do it?"

"Both. Six thousand is a lot of money for you to forget about. And if you did choose to remember, you don't have the means to pay me back."

"I need this loan. Remember that group home I told you about? The one I grew up in?"

"How could I not?"

"My kids are there; gotta get them out."

Killer sighed. That statement was painful to his ears. "For Secret and Junior, if I had it, I'd give it to you. The problem is I just don't. I'm in the red. You of all people know how it is."

"I understand." GP tugged on his goatee. "Yo, Killer, go outside and tell Smitty to come to the phone."

"Just saw him no more than fifteen minutes ago. He went over to Terminal Tower for some burgers. He left his mannish-ass daughter to run the booth, and I'm keeping an eye on her. Call back in a little while; I'll make sure he's around." Killer glanced at the digital clock on his cash register. "Some white kid came looking for you this morning."

"White boy?" GP put a finger in his ear to block out the surrounding noise.

"Yeah, some older kid dressed in a mean suit. He called himself Mr. Lee. Said he had something important to talk to you about. I didn't tell him your business. I did say you might be gone a few days, though."

"All right. Good looking out. I'll hit you back later."

"Stay up." Killer stared at GP's empty booth through the costume shop's showcase window.

§ § §

"They're coming." Secret stuck her tongue out.

"Are not!"

"Are too, punk."

"Not, sissy." Junior plopped down on Secret's bed, slipped on a sneaker, and began to tie it.

"Mom and Dad know we need them, so they *are* coming home soon." She froze when a noise came from the first floor. "Did you hear something?"

"No, retarded. You didn't either." He stuck a foot in his sock and heard something himself. He jumped up and dropped the opposite sneaker. "They're home!"

"Told you. When are you gonna listen to me?" Secret was ecstatic that their dilemma was over. She followed Junior into the hall. They hadn't quite made it halfway down the stairs when a sheriff appeared at the bottom of the flight.

§ § §

Sheriff Colin Edmund parked in front of 2197 Miami Street.

He lugged a toolbox from the Oldsmobile's trunk, then followed the driveway to the property's back door. From the exterior's appearance of the property, he was sure the Pattersons would miss the Upper Valley home. He secured a *Foreclosed* and a *No Trespassing* sign to the door with a cordless screwdriver. Then, he fastened a folding hinge to the doorframe and rested a Master Lock on the hinge. Before he could bolt the rear entrance, he was required to make sure that there were no people or animals inside the property.

He gathered his tools, went to the front entrance, and repeated the process—only this time, he opened the door and went inside. *Good thing they moved some of their belongings.* He crossed the empty living room and began to lock every window on the first floor. He studied the Pattersons' family portrait mounted above the fireplace and wondered why bad things seemed to happen to good people. He backed away from the attractive photo and banged against an end table, causing it to open, sending his toolbox crashing to the floor. "This isn't going to be a good day."

He began tossing the tools back into the metal box, resonating a clatter throughout the residence. He fastened the lid, double checked it, then headed for the stairs. He gripped the banister, looked toward his destination, and flinched. "You kids startled me, liked to gave me a freaking heart attack. Is there anyone else in the house?" He put a boot on the next step.

"We're not going back." Secret tugged Junior by a shoulder and backed up the stairs.

He took another step. "I have to remove you from the property. You have to go somewhere."

Secret's foot hit the landing.

"Don't make us go." Junior shook his head.

"I have to." A third step.

Secret yanked Junior and they dashed to their room. She locked the door with a sliding lock. "I knew they would come for us, but damn."

The sheriff climbed the remaining stairs. "Not a good day at all." He faced a door with a sign on it that read: *Leave Me Alone. I'm Concentrating.* He pounded on the door with the side of a closed fist. "Come out of there. Don't make this harder than what it is."

Junior and Secret eased away from the vibrating door.

Junior stared with fright. His young heart thumped each time the Sheriff hit the door. "He's going to break it open."

The doorknob spun in both directions.

"I don't have all day to fool with you kids. Come out of there now! Or I'm coming in."

"Help me." Secret struggled to push the huge dresser toward the door.

Junior joined her efforts.

"I can't go back, Junior." She began to cry.

More door banging.

"We don't have to go back."

Secret sat on her butt, leaning against the dresser. "We're stuck in here. You even said it yourself; that policeman is going to get in." She could feel the heavy door pounding in her back through the vibration of the dresser.

"You promised me that we wouldn't go back, so we're not." He opened the window and lifted the screen. "It's not high as you think. Don't be a sissy." He poked his head out and looked down to Mr. Irvington's driveway. It really was high. "You can do this, Secret; we practiced this fire drill route with Mom and Dad enough."

"But I'm the only one who'll get trapped in a fire if I'm upstairs." She gazed through the open window in horror. "It's too high."

The sheriff aimed a shoulder at the door and rammed it. The wood splintered.

The force was too much for Secret's small back to absorb. She detached herself from the dresser.

"You're not getting trapped today." Junior pulled a wooden case from under the bed.

Sheriff Colin rubbed his aching shoulder. *I'm too old for this freaking bullshit.* He positioned himself to ram the door again.

Junior secured the fire ladder on the windowsill like GP had taught him, then tossed the ropy rungs through the window.

A portion of the sliding lock fell to the floor. Secret's knick-knacks rolled from the dresser top.

"Come the hell out of there!"

Junior started down the swaying ladder. "Come on, Secret. Don't get caught and leave me by myself."

The dresser began to move as Sheriff Colin pushed.

Secret took a deep breath and backed out of the window, searching blindly to gain footing on the ladder.

"See, it's easy." Junior lowered himself. "Don't look down."

She looked to where she had just come from and screamed when Sheriff Colin stuck his head through the window.

§ § §

Smitty hated to say no. His character flaw was that he'd been generously irresponsible for years. He shook his head with the phone receiver on his ear. "Bad as I want to say yes, GP, I just can't. Right now I don't have that type of money. Times have been real hard for me. Ends are not meeting. I need to be asking you for the money you owe me."

Killer tapped Smitty when the gorgeous lady strutted through the door wearing a pea coat that showed nothing but a set of long legs in a pair of fishnet stockings.

"Thanks anyway, Smitty." GP hung up.

The Ebony Lady stood in front of the counter and let her pea coat fall to the floor. The nurse outfit hugged her spectacular body like taut skin. A stethoscope swung from her neck. "I was told that there was a sick little boy here who's in dire need of medical attention."

Killer grabbed Smitty's hand and placed it on his own forehead. "See, Smitty, I told you I had a fever, but you wouldn't listen." He led Smitty to the door.

"Hey, what's the rush? I—"

"I got the flu. A nasty one. Trust me; you don't want to catch it." Killer locked the door and turned to his nurse. "It hurts all over."

§ § §

Suzette scanned house addresses as she spoke into her cell phone. "Todd, what more do you want me to say? I apologize. It slipped my mind. Let's reschedule; I'm really doing something important."

"And trying to save our marriage isn't important?"

"Don't do that to me. It's not fair." She was getting closer. "I told you that I'm helping someone out."

"Jesus fucking Christ, Suzette! That's always the case with you. Your priorities are totally screwed up. What's important is home; not every Tom, Dick, and Harry. You can't save the Goddamn world."

"Give me an hour, Todd. One hour and I'll be there."

"So help me God, Suzette, if you don't come now, forget about the marriage. I'll have my lawyer fax you the divorce papers."

Suzette sighed at the same time as she found Kitchie's address.

"Must you be stubborn...all..." She saw two children coming down a flimsy ladder. "I'll call you back."

"Don't bother. Let the record show that I tried. You just became a waste of my time. Have a ball saving the world." He hung up.

Secret screamed.

Suzette saw the older white man in the window above the children. She jerked the Ford in Park and rushed across the yard.

Junior's feet hit the ground. He helped his trembling sister off of the ladder.

"Secret, Junior," a frail white woman called out as she ran toward them.

They cut through the tall bushes in their backyard, running as fast as possible.

Sheriff Colin watched from above. "Crazy bunch of kids." He unhooked the ladder. It fell to the ground. He locked the window after it.

$$\text{S S S}$$

Hector came out of Mr. Doughnuts sipping an espresso.

Detective Thomas leaned against a mailbox. "Hector Gonzales." He flashed a badge. "Mind if I have a few words with you?"

Hector grunted and turned in the other direction.

Detective Crutchfield stepped out of a phone booth and produced a badge. "Maybe you're more comfortable with talking to me."

Hector stopped in his tracks. *Crutchfield*.

Detective Thomas guided Hector to the phone booth, kicked his feet apart, and frisked him. Thomas took a bag of dope from his own pocket and held it up to Hector's face. "You know better than this. You could have at least tried to hide the shit."

Crutchfield stepped closer. "Looks like you're on your way back to the joint with a new case and a parole violation."

"What the hell you want from me?" He eyed Crutchfield, then Thomas.

"Now that's what you call a freedom question." Crutchfield grabbed Hector by an arm. "Let's go downtown and talk about it."

§ § §

"Where's your other shoe?" Secret huffed and puffed.

Junior paused. "In the house. We gotta keep going. They have people looking for us like we broke out of prison." He led the way through the woods.

"We did. Are you sure this is the way?"

"Me, Rasheed, Rashaad, and them come in these woods all the time to find salamanders. The street is straight ahead." His once-white sock was beyond cleaning.

"We have to get something to put on your feet." She dodged a tree branch.

"Buy me some shoes at the shopping center."

"Can't."

"Why?"

"I left the money in my other pants. I should've put it in my sock again."

Junior stopped. "So what am I supposed to do? We haven't even ate."

"Don't look at me like that. We'll figure something out." Secret could see the traffic on Green Road through the trees a few feet ahead.

"Told you this was the way." Junior walked with a limp.

"Bet Mom and Dad don't know you and the twins be in the woods this far. They told you not—"

"Only way they'll know is if you tell them—if we ever see them again."

"Get that out of your fat head; we'll all be together soon."

"You hope." He paused and leaned against a tree. "My foot hurt."

They left the woods behind them and started their journey to the bottom of Green Road.

"Aunt Jewels will get you something to put on your feet when we get there. It's not that far from here. Will you be all right until then?"

"Do I have a choice?" Junior detoured around some broken glass on the sidewalk. He stopped when he saw more ahead. "Gimme a piggyback ride."

Secret drew in a breath and squatted. "I swear, you're lucky."

Junior poked his tongue out at the back of her head while climbing on. "Secret."

"Huh?"

"I don't really think you're a sissy. What if Aunty ain't there?"

"Then we'll wait until she comes."

A Ford slowed to a snail's pace beside them. Suzette lowered the power window while keeping an eye on the winding road. She shouted through the front passenger window. "Listen to me, Secret, your—"

"Why don't you leave us alone?" She started taking backward steps. "You're not taking us back."

A city bus was almost kissing Suzette's bumper. Its husky horn was blown. Secret and Junior ran for the safety of the woods.

"How long has he been in there?" The captain observed Hector in the interrogation room from a two-way window.

Crutchfield kicked his feet up on a desk. "About eleven hours now."

"Then question him or turn him loose." The captain sipped a cup of coffee laced with vodka.

Thomas pushed Crutchfield's feet off the desk, then sat on the cleared area. "Crutchfield likes to make their imaginations drive 'em crazy, Captain." He pointed to Hector, who seemed to be taking it well.

The captain raised a brow. "How much longer do you plan on leaving him in there?"

"Patience is truly a virtue." Crutchfield smiled. "He'll be good and ready to talk by morning."

The Captain sighed, then left to refill his drink.

§ § §

Darkness threatened to consume the sky. Junior and Secret sat back to back on a large oak stump.

Junior rubbed his sore foot. "Do you think Daddy talks to Mommy the way that Brandon guy talked to Shea? You know, when they..."

"They what?"

"When they get ready to do the oochie coochie."

Secret shrugged. "After hearing them, I don't ever want to do it to nobody. That's nasty. No boy can ever talk to me like that."

"So, am I supposed to say to a girl: Suck my you know what, and let me hit that p-u-s-s-y?"

She shrugged again.

"I'm hungry." He scooted next to Secret. "And I'd rather go back to Mr. Reynolds's than stay in these woods at night."

"It is getting dark. I'm hungry, too, and I have to pee."

"The tree is free."

"Imagine that."

"Then pee on yourself. Let's eat at Pizza Hut at the bottom of the hill." He lifted Secret's pant leg.

"What are you doing?"

"Let me have your socks."

"We can't eat pizza. I told you that I left the money at home." She kicked her shoes off.

"We don't need any. I saw this movie where these high school kids ordered a bunch of food, ate it, then one by one they pretended to go to the bathroom and snuck out. We can do it, too. I'm hungry for real."

"That's stealing." She slipped her shoes back on.

"Daddy does it when he has to." He put both of Secret's flowered socks on one foot. "Let's go eat. That lady ain't looking for us no more. Well, for a little while anyway."

§ § §

"You little bastards!" The Pizza Hut manager waved a fist in the air as Secret and Junior ran down the avenue with full bellies.

CHAPTER 8

Thursday morning, Jewels exited a Greyhound bus and stretched her limbs. She took the pillow from beneath Ndia's arm and gave her a handful of change. "Call us a cab while I get the luggage."

"I'll check out front first. There might be one already available."

"Handle it, then, baby." Jewels smacked Ndia's globular ass.

She giggled and sashayed away.

Jewels stuffed the pillow in a nearby trash receptacle, then claimed their luggage inside the terminal.

"Jewels!" Ndia called out from the terminal's entrance. "There's a cab here."

Within minutes they loaded the taxi's trunk space with stolen merchandise. Then, they snuggled in the back seat and enjoyed the scenic route home.

Ndia picked a piece of imaginary lint from Jewels' sweatshirt. "I can't wait to take me a long, hot bath. You wanna soak with me?"

"I need a rain check. There's a few things I have to take care of before my call comes through." She thought for a split second. "Which reminds me: I misplaced my damn cell phone."

§ § §

Crutchfield kicked the chair over that Hector was shackled to. "Tell me where the body is. Cut the games; I don't want no shit outta you."

"I'm starting to feel like a broken record. I don't know what the hell you're talking about." Hector peered at Crutchfield and Thomas from the floor.

"Too bad you don't." Thomas squatted beside him.

"Fuck him." Crutchfield undid the button at his shirt collar. "I'm tired of tongue-wrestling with this burrito-eating spic." He turned to Thomas. "Charge him with the dope; send his ass back to Lucasville. Save me the trouble of finding this crud ball when I have enough evidence to charge him with murder." He went for the door.

"I asked you not to piss on his Cheerios, Hector. It'll take him a week to find a good mood. Now I can't help you." Thomas sat Hector upright. "There's nobody to blame but yourself. I don't understand your loyalty. It intrigues me. You're going to prison to share a cell with another man, basking in each other's anus gas. In the meantime, Squeeze will be laid up in his penthouse every night with a soft woman, and he'll spend his days driving around town in one of his fancy cars, courtesy of the chop shop. We know about that, too."

Hector lowered his head.

"Tell me something that'll make Crutchfield smile again. You don't have to take this hit; it's Squeeze we're hard up for."

"A piece of chewing gum and leniency. Yeah, I'll bargain for that." Hector stared at his soft-bottom Kenneth Coles.

Thomas waved at the two-way mirror.

Crutchfield entered the gloomy room. "Why are you still wasting your time with this mutt? Book his ass and throw him in the holding tank."

Thomas whispered into Crutchfield's ear.

Crutchfield looked at Hector, left the room, and returned a minute later with a pack of Juicy Fruit.

Hector stuck two pieces of gum in his mouth and let the wrappers fall to the floor. "I didn't have anything to do with it. You gotta believe me. When I got there, he was already dead. I swear…"

§ § §

"Too Tall, I know that ain't for me and you." Jewels took the last bag from the trunk. "Come help us carry these bags up to my place, while you sitting out here looking silly."

Too Tall dragged his feet as he left the bench.

"Punk, quit tripping…I'm gonna break you off something."

He moved much faster now, collecting the luggage from the pavement, and he relieved Ndia's load by one bag.

"Thank you." Ndia slung her wide hips as she strutted toward the building.

The trio climbed the last step and rounded the corner.

Jewels hesitated. Fear and confusion were having a good time playing tug-of-war with her. There was no logical reason for the bone-chilling sight before her. She dropped the luggage and ran in the direction of her apartment.

§ § §

Crutchfield was aggravated as he watched Hector take his time preparing to put the gum in his mouth. Crutchfield's patience was shop-worn. To him, it seemed like it took two lousy gum wrappers four hours to hit the floor from the time Hector had discarded them.

"I didn't have anything to do with it." Hector looked at his reflection in the two-way glass. "You gotta believe me. When I got there he was already dead. I swear. All I did was throw a few shovels of dirt on him."

Crutchfield smiled. "Where's Jap buried?"

"I don't know." Hector blew a bubble until it popped. "I'll take you to the body I buried."

"That wasn't so hard." Thomas patted Hector's shoulder, showing approval. "I can go for a ride."

"Uncuff him." Crutchfield was about to score one for the good guys.

Thomas let the shackles fall to the floor and shoved the cuffs in a carrier fixed to his waist. "Let's go see this body."

Hector only moved the muscles it took to chew his gum.

"Before I change my mind." Crutchfield gave him a look of contempt.

"I already changed my mind." Hector shifted his eyes between the two. "Somebody needs to make me trust again...or forget about it."

Crutchfield sat across from him. "What is it you want?"

"For starters, I don't recall having a dope case. Do either of you?"

Thomas took some papers from his pocket. He showed Hector his name on the police report. "No one ever knew about this but us and God." He used his cigarette lighter to set the report afire. Once the flame grew, he dropped the inferno inside a wastebasket.

"You're smoking cigarettes again?" Crutchfield shook his head.

"Off and on. It's your fault that I started back."

They all watched the flame die out.

Crutchfield ran a hand over his beard stubble. "What now, Hector?"

He stood up. "I'll think of the rest in the car."

§ § §

Secret and Junior were lying on Jewels's welcome mat, cuddled in a human knot, asleep.

Jewels's eyes threatened to water when she saw Junior's bare foot. She bent down and shook the knot. "Secret, Junior, wake up."

Junior lifted his eye lids. "Aunty." He jumped up and wrapped his arms around her. "What took you so long?"

Secret yawned, still drugged with sleep. "Where you been? This floor is hard."

"One question at a time."

Ndia reached out to Secret. "How long have y'all been in this trifling hall like this?"

"Since yesterday." Secret got her balance.

"Where the fuck are GP and your mother?" Jewels felt her anger mounting.

"In jail." Junior scratched his head.

Too Tall cleared his throat. "Let me get mine so I can go."

"Motherfucker, don't you see I'm having a family problem here? I said, I got you. Sit my shit down and come back later after I get my people in order."

He set the bags down and left. *I'll fix you.* He stopped on the first floor and knocked on Apartment 114.

"What?" came from the other side of the metal door.

"Let me in. It's Too Tall."

The frail woman eased off the threadbare sofa and opened the door. "You got a little something to give me a kick-start, TT?"

"I will after you let me use the phone."

She stepped aside.

TT maneuvered through the dim apartment to the phone. "Sometimes I think you're a vampire."

"You're gonna find out for sure if you try and play me."

"Chill, Meka. I'm on the level." He removed a piece of paper from his pocket and dialed the number written on it.

The phone rang.

Meka stared at him.

"Hello?" Trouble turned over and realized that the room he was in was unfamiliar. To add to his confusion, the snoring woman beside him was a complete stranger. "I got to stop drinking."

"That's what we all say," TT echoed in his ear.

"Who this?" Trouble took a peek beneath the covers. *Damn, that Hennessy sure can pick a woman.*

"It's Too Tall."

"Yeah, what's good?"

"Jewels is back."

Six figures and corporate numbers popped into Trouble's mind. "Where is she now?"

"At home; helped carry her bags myself."

"Good. Good." Trouble swung his feet to the floor and noticed a used condom.

"You still gonna look out for me?"

"Yeah. Meet me in front of the convenience store in ten minutes. Wait a minute." He shook the woman. "Get up, hoe. Where am I?"

"Seventy-ninth and Saint Clair." She reeked of alcohol. "Don't be calling me out my name."

Trouble's stomach churned when he saw her rotten teeth. He hoped that the Hennessy hadn't convinced him to kiss Yuck Mouth. "Make that twenty minutes."

"You still owe me for yesterday's watch." TT grinned at Meka.

"I'll take care of it in twenty." He hung up.

TT headed for the door.

"Where you think you going?" Meka put hands on what was left of her once-bodacious hips.

"Meet a friend of mine so I can get something to kick-start us both."

"I'm not letting you out my sight. You ain't to be trusted." Meka stepped into her shoes and pulled her wild hair into a makeshift ponytail. "Let's go."

§ § §

Kitchie felt as if her breakfast was protesting in her stomach. "Thank you for everything, Suzette. I'll call you back this evening."

"I tried...I really tried, but they kept running from me." Suzette paced her den floor while holding her toddler on a hip. "I'll keep looking. We'll find them."

"I know." Kitchie hung up and hoped that the shower would relieve some tension.

From the other side of the day room, Logan watched Kitchie go to the shower stalls. Logan whispered in the ear of the woman sitting to her left. The woman excused herself from the card table and went into a cell.

The water felt marvelous crashing into Kitchie's curvy body. But it had no positive effect on her mood. Suzette had left her with unanswered questions that promised to drive a loving mother insane. Where are the children? Where'd they sleep last night? Are they hurt? Are they hungry? Are they safe? Her wet, silky hair stretched to the center of her back. The water camouflaged her tears.

"Mind if I share the mist with you?" Trish closed the space between Kitchie and herself. Their naked bodies touched.

§ § §

Thomas unearthed the first shovel of dirt. "I can't believe you'd bury a body in a public park. Anybody can stumble across it."

"Had to put it somewhere." Hector admired the ambience of the park as he wiggled his wrists inside the cuffs, searching for comfort.

"It's gonna be a hot one." Crutchfield wiped his moist forehead.

More dirt.

"For a bunch of white cops, you guys aren't that bad."

"You lived up to your end of the deal; you have my word that I'll honor mine." Crutchfield watched the dirt pile grow.

"Thank you, Crutchfield. He was already dead when I got there."

"Don't worry about it. Your cooperation, statement, and testimony will work in your favor."

The shovel's tip struck a flat object. "Got something." Thomas' shirt was spotted with perspiration. He dropped to his knees and pushed the dirt away from the object with his hands.

Crutchfield gave Hector a pat on the back. "Good job." He moved in closer to see what Thomas's labor would reveal.

Hector spat out the chewing gum and replaced it.

Thomas pushed the remaining earth away from a shoe box that had *Nike* printed across the top. He looked at Crutchfield, then they looked at Hector.

"That's how I found him."

Thomas pulled the box from beneath the earth and set it on level ground.

Hector closed his eyes when Thomas glanced at him.

Crutchfield prepared himself to see what was inside. "Open it."

Hector turned away. He couldn't stand to see the remains again.

§ § §

Kitchie threw her arms across her breasts and backed out of the water. "Trish, you dumb bitch. I told you I'm not on that homo shit. Bitch, you're gonna force me to step in your ass. Now get the fuck from around me."

Trish's eyes locked onto a butterfly that was tattooed right above Kitchie's vagina. "That's pretty." She squinted and turned her head sideways to read the calligraphy below it. *Greg.* "That's sweet. Think he'd mind if—"

"Back the fuck off." Logan tossed Kitchie a towel. "It ain't hard to tell she doesn't want to be bothered with your shit."

Kitchie covered herself with the towel and folded her arms beneath her breasts. "Thank you." She removed wet hair from her face and noticed two of Logan's buddies guarding the entrance.

Trish stood her ground. "One way or the other, you're gonna stay out of my business. This dorm is too small for the both of us."

"Then claim your title or holler at the guard so you can conduct your business elsewhere. I'm here to stay, and as long as I'm here, I'm the producer of this video." Logan turned to Kitchie. "Go on and get your shower. I'm holding you down now. Trish is leaving…ain't she?"

"No, no, I'm okay." Kitchie adjusted her towel as Trish brushed by.

Trish found her payment on her pillow. She cuffed the heroin, then went to a stash for her syringe.

Logan walked Kitchie to her cell. "You have to pay more attention to your surroundings. You don't have the slightest clue of what's really going on around here, do you?"

"I'm not into this jail nonsense." Kitchie closed the door behind them. She could see Logan's two shadows loitering outside her cell.

"In here, everybody wants something. Everything is gonna cost you something, and no one does something for nothing." Logan sat on Kitchie's bunk.

Kitchie's skin crawled when the two shadows entered the small cell.

Logan laughed. "Right about now, you're asking yourself what do I want for helping you out of that tricky situation?" She glanced at her buddies. "For starters, I want my towel back."

A dark-complexioned woman towered over Kitchie, then snatched the towel away.

"Why?" Kitchie backed into a corner. "Why are you doing this?"

"Because you're sexy." Logan ran a hand over the bed as if she were removing the wrinkles. "We like sexy. And, as you now know, I didn't come to your rescue for nothing. Now come over here, lay down, and close your eyes so you can pay me back. It'll be fun for the both of us...all of us." She gestured toward her buddies.

"I'm not into women. Nothing against—"

"Get into it! Bring the bitch over here so I can break her in."

The bigger of the women started toward Kitchie.

The other woman held up a hand, stopping everyone's actions, and listened. "I hear keys." Now she was looking through a small window, out into the wing's main hallway. "The police is on the block."

"Who?" Logan stood, never taking her eyes off of Kitchie's trembling body.

"That fucked-up broad, Lieutenant Proctor."

The bigger woman was standing inches away from Kitchie. She could feel Kitchie's fright, the rapid movement of her breath. She licked her lips. "Logan, Proctor is on some real police time. She's gonna pop her head in every cell."

§ § §

Lieutenant Proctor was a sexually frustrated woman who found it exhilarating to use her authority to be a hard ass. It was her way of exacting revenge for being bullied in her buck-toothed, ugly-duckling days.

The prisoners fell silent when she entered the dorm.

"Those pants have been altered; make sure I have them in my hand before I leave."

"Come on, Lieutenant, I'm pregnant. I had to hook them up. I'm in my second trimester." She caressed her huge belly.

"I want them. Sign up for sick call; medical can see to it that you get some maternity pants." Her keys sounded off as she left the expectant mother. She pointed at two women. "Find a cell; this isn't a beauty salon."

"You need to find you something to do," someone called out. "Don't take it out on us 'cause your batteries died last night."

"Coward, say it to my face. Woman-up and make it known who I'm conversing with." Proctor's small shoulder-pack radio squawked. She switched to a private channel and received the message. She clipped the radio back on her shoulder. "Kitchie Patterson, pack it up. You made bail." She turned to a woman watching an episode of *Divorce Court.* "What cell does Patterson lock in?"

She pointed.

The woman watching the day room's happenings from the cell looked over a shoulder at Logan. "She's coming this way."

Logan nodded at the big woman who had Kitchie cornered. Big girl was swift and precise with her actions. She pinned Kitchie against the cell wall. As Logan came closer, Kitchie clamped her eyes shut.

Logan kissed Kitchie on the mouth. "This ain't over until I have you my way."

"She's coming, Logan."

The door swung open and the women were having a conversation as if things were fine and dandy. All with the exception of Kitchie who, for the first time in days, was thankful to be in the presence of the police.

Proctor was no fool. She eyed Logan with scorn while she addressed Kitchie. "Get dressed. You made bond."

§ § §

"Daddy!" Secret and Junior said in unison. They rushed him when the elevator opened.

GP wrapped his arms around them both. It was rejuvenating to know that his children were safe. "I missed y'all so much. I'll never let us get separated again. We're gonna have to send the lawyer a thank-you card for getting y'all out."

"Not exactly." Secret nestled her head against his stomach.

"What do you mean?" He put a finger under her chin to lift her head.

"You look like shit." Jewels gave him the once-over.

"I felt like it until now. Thanks for getting me out."

"Fool, you got me fucked up. Don't motherfucking thank me; tell me what the hell is going on. You got my niece and nephew out here living trifling. Some cracker beating on Secret; chattel slavery is over." Jewels pulled up Secret's sleeve, allowing the bruises to speak for themselves. "On top of that, they pulled a Harriet Tubman on Whitey and got exposed to some shit they ain't have no business around."

GP dropped to his knees and hugged Secret tightly, wishing he could transfer everything she had endured onto himself. "I'm sorry. I'm really sorry, baby." *That you are, Greg,* Mr. Reynolds confirmed in the privacy of GP's head.

"Let me see your tattoos, Daddy." Junior tugged on GP's Street Prophet shirt.

GP feigned a laugh to conceal his hurt. "You know I don't have tattoos."

"Lil' Eric's dad said people in jail get muscles and tattoos."

"Are you sure he's my brother?" Secret draped her arm over GP's shoulder. "He says a lot of stupid things."

"Shut up." Junior stuck his face in Secret's. "If I'm stupid, why are you the one failing math?"

Junior smiled. GP and Jewels looked at Secret.

She shrugged. "It's hard."

"We'll talk about this at home." GP pulled Jewels to the side but kept an eye on the children.

Jewels shook her head in disgust when they were out of earshot. "I'd like to know what home you're talking about?" She noticed a smudge on her pink Timberland boots. "Your crib is padlocked."

"We wasn't supposed to be out until tomorrow."

"Well, you're out now."

GP fell into a long silence. "Mr. Reynolds is still on some abusive shit. I swear I wish something bad would happen to his fat ass."

Jewels was taken aback. "You mean—"

"Yeah, the same one."

"You some cold shit, GP. I knew I should have left you locked up. No wonder they ran away."

He looked at Jewels, then across the waiting area at the children. "What you mean, *ran away?*"

"Didn't you hear me when I said they pulled a Harriet Tubman? You heard right."

"How long before Kitchie—"

The elevator chimed.

The children greeted their mother with the same affection, if not more, than they had shown their father. GP joined the family's reunion hug. Kitchie couldn't speak because of all the crying she was doing.

CHAPTER 9

Detective Thomas flicked open a four-inch Harley-Davidson blade and cut the tape securing the Nike box's lid with caution.

Hector stuck his tongue through the gum and blew a bubble.

Thomas eased the lid off and jumped back in disbelief. "What the…goddammit! What the fuck is this?" His arms spread wide.

Crutchfield took a peek inside the box. His blood pressure reached its apex. He clenched his fists until his knuckles turned whiter.

Thomas shot to his feet with the shovel cocked. "You had me dig up a dead goddamn goldfish…a stinking fish!" He swung the shovel, dislocating Hector's shoulder.

Hector yelped as the pain registered. "I thought that's who you were talking about." He held on to his shoulder. "My fucking arm… I think you broke it. That's the only body I know about."

"Smart ass, you think you can toy with us like we're some clowns?" Thomas drew back with the shovel.

Hector tried to shake the pain. *Does he really want me to answer that?* "I did what was asked of me. I showed you the only body I know about. I came home a week ago and found Pablo floating in his bowl. I had him for years. He was my main man, you know. It was only right to give him a proper burial."

"Who does this murderous…asshole think he's talking to?"

Crutchfield saved Hector from a second blow. "Fuck him, Thomas. He'll slip up on his own or by my design. Either way, we'll get him…" He tugged on the cuffs with a force that sent shock waves of excruciating pain through the damaged limb. "…And we'll bring Squeeze down."

Hector fell and soiled the knees of his designer slacks.

§ § §

Jewels wheeled the Escalade onto the avenue leading to GP's home.

Kitchie shifted Junior from one side of her lap to the other. "You shouldn't do this. I don't want us to get into any more trouble than we're in, Papi."

"What else am I supposed to do? None of us have any clothes and there's a couple hundred dollars in there, which we need. Unless you have another suggestion, I'm going in."

"There's fifty dollars in my pants pocket on my bedroom floor, Daddy." Secret leaned on Kitchie, holding on to her hand.

A crease stretched across Kitchie's forehead as her brow furrowed. "Where did you get that type of money?"

She explained her possession of the money to her parents.

"Kitchie, everything is gonna be all right. I'll be in and out like a heist."

"In reality, that's exactly what you're doing." Jewels parked in the driveway. "But what's fucked up is you're breaking into your own house to steal your own shit."

GP looked at the children's bedroom window. "I sure would've liked to watch my baby make that climb."

Secret smiled.

"She almost peed on herself, Daddy."

"Shut up. You're lying."

Their meddlesome neighbor, Mr. Irvington, strolled his compact lawn mower down his drive with his nose in the air. He paused, looked over the shrubbery dividing the two driveways and into GP's aggravated face, then scanned the other members of the Patterson family.

"Let's go." GP released the door handle. "Nosy old bastard has diarrhea of the mouth."

"Mommy...I asked Secret, but she didn't know. Does Daddy tell you..." He whispered the rest into her ear.

Kitchie's eyes widened; her mouth fell open. "Boy, you have no business. Don't you ever, ever let me hear you say that again. Where did you learn that...filth?"

"Me and Secret heard that man, Brandon, say it to his girl-friend, Shea. I saw her titties, too. They're big."

Jewels frowned at Junior through the rearview. "I told you to leave all that out for now."

GP turned in the seat. "How did you see her chest inside his car?"

Junior lowered his head.

GP shifted his gaze to his daughter. "Secret, tell us everything, and this time don't leave nothing out."

§ § §

Mr. Irvington noted the Escalade's license plate number as it backed out the drive. He went into the house and removed a business card stuck to the refrigerator by a banana magnet.

He put on his glasses to make out the blurry numbers on his telephone's keypad. He punched the extension in.

"Department of Social Services; how may I direct your call?"

Mr. Irvington adjusted his hearing aid. "Child Services, please."

"One moment."

Eight seconds later, a man's voice was on the line. "Child Services."

"Uh, yes—" Mr. Irvington read the name on the card. "May I speak with Nancy Pittman?"

"Nancy, line two!" he yelled to a cubicle to the right of him.

"Got it." She picked up. "Hello."

"Ms. Pittman, this is Carmichael Irvington. I met with you yesterday evening."

"Good afternoon, Mr. Irvington. I take it that you thought of something that'll help me locate the Patterson children."

"Better than that; I know exactly who they're with."

§ § §

"I'm gonna give somebody hell if I catch their fiending ass smoking that stinking shit in this hall." Jewels checked her mailbox and fanned the crack smoke.

"Achoo! Achoo!" Junior pinched his nose. "That smells like the same stuff Brandon and Shea was smoking."

"Junior, you and Secret go upstairs with your father. Let Mommy talk to Aunty Jewels for a minute."

GP held the vestibule door open for the women. "Can't y'all—"

"GP, please."

"Come on." He led the children up the stairs to Jewels's apartment.

Jewels leaned against the mailboxes. "What's up?"

"Thanks for everything."

"Don't sweat it. Y'all would have done the same for me. Girl, I know you didn't want to thank me for that in privacy."

"You're right. I've asked you not to encourage my children to do wrong. Secret looks up to you. You teach her to fight, use foul language, and, now, you've overstepped the boundaries of your influence when you advise my children to hold back information from their parents."

"Damn, Kitchie, don't trip. I don't feel like going through this with you again." Jewels threw her hands up. "I only told them to keep their mouths closed for a while; I didn't want them to rattle your nerves with a bunch of shit none of us can do anything about. Seeing all that you've been through, I was trying to let you get your pain in small doses. Y'all got enough to worry about, other than some dude getting his dick sucked."

Kitchie folded her arms and sighed. "You have a point, and I appreciate your concern. Always have. You're special to all of us. But let GP and me be the parents."

§ § §

"We had to eat." Secret pouted. "What else were we supposed to do?"

"You're getting mad at us for stealing; we only did what you do." Junior's innocence oozed from his gaze.

GP sighed. "I'm not mad."

He wasn't angered at all, but he had just been wounded by his son's words.

"I know why you did it. All I want you to understand is that stealing is wrong. No matter why you did it."

"Then why do you steal? Why is it wrong for us but not for you?" Secret folded her arms.

At this moment, Secret reminded GP so much of Kitchie. Her cocky, inquisitive attitude. The prove-your-point attitude her body language communicated. Like mother, like daughter.

"Just because I'm known for doing some things in the past doesn't mean it's cool for either one of you to do it."

"Aaunk! Wrong answer." Kitchie strolled into the room with Jewels close behind. "Answer her question. I want to know, too."

Junior rested an elbow on the arm of the couch. "Well, Dad, why *are* you allowed to do it?"

"This ought to be good." Jewels plopped down onto the love-seat. "Your own kids got you on the ropes; going to your body real good."

GP visited each set of eyes staring at him for a brief moment. "Stealing is wrong for me, too. It's not something I'm proud of. Stealing is self-centered. When you take something that doesn't belong to you, you're only concerned with the benefits you get." He took Junior's hand. "Stealing one small thing can hurt a lot of people in a big way."

"So, you don't care about other people when you steal, Daddy?" Junior bit his bottom lip.

GP looked at Kitchie, hoping that she would come to his rescue.

"I won't help you." She shrugged. "I told you that you'll be confronted by this one day."

"Man-up, homeboy, 'cause you're definitely on front street."

GP scratched his head. "No, Junior, I don't. The times I've stolen, at the time, there wasn't anybody I cared about but your mother, you, and Secret. That's wrong for me to think like that."

"If you know all of that—" Secret stretched. "—then why do you do wrong?"

"Oomph, good goddamn question." Jewels leaned back on the loveseat. This was getting good.

"My teacher said, 'Once you know something,'" Secret said, "'you're held accountable for what you know.'"

"Your teacher is a very smart woman." GP shifted his gaze from Secret to Junior. "Tell you what: I'll make a deal with you. You won't ever hear about me stealing anything again. But you have to promise me that neither of you won't ever take something that doesn't belong to you unless your life depends on it."

"Deal." Secret kicked her shoes off.

"Throw my bike in there and you got yourself a deal, Daddy."

"Bet." GP shook his son's hand.

Jewels turned the TV on. CNN was doing a news brief on yet another entertainer turned pedophile. "Freak is going to jail this time. They finally got his confused ass trapped off."

Kitchie sat down beside her. "You think he's guilty?"

"You motherfucking right! Ain't no question. He lucky it ain't nobody I know, 'cause I'd break his ass off—literally. Show him how that shit feels. Anybody that tampers with kids in any type of way deserves to be done in. Fuck him, perverted queer." Jewels turned the channel. "It's some bags on my bed. Some of the hottest gear out. It's something in there everybody can wear. Y'all take whatever you need. It might be a minute until things is back right."

"Booyah!" Secret sprang up and darted toward the bedroom.

GP threw up a hand, stopping her. "Hold up a minute." He turned back to Jewels. "You need to hustle those clothes so—"

"Don't sweat it. Y'alls bond money already set me back. I'm a player, though. I'll get another opportunity to make some major paper. Them stolen clothes don't mean shit to me. Take them all and get right. Family comes before money."

Junior turned. "Aunty, you stole, too?" His brow rose.

"Boy, don't you even go there with me. Ain't no telling what Aunty might do. Steal, kill, wheel, and deal."

§ § §

The following morning, Nancy Pittman was being escorted by a plain-clothes officer to an address that the Department of Motor Vehicles had matched with the license plate number provided to her by Mr. Irvington.

"After you." The chubby officer opened the vestibule door.

"Thanks…" Nancy looked into the face of a dusty black man steadying a flame to the tip of his glass pipe.

"Come in or close the damn door." Smoke escaped Too Tall's nostrils. "What y'all white folks doing down here?"

The door slammed shut behind the officer's wide load. He shoved a badge in Too Tall's face. "Break it or I'm hauling you in."

"Ah, come on, man. All the dope I got is in here." He held the pipe up, then bolted out the door, nearly knocking Nancy over.

"You okay?" The officer held her in his arms.

A strange feeling ran through her. She felt a connection that had abandoned her years ago. "I'm fine, Officer Howard." She looked at the paraphernalia littering the building's interior. "It's on the third floor."

Howard could just about tell what she was thinking from the expression etched on her face. "What you just witnessed and what you see..." He pointed to an empty crack vial. "...is almost considered normal in this type of area."

"This is no place for children to be."

Howard studied her slender frame as she climbed the stairs. "No one should be forced to live in an environment such as this, but unfortunately, this is the best some people can do."

"Why doesn't the police force come through places like this and rid it of people like...that guy who tried to run me down? That way the families who are economically challenged, that must stay in places like this, will have a halfway decent place to live?"

"Addicts aren't the problem. They're part of the equation, but not the majority of the problem. Sure, we can arrest them on bullshit charges, which won't amount to nothing more than a county sentence." He was really impressed with the way Nancy's long legs performed in her business skirt. "From experience, my opinion is we shouldn't concentrate on punishment for addicts; we should direct that energy into getting them help. And crack down hard on the dealers responsible for poisoning these people—starting with the government."

They stopped in front of Apartment 302.

"Here we go. Uh...Nancy..."

She looked into his boyish eyes.

"I know this is bad timing, but would you like to go out some time?"

Jewels tugged her door open and was headed to the store. She was startled when she found two strangers standing there making goo-goo eyes at one another.

Nancy looked at the huge, brown-complexioned woman, and the people camped out on the living room floor. "Is Jewels Madison here?"

"Who wants to know?" Jewels became nervous when the uppity-looking white woman used her full name. "If you're here to collect some money, she ain't got it. The bitch still owes me."

"I'm Nancy Pittman with the Department of Social Services." She extended her hand. "This is Officer Howard."

He flashed a badge.

Jewels eased the door up, blocking their view. She gestured toward Nancy's hand. "It's against my religion to shake hands. Jewels ain't here. What y'all want?"

Secret opened the door before it could close all the way. "Aunt Jewels, Mommy said bring back a dozen eggs, too."

"Good morning, Secret. Remember me?"

She slid behind Jewels for protection.

§ § §

Both men hushed themselves when the eyesore waitress wobbled to the horseshoe-shaped table with their meals. "Can I get you anything else?"

Hector waved her off.

Well, fuck you, too. She feigned a smile because policy said so. But she was just about fed up with the customers-are-always-right cliché. Nine times out of ten they were wrong. And she was tired of dragging herself in to work every day to wait on ignorant people hand and foot. Not for one minute did she like plastering a smile on her face as if she approved of *their rudeness*.

Being that Hector was right-handed, and his right arm was resting in a sling, it was a difficult task to eat with his left. He stuck his chewing gum on the edge of his plate of tater tots. "If you would have let me waste Miles when I wanted to, the police wouldn't be breathing down our necks. I can't even take a whizz in peace."

"Chill out, my friend." Squeeze leaned forward. "They don't have nothing; there's no way for them to get anything." He spooned a mouthful of scrambled eggs, then rinsed them down with a swig of Sunny Delight. "You act like you don't understand that citizens honor a different set of principles than criminals. It's no surprise that he went to the cops and told what he assumes. That's what law-abiding citizens do. Our tracks are covered. Relax and enjoy your food."

Hector jerked a thumb toward the parking lot. "Them cops tried to send me back to—"

"May I refill your drinks?"

Hector lost it. "Did we fucking ask for refills?"

The collective chatter of conversations and knives and forks scraping against plates came to a stop. The diner full of customers zoomed in on Hector.

"Don't fucking bother us again unless I fucking ask you to." He took a ten-dollar bill from his pocket and slammed it hard against the tabletop. "This is the only reason you're proving to be a fucking pest. Take it and stay the fuck away!"

"Don't take it personal." Squeeze looked at the wounded waitress. "He hasn't taken his angry pills yet."

And I'm supposed to smile. The customer is always right. "Kiss my ass." She took her apron off, tossed it in a trash can, and walked out the front door. "I'm not putting up with that bullshit anymore."

Hector pushed his plate to the center of the table. "I don't need Crutchfield watching my every move, looking for an opportunity to make me violate parole." He glanced through the window with contempt at a dark blue Caprice.

"You're not gonna eat this?" Squeeze wasn't the least bit bothered by the detective's presence.

When Hector didn't respond, he pulled the plate to his side of the table. "If Miles winds up on the missing list, the cops will really be on us. This here will pass if you let it. There isn't even the slightest possibility that they'll find Jap. It's a cold case." He sprinkled salt on Hector's tater tots. "Go home and fuck your old lady; relieve some of that build-up, then meet me tonight at six. Cutty has a Maybach he wants me to check out. Lifted it in Solon. If I like it, I need you to drive one car back."

Hector grunted. "We need to shake this nasty flea first."

"Relax. He'll shake himself. The more I talk to you, the dumber it feels like I'm getting." He cut away the last portion of meat from the T-bone. "You have no understanding."

"Understanding of what? Don't start with your philosophical babble."

Squeeze laughed. "You're giving Crutchfield exactly what he wants. He's fucking with you and you're letting him."

Crutchfield walked directly to their table. "Squeeze. Hector, I hope you're taking care of that arm. Mind if I sit down and ask you two hoods a few questions?"

CHAPTER 10

The ruckus echoed throughout the narrow hall. Nancy struggled to hold on to Secret.

Kitchie tugged Secret's arm. "Let her the hell go, lady. What the fuck is wrong with you? This is my baby; you can't take her!"

"I assure you I can, and I am." She got a firm grip on Secret. "These children are custody of the state, and as it stands, you're harboring runaways."

GP stepped between Junior and Officer Howard. "*Runaways*, we're their parents. My kids ain't going nowhere."

"Fuck that shit. That bastard, Reynolds, put his hands on my baby." Kitchie pulled up Secret's sleeve. "You see these fucking welts? I don't whip her like this. I'll be damned if somebody else is going to do it. Bullshit!"

"Look," GP said. "Go back to your ideal worlds and get the hell away from us. My kids ain't going nowhere. Not today." He aimed his eyes at Officer Howard like a double-barreled shotgun.

Officer Howard unsnapped his side holster. "Don't make this situation any worse than it is."

"Get the fuck out of here, then. You're making it worse." GP punctuated his words with his hands.

"Mr. Patterson, please—"

"Please, my ass."

"Mr. Patterson," Nancy said, "think about the behavior you're displaying in front of the children." She had had no idea that she would be confronted with this much resistance.

"My *behavior* is because of my kids. Instead of concentrating on putting mine in a home, you need to get the rest of them kids out of that place. Y'all smart motherfuckers is the dumbest motherfuckers in the world. But y'all swear you got all the right answers for everybody else."

A neighbor stood in her doorway, watching the commotion while relaying it to a third party on the telephone.

§ § §

Jewels was ticked off and growing more vexed each time she flushed a portion of her drug supply down the toilet.

§ § §

"Mr. and Mrs. Patterson, there is a right and a wrong way to go about this." A spasm of irritation crossed Nancy's face.

"Don't let them take me, Daddy," Junior spoke with bitter resentment. "I wanna stay with you."

"Mrs. Patterson, get a hold of yourself." Nancy pulled Secret free of Kitchie. "Is this the behavior you want reported to the judge? This display of aggression will not act in favor of you regaining custody."

"Please, Mommy, I don't want to go." Secret bit down hard on Nancy's arm.

"Ow! You're hurting me!" She pried her arm from the set of teeth. "That wasn't nice, Secret."

"Enough is enough. I've had it." Howard took out a set of handcuffs. "There's room in the car for the two of you." He pointed at GP, then Kitchie. "Whatever your problem is with juvenile court is not my concern. We're here to do our jobs. The next time either one of you interferes with Ms. Pittman or myself, I'm taking you in for obstructing official police business."

"*Mierda*! This is bullshit. You—"

GP gave Kitchie a look that screamed out, *Would you please shut the hell up?*

"Here's my information." Nancy thrust a business card toward Kitchie. "I'll personally see to it that you and Mr. Patterson see the judge tomorrow. If you want custody back, court is the standard operating procedure."

Kitchie dropped to her knees, hugging Secret around her waist. "I love you."

"Come with me, Mommy." Secret's lips quivered. "Don't make me go; he's gonna beat me again. Please come."

"Let's go, son." Howard offered Junior a hand. "You'll be back with your parents before you know it."

Junior viewed the white hand as everything but friendly. He squeezed his father's hand tighter. He looked into GP's pained face, shaking his head. "Beat him up, Daddy. I wanna stay with you and Mommy. You...you said that you was gonna protect us."

GP died inside. He lowered his head in defeat, dodging Junior's gaze. "I'll be there first thing in the morning to get you. I promise."

Howard tried to cut the tension with a smile. "It'll be fine." He grabbed Junior while gauging what he could of the family's hurt.

Junior snatched away from Howard and turned to his father. His eyes narrowed with contempt. "I hate you. All you do is lie to us. I wish I had another daddy."

GP died for the second time in less than two minutes. He looked as if he wanted to cry. "I'm sorry, I'm sorry." His words were delivered at a whisper.

When Nancy and Howard led the children away, Kitchie

broke down with a hysterical cry. Tears dripped from GP's chin as he watched Junior stomping away. The child looked as if the only thing that would make him happy again was GP's death.

Jewels came to the door and witnessed the aftermath.

"Honey child, them crackers just took them poor children away." The neighbor held the phone between an ear and a shoulder. "Sure did."

"Mind your fucking business." A vein formed in the middle of Jewels's forehead. "Go in the house and shut the door before I stall that pump in your chest. My conscience won't bother me if I let your old ass have it."

The neighbor's door closed without hesitation.

"GP." Jewels knelt beside Kitchie. "GP...GP! You fucking hear me!"

GP was still staring at the area from which the children had been taken.

"GP!"

"Huh?" He finally snapped out of it.

"Help me get Kitchie in the house."

§ § §

"Look what the cat dragged in." A tall girl nudged Nise, then pointed into a courtyard.

Secret and Junior climbed from the backseat of Nancy's SUV. Nise thought about how easy Secret had broken her nose. "Yeah, I see." She adjusted a cheap pair of sunglasses on her face, which did a piss-poor job of concealing her black eyes.

"What's up, then? Now you can get some get-back. You know I got your back."

"Nah, I'mma let it go." Nise turned away from the window

overlooking the courtyard when Secret and her little brother were escorted up the cobblestone walkway.

The tall girl sucked her teeth. "I can't be madder than you are. If you're cool with your beat-down, then I'm cool with it, too."

"Fuck you! If you have my back, you would have had it then!"

§ § §

Nancy pushed Mr. Reynolds's office door open. "Look who I found."

He turned away from the computer screen. "Oh my, you two really gave me quite a scare." He came from behind the desk. "I was worried sick about you two."

"They scared all of us," Nancy said.

Mr. Reynolds ruffled Secret's curly locks. "It's a blessing you're all right."

"Keep your hands off me." She pulled away from his reach and held Junior as if to protect him.

"Uh, Mr. Reynolds, may I have a word with you?" Nancy nodded her head in the direction of the hall.

"Sure. Sure." He followed Nancy and pulled the door closed behind his dump truck.

"Secret claims you beat her. They're both frightened to stay here. She has belt markings on her back and arms. Can you explain that to me?"

"You're aware of how creative a child's imagination is. They'll say anything to get their way. The last time I saw Secret, there was not a scratch on that child, Ms. Pittman. I assure you."

Nancy didn't enjoy the vibes she was feeling. All she could register was the full-of-shit air he had about himself. "Our office has received complaints in the past on the way you care after these children."

"If somebody wasn't talking about me, Ms. Pittman, then I'd feel like I wasn't doing my job. I've been in this business nearly thirty years. I know exactly what I'm doing."

"For your sake, and the children in your care, I hope so. Secret and Junior just went through a very emotional experience. Make sure they're comfortable."

Mr. Reynolds smiled. "That's my job. They'll be taken care of well."

She turned toward the exit. "I left a copy of their file at the front desk."

Mr. Reynolds listened to the click of Nancy's Payless high-heels until they left the building. He wobbled into his office with a scowl on his fat face. "To run away is to break the rules."

§ § §

Friday morning had taken forever to arrive, and time was still moving too slowly for GP. He paced the marble floor in the crowded hall of the juvenile court building. "What's taking so long?"

Kitchie opted not to answer. Instead, she glanced at him from a bench seat, then shifted her eyes back to the floor.

Jewels came down the hall, soaking wet. "I had to park two blocks over." She stood there, dripping puddles.

A lady seated beside Kitchie watched the water accumulate around Jewels's alligator boots. "It's raining out there?"

"Nah, I'm standing here pissing on myself."

The courtroom's oversized mahogany door swung open. A peanut-shaped-head bailiff with a wrinkled uniform rubbed his stubble beard. "Mr. and Mrs. Greg Patterson."

GP signaled Peanut-head with a wave; Kitchie started toward him.

"The judge would like to see you in his chambers. Follow me, please." He held up a hand to Jewels. "Where are you going, sir?"

"She's family." Kitchie pushed past him.

Peanut-head examined Jewels closer. "I apologize."

Inside the judge's chambers, the air conditioner's cold hiss gave Kitchie goose bumps; perhaps she was a little nervous, too.

Judge Brooks sat hunched over in a leather chair as if his back were causing him a great deal of pain. "Have a seat." He motioned toward several empty chairs around the table.

"Good morning." Nancy tucked a lock of hair behind her ear as Judge Brooks suffered a short coughing attack.

"Pardon me," he said. "Why don't we get this over with? My caseload is already behind schedule today without the extra-curricular work, Ms. Pittman."

"My apologies, Your Honor." She handed him a manila folder. "The Pattersons were released from jail, as you will notice there, and I would like to get their children back in the home ASAP. They're runners."

He took the folder. "I didn't give you a choice in the matter. Have a seat." He stared at Jewels.

Jewels followed the order—this time. *Old motherfucker, swear he tough. Punk! I'd like to catch his bitch ass in the street; bet he'd change his tone.*

He coughed the entire time he studied the contents of the folder. "Mr. and Mrs. Patterson." He never looked away from the folder. "I'll relinquish custody from the state back to you in this matter, providing that your residence passes a home evaluation and inspection."

"But, Your Honor, we recently lost our house to foreclosure." Kitchie eyed him with the hope of a worried mom. "We're staying with the children's aunt." She gestured toward Jewels. "It's a temporary arrangement until we get back on our feet and save enough money to get our own place."

After what sounded like a painful cough, Judge Brooks cleared his throat. "This isn't the same residence the children were found in yesterday, is it?"

GP didn't like the negative connotation in the judge's question. "Yes. There's enough room for us and we're welcomed."

"I'm enjoying their company; gives me the chance to spend more time with my niece and nephew." Jewels settled on the back of the chair. "If—"

Judge Brooks threw up a vein-ridden hand. "Ms. Pittman has concerns about the area the children were found in, and I'm well aware of the things that go on around your apartment, Ms.... I never caught your name."

Jewels sighed. *Here comes the bullshit.* "Jewels Madison."

"Ms. Madison, I can't understand how you endure, unless somehow you're involved in the drug activity there. The environment you stay in is unhealthy for the children. Hell, Cliffview Gardens is unhealthy for adults."

"I'm being stereotyped because of where I live. What goes on outside of my building doesn't have anything to do with us or the kids. They're in good hands and have more than enough supervision between the three of us."

"Excuse me, Your Honor." Nancy tapped her ink pen against the table top. "Things are not only going on outside of her building but on the inside also."

I can't believe this shifty bitch. Kitchie burned a hole through Nancy with a narrow gaze.

More ink pen tapping. "When an officer escort and I went to Ms. Madison's apartment, there was an addict smoking crack in her hall, who incidentally almost hurt me trying to flee. There was even drug paraphernalia littering the hall floors."

Judge Brooks passed a hand over his ash beard. "Relatives get first priority. I'd much rather place the children with family than to leave them in the custody of the state at the taxpayers' expense. Is there someone else?"

GP focused on the judge. "Here in Cleveland, all the family we have is right here in this room."

Nancy crossed her skinny legs. "The children have grandparents in the state of New York, who maintain on a fixed income and are not capable of taking care of the children for any period of time."

Judge Brooks sighed. "It's final. The children remain in the custody of the state until Mr. and Mrs. Patterson can provide appropriate living arrangements in a proper environment."

"Your Honor." GP shot to his feet.

"It's final."

Kitchie's eyes began to leak.

"Dammit! You can't leave my kids in that home." GP snatched his shirt off. "You see this? This happened to me there." He turned his back to Nancy and Judge Brooks.

Nancy gasped and threw a shaky hand over her mouth. His back was reminiscent of a picture she had seen of a slave who had been repeatedly lashed with a whip. "My God, that's terrible."

Judge Brooks thought he had seen it all. He avoided the sight of GP's keloid-riddled back. "Put your shirt on, son. If that happened to you while you were in custody of the state, it should've been addressed then. I assure you, that type of abuse isn't happening today. If you want your children out of the Eastside Group Home, I'd suggest you provide them with a decent home to come home to."

§ § §

Jewels's apartment was sweltering from summer's oppressive heat. There was less than an hour of daylight left, and for some reason, it seemed that as night approached it became even hotter.

"Don't touch me." Kitchie moved to the opposite end of the couch. "You never listen; not one fucking time."

"Kitchie—"

"Kitchie my ass." She scorched GP with a penetrating look. "If you would've taken us into consideration, the kids would be here with us now."

"Uh-uh, if you wasn't so hotheaded and knew how to keep your hands to yourself, the kids would be here."

Kitchie buried her head in her hands and cried. "I'm sick and tired of crying for you…because of you, GP. I'm just about cried out."

"Mami Chula, I apologize. We're not going to get anywhere blaming each other." He scooted next to her. "We need to—"

"I meant what I said; *don't* touch me." Anger seeped from her presence as a profound silence fell on the room. She turned to GP. "So now what, Mr. Street Prophet? What brilliant, get-by tactic do you have to get us through this shit?"

More silence.

"Just like I thought." She took a container of pepper spray from her purse and started for the door. "You don't have a clue." She paused at the door. "You know what your main problem is? You need to stop trying to get by and figure out a reliable way for us to make it."

GP watched the heavy door close behind Kitchie. He went and knocked on his friend's bedroom door. "Jewels, let's talk."

"Come in." She lay across a set of satin sheets with the phone up to her ear. "What's up?"

"Hang up and put something on."

"Punk, don't come in here running off a list of orders. This is how I relax—in my drawers. It's hot as fuck. If you don't like it, close my door in your face, and take your stressed-out ass back in the living room."

"I'm dead-ass, Jewels."

She spoke into the phone. "Ndia, baby, hold that thought…and that position. I'll call you back in a minute." She returned the phone to its cradle, then slipped a pair of boxers over her men's briefs.

GP flopped down beside her. "Promise me won't nobody get hurt."

"Motherfuckers get hurt every day, and I ain't a stranger to hurting a motherfucker. Now that we have that clear, what are you talking about?"

"I want to get my kids back immediately. I…I just don't want nobody to get hurt in the process."

"Psst. Fool, you taking a beating. Fucking with you, I'm taking one, too. It cost me fifteen grand to bond y'all out. I flushed four ounces of coke and a pound of herb. Half the shit we knocked off in N.Y. was given to y'all to put some clothes on your back. Your hard times have rubbed off. I'm fucked up. I don't have the money to get you an apartment; not now anyway."

"I'm talking about that hundred-thousand-dollar move you was telling me about last week."

"What, you got selective hearing or something?" She feigned a display of sign language. "I said, I'm fucked up right now. That move is supposed to go down tomorrow night. I'm lucky if I have five hundred dollars to my name."

"Put me in the know. Tell me what the deal is. I wanna know what's up with it."

She fell back on a large pillow. "I can't believe you jacked off a phone-sex session for this. What's the point? It's only gonna piss me off thinking about all the money I coulda had."

"Get pissed off, then."

"You about to get on my fucking nerves." She laced her hands behind her head and stared at the ceiling. "It's a credit card scam. A hundred grand will get me a package deal."

"A deal on what?"

"Ten major corporate account numbers with a history of a spending habit from anywhere, say, between two hundred-fifty grand and a million."

GP lowered his brow as he thought. "What good is having the corporate numbers? You can't access their accounts."

"You can with a credit card. Platinum cards, homeboy. All the equipment to make the cards comes with the package. All I would have to do is let my girls work with the cards."

"How much would you make?" GP scratched his head. "You know, if you had the money to buy the package."

"Well…like I said, each card will be worth at least a quarter of a million, but that doesn't mean I'll get that much."

"Why?"

"'Cause the company can red flag the account at any time. Then, it's dead. Two-fifty times ten is two-and-a-half million. Out of that, I would see about one-point-two million in merchandise. Then, when my girls and I hustle it in these streets, I'll take home six hundred grand—easy."

"One more question."

"You working my nerves, but spit it out so I can get back with Ndia."

"If you had the front money, how long would it take to make it back?"

"Sheeit, I got at least a hundred-fifty grand worth of orders now. All I need to do is come up with the merchandise. I could have the front money back in three weeks tops. Why you interested in all this?"

GP flashed a business card. "We split the profit down the middle, and I'll get you the money."

"Get out my room."

"Fifty-fifty."

For the first time in their eight-year history, Jewels saw desperation in her friend's eyes. "Get it and that's a bet."

GP and Jewels touched fists.

CHAPTER 11

S queeze watched the clock as it changed from 8:36 to 8:37 a.m. "I have a deep respect for a man who rises with the sun to take care of his business. It's a display of...character." He stood at a wet bar, adjacent a floor-to-ceiling wall window that overlooked the lake. He fixed himself a stiff drink, then offered GP one.

"No thanks."

"A hundred stacks is a lot of cash to borrow on an artist's salary." Squeeze threw back the alcohol as if it were a glass of water. "What's your gamble: cocaine, hoes, guns, heroin, blackjack?"

GP was watching the big Spanish guy shifting his weight from one foot to the other, smacking on chewing gum. "Your concerns are out of order. What I do with the money ain't your business. I thought, in your line of work, pay day was your only concern."

Squeeze laughed as he stared through the window, one hundred stories down. "Three weeks. Thirty-five percent interest. Five thousand-dollars-a-day late fee. My suggestion to you, old friend, is to be as punctual in paying me as you were in picking the cash up. You'd hate it if we fell out." He nodded at Hector.

Hector left the room and returned in less than a minute with ten crisp stacks of money.

GP shoveled the money into a drawstring nylon bag. "Thanks, man. I really appreciate this."

"I hope so." He turned away from his endless view to watch GP being ushered out the door. He poured himself another drink.

Hector closed the door behind GP, then looked back at Squeeze.

"Follow him. Find out what he's into and who he's doing it with. Find out where he and that pretty woman of his rest their heads at."

Hector grunted and headed out the door.

§ § §

Kitchie rested her hands on her curvy hips. "What are you two up to?"

GP and Jewels turned to face her.

GP averted his eyes to the kitchen clock. 3:17 p.m.

Jewels had no shame. She matched Kitchie's questioning gaze. "Girl, we ain't fucking. I plead the fifth." She had the nylon bag cuffed behind her back.

"GP." Kitchie put her face up to his, forcing him to look at her.

"It's nothing, Mami."

"GP!"

"If you don't want me to lie, then don't ask me again. It's nothing; trust me."

"Uhm-hm, I suppose there's nothing in the bag either."

"Chill, Kitchie." He stroked the side of her face. "Let's go; visiting hour is about to start." He paused. "And when we get there, keep your cool. Please don't forget for one minute that we have to leave Junior and Secret there. Don't start no shit."

"I'll bite my tongue for now. But I swear to God, GP, the day we bring my babies home, I'm going to dig deep and hawk spit in his face."

Jewels took a set of keys from the top of the refrigerator. "I'm gonna drop y'all off and go cop me a new cell phone. I like that new BlackBerry phone; it does everything but talk for you."

"I meant to ask you," GP said. "Who was that answering your phone last week?"

"I don't know. I lost it somewhere."

"Nah, this dude said you left the phone with him while you were gone. I left a message for you with him."

Jewels pulled the key out of the door. She stood still, thinking. "They said that I gave them my phone?"

"Yeah. Said that y'all was handling some business together. I thought that's how you knew we were in jail."

"That's strange." Jewels walked out of the building into the sunlight. "I wish I would find the motherfucker who was finger-fucking my phone bill. I'd break my big toe knuckle deep in his ass."

Kitchie climbed into the front seat of the Escalade. "How'd you know we were locked up, then?"

"I didn't until I found Secret and Junior sleeping in front of my door. Not to mention a hundred crying-ass messages from your husband. *Come get me, I can't take it in here. They're so much bigger than me.*" Jewels laughed.

"Stop clowning." GP joined in her humor.

"I don't know what y'all are laughing at. That shit is not funny whatsoever." Kitchie watched the scenery from her window.

§ § §

The hatred shared between their silent exchange caused Kitchie's skin to crawl. Their silence seemed to communicate more than words possibly could. For Mr. Reynolds, the loathing had begun when GP was only nine years old. He'd discovered that GP had stolen a family heirloom of coins to buy a damn Van Gogh drawing pad and a set of thirty-six prisma-color oil pencils. The handful of coins turned out to be worth over a million dollars. For GP, the loathing began when the beatings and various forms of mental torture wouldn't stop. The way Mr. Reynolds felt about the whole situation was that GP had stolen his express pass to the good life.

"What the hell do you want?" Mr. Reynolds shattered the profound quiet, stepped out onto the platform porch, and pulled the door closed behind him.

Kitchie stuck her hand out. "I'm Kitchie Patterson and this is my husband. We're here to visit our kids, Secret and Greg Jr." She withdrew her hand; it was obvious that Mr. Reynolds wasn't interested in being cordial.

"The Patterson children are yours?" A wicked smile stretched across his chubby face. "I should've known that misfortune would strike me twice in the same place. Come in."

GP began to feel as though he had made the wrong decision in going there. He should've never revealed that Junior and Secret were connected to him. The sound of Mr. Reynolds's hard bottoms clicking in front of him brought back memories that he and the walls had often tried to forget.

"Is that for the children?" Mr. Reynolds pointed at the bag in Kitchie's hand.

"Yes. It's a few more outfits and a math book for Secret."

"I'll take it." Mr. Reynolds pushed the door open to a living room that had been converted to a visiting room.

"I wanted to—"

"Either I take the package for inspection or you can leave it at the desk and pick it up when you leave."

Fat Bitch! "No problem." Kitchie gave him the bag. "GP, forgive me." She looked at Mr. Reynolds. "If your fat ass ever puts your dick-beaters on either one of my kids again, I will blow your fucking head off."

Mr. Reynolds laughed. "Your foul mouth is not appropriate.

I've never touched your children. I don't have the slightest idea of what you're speaking about, Mrs. Patterson."

"Play dumb if you want. I'll repent for my sin later."

"That's enough, Kitchie." GP shook his head. *Will you ever keep your mouth closed?*

"You have thirty minutes to visit. Have a seat." He looked at GP. "Secret and Junior, *Greg Jr.*, will be down shortly."

If looks were fatal, GP would've been brutally murdered.

🔊 🔊 🔊

"Sticky, what's up?" Jewels walked out of a mom-and-pop store talking on her new BlackBerry.

"I'm just shooting my regular. Everything is everything and I'm with anything lucrative."

"I take it it's still on for tonight."

"If your purse is right."

"When have you known me not to come correct?" She leaned against the Escalade and watched a chocolate girl's fat ass in a pair of Apple Bottoms jeans. Jewels tried to picture the jeans hitting her bedroom floor.

"After tonight, you're no longer a petty hustler."

"Take my new number and get at me if something changes before my graduation."

🔊 🔊 🔊

"Daddy!" Secret ran at top speed and jumped into GP's arms. She leaned over and kissed Kitchie's cheek. "You and Mommy came to take us home."

GP looked at the room's entrance. "Where's your brother?"

"He's coming. So we're going home with you and Mommy, right, Daddy?"

"Look at your hair." Kitchie pried Secret from GP's arms. "Come over here and sit down. Let me do something with this mess. Your father bought you a math book."

"We're not leaving, are we?" Secret's hopes started to fizzle.

Kitchie took out a comb, brush, some barrettes, and hair grease from her purse. "Not today but soon."

"Yeah, baby. Daddy promises to get y'all out of this place. I promise to—"

"Get me a bike, Secret a puppy...and new clothes." Junior eased into a chair, six seats away, with his arms folded. "Mommy's gonna get a big house. You always promise us stuff we never get. Secret, stop asking. We ain't getting nothing and we ain't going nowhere, just like everybody else here." He stared at the wall to his left, avoiding looking in the direction of his family.

Kitchie turned her wounded eyes on GP, then began to get up.

He stopped her. "No, I need to. This is about me." GP took in a deep breath, then sat beside Junior. "You have every reason to be upset with me. I've let you down." He shifted his gaze between the three of them. "I've failed all of y'all several times, and I'm not proud of it. Junior, when I promise you something, I have every intention of making it happen. I try to make y'all as many promises as I can, so I work real hard to get it."

"But we never get anything except the promise." Junior swung his feet back and forth.

GP noticed Mr. Reynolds standing at the entrance. He could hear the voice shouting in his head. *You're just another black whore baby who'll never amount to nothing.* He clamped his eyelids, forcing Mr. Reynolds out. When he opened them again, Mr. Reynolds was doing a penguin walk down the narrow hall. "Listen to me,

Junior. I won't make any more promises to any of y'all that I'm not prepared to deliver."

Junior looked at GP for the first time. "Should I play pretend? You even break your own promises. You said that you'll always protect us."

"I will. You can count on that."

"How can you protect us from Mr. Reynolds, and the rest of these mean people, if you're at home and we're here? Mommy, I wanna go back to my room."

§ § §

Night had come quicker than usual, at least that's how Jewels felt about it as she eased the Escalade into the congested lot of the Improv Comedy Club. She spoke to her reflection in the rearview mirror. "Let's get paid, girl." She blew herself a kiss, then climbed from behind the steering wheel.

The door to the club opened and laughter poured out.

Jewels looked into the sky at the endless scatter of stars, and that's when she was forced to see a few stars of her own.

§ § §

"You don't know? What the hell you mean, you don't know what you're gonna do?" Kitchie punched GP in the chest, then climbed through the window and sat on the fire escape.

He kneeled by the window. "Kitchie—"

"Kitchie my goddamn ass." She rattled off a few more cruddy sentences in Spanish. "Our children have been taken from us. They don't want to be there, and I sure as hell don't want them in that place. And all the fuck you can come up with is *you don't know*."

"Take that shit back in the house! You blowing the spot up with your loud-ass mouth!" a hustler yelled from the parking lot below.

"Kiss my ass, panocha!" Kitchie held up a middle finger.

"Come inside," GP said.

"I don't feel like being bothered with nothing or nobody but this breeze."

"I said, get your ass in here."

"When I—"

"Now, dammit! I'm tired of your bullshit!"

Kitchie understood that he meant business.

He stepped aside and helped her through the window.

"You're worried about me cussing out some punk. Your concern should be focused on the anger your son has built up toward you. He doesn't even respect you anymore. The sad part is I don't blame him."

Her words cut through GP. He drew his hand back to slap her with all of his might.

"So that's what it is now, GP? You're gonna hit me, mother-fucker? Go ahead, go on, kick my ass real good because you're only gonna get one chance to do it. I hope you're real satisfied with the outcome."

He looked at his hand, fingers spread wide, and lowered it in guilt.

"Ten years, GP; ten years. I've let you drag me and my kids through every shit hole in this city. I supported you in everything and gave up a career to help you skip down your dead-end, yellow brick road." A tear rolled off her cheek. "If you ever, I mean ever put your goddamn hands on me, you'll lose me faster than you're losing your son."

This time when she went out to the fire escape, she shut the window behind her and walked down to the parking lot.

"Hey, Little Mama, mind if I conversate with you for a few?"

Kitchie inspected the handsome, rugged hustler from head-to-toe. She hoped GP was watching from the window above. "What are we talking about, stranger?"

"I'm Desmond." He offered a hand.

"I'm—"

"Kitchie, I already know. I guess that means we're not strangers anymore."

She withdrew her hand and raised a brow. "How'd you know my name?"

"Everybody knows who you are. The walls in these buildings are paper thin. You and your man…" He jerked his head toward GP in the window. "Y'all broadcast your business to the whole 'hood."

"And this is what you wanted to talk to me about?"

You are so pretty is what he wanted to say but knew it would be inappropriate. "Nah, ma, not at all. I just want you to know I feel your pain. Me and my little sister was shipped from group home to foster home until I said fuck that shit. We came a long way. Now I'm able to send her to college." He pulled out a knot of money. "I hope this will help you and your man get them kids back."

"I can't take this."

"Trust me, ma, it's nothing. If I didn't have it to give, I wouldn't offer it. And as it stands, you don't have the luxury of turning it down."

"Kitchie, what the hell you think you're doing?" GP howled into the night from the fire escape.

She rolled her eyes and turned back to Desmond. "Thank you. This is very kind of you."

"I just wore them boots before, ma; that's all. Don't let your pride get in the way. If y'all need anything, I live in the apartment above Jewels." He pointed to GP, who was coming across the grass. "I think you better go. It looks like your man is foaming at the mouth."

§ § §

Trouble tapped Dirty and pointed. "There goes that bitch right there."

They both watched Jewels back the Escalade into a parking space.

"If this bitch buck at all, kill her." Trouble eased out of the car with his weapon, then blended into the night.

Dirty followed.

Jewels climbed from behind the steering wheel and stepped into the excitement and energy of the Flats district's nightlife. From forty yards away, she could hear people enjoying themselves and laughing it up inside the comedy club when the door swung open. She looked at the open sky and pondered on the stars' beauty.

Trouble cocked back and crashed the butt of his gun against Jewels' skull. "You ain't so tough now, is you, bitch?"

The words never registered; Jewels was unconscious before she slammed into the asphalt. Her key ring slid a few feet away.

Dirty retrieved the keys.

In less than a minute, Dirty had searched the Escalade. "It's not here."

"Kiss my...fuck!" Trouble kicked a dent into a Hyundai, then cast his annoyed gaze on Jewels. He began to search her. "Whatever this bitch is made of, it's heavy and solid. Help me turn her over."

"Like she got a hundred grand on her."

"We can tongue-wrestle later; help me turn this hoe over."

They turned Jewels onto her back as the BlackBerry in her pocket began to ring.

Trouble lifted her shirt and saw the money belt strapped around her waist. "Pay day."

"Goddamn, now that's what I call a six-pack." Dirty pointed to her defined abs. "Her shit look better than them body-builders in the magazines."

Trouble removed the money belt. "Muscle can't help her now. Fuck this bitch." He kicked her in the ear as hard as he had kicked the Hyundai, then walked away.

Jewels's BlackBerry was begging to be answered.

Dirty froze in his tracks. "Where you going? The ride is this way." He pointed.

Trouble never broke his stride. "We came to get paid, right?"

"We got it, let's roll out."

"Nah, you got it fucked up. It's still some money waiting for us on the inside. You ain't pussy, is you, chump?"

"Watch your mouth."

"Let's go get it, then." Trouble turned in the direction of the comedy club.

§ § §

GP grabbed Kitchie. "What did he give you?"

"You're hurting my arm." Her attempt to break free was useless.

"I asked you a question."

"A few dollars; that's all."

"What he giving you money for? Huh?" He shook her one good time.

"He was just looking out." Kitchie saw the devil in GP's eyes.

"You're giving it back. Give it to me."

"I'm not. We need this money. I said you're hurting me. Now let me go, GP!" She snatched away from him and went inside the building.

GP turned toward Desmond. "Uh, let me holler at you, main man."

Desmond leaned against a Dumpster under a street lamp as GP approached.

"You know my wife from somewhere?" He connected a solid fist to Desmond's jaw. "Stay the hell away from her."

Desmond countered with a two-punch combination, which sent GP to the glass-ridden pavement. "Don't come down here with that fake gangster shit, you clown-ass chump." He flexed his lower jaw, working the pain out. "I don't want your girl; and if you wasn't putting your business in the street, I wouldn't be in it."

GP threw a hand in front of his eyes to block the glare of the street lamp. He balanced himself on a knee.

Desmond yanked out a .9mm. "Fool, stay down. I didn't tell you to get up." He clicked the safety. "Don't force my hand. I ain't that big on violence, but I'll fuck you up if you push me."

The mechanical sound of the safety echoed in GP's ear. It scared the shit out of him.

"I respect the fact that you're trying to do the right thing. Being broke is hard. I admire honest motherfuckers like you. I wish I didn't have to make my living in these streets." He spat a mouthful of blood into the Dumpster. "You don't know nothing about waking up every morning, thinking today is the day I'll be murdered or thrown in jail, or that maybe I'll have to kill a stupid motherfucker like you. Maybe I was out of line for giving your woman money toward your hardship. So what! What you gonna do about it? Your broke ass need all the help you can get."

A car engine started.

"My business ain't—"

"Shut up. You need to get your seeds. I wore them boots before. If it's ever a next time, I'll make it my business to put the money in your hand. And don't be one of them proud motherfuckers. You need something, ask. I'm always out here." Desmond stuffed the gun in his waistband and reached out a hand. "Get up. Don't you think you've been down long enough?"

Hector put his foot on the gas pedal and eased out of the lot.

§ § §

A security guard was searching patrons at the Improv's entrance. Dirty could feel the .40 caliber's heft in his Evisu jeans. "We'll never get by dude. Fuck them numbers. We came off; let's roll out."

"Stop crying and come on." Trouble rushed over to the guard. He was breathing hard as if he'd run a marathon.

"Twenty-five a head with identification," an awkward-built guard said as he inspected the duo. "If you don't have IDs, you two look like you can afford seventy-five a pop."

"Man, you trying to rob us and you got a dude in the parking lot having a heart attack." Trouble acted as if he couldn't catch his breath as he poked a finger toward the lot.

The guard's eyes bulged. "You left him there…alone?"

"You damn right. I got two felonies. I can't wear a murder rap."

The guard stepped from behind the velvet rope. "Where is he?"

Dirty pointed. "Stretched out on the ground beside a blue Escalade. Hurry up before the dude die."

The guard sprinted toward the lot in search of an Escalade.

Dirty and Trouble went inside the club, armed.

CHAPTER 12

S teve Harvey was on stage, showing his ass. He was having himself a good time acting a fool. The crowd responded with gut-busting laughter.

Sticky Fingers and an associate sat in private loft seats taking advantage of the bird's-eye-view. Sticky Fingers appeared to be in his mid-forties with thinning hair and sunken cheeks, compliments of his strict vegetarian diet. He wore a designer shirt with two buttons unfastened at the collar, which showed off his gray chest hairs and the darkness of his rough skin. He shut the cell phone's power off. "She's not answering. Give her a few more minutes. Jewels will be here. She's thirsty."

A soot-colored man with wire-rimmed glasses and a bald head sat beside him at the table. "I've given you more time than I was willing. You're washed up, Sticky. You don't have that...that winning drive anymore. It's like you've lowered your player standards. You'll deal with anybody to turn a buck. I can no longer vouch for you."

"Fats, relax and enjoy the show. My friend is stand up; she'll be here."

"That was the same Parker Brothers you threw at me last month." Fats stood to leave. "My business doesn't thrive on practice runs. This is the second time I find myself rehearsing with you. Lose my number, immediately."

The door to the loft was opened.

"Pump your brakes and park your ass back in that chair." Dirty steadied his gun on Fats. "Stay and enjoy the party, old-timer."

Sticky Fingers shifted his sight between the two strangers.

"The Legendary Sticky Fingers." Trouble seated himself directly behind the stunned men. "Jewels told me that I would find you here. She also said that one of you two players would have some numbers that I would be interested in." He looked at Sticky, then pointed at Fats. "I think that would be you."

Dirty waited with his weight against the door, preventing anyone else from entering.

"Listen here, youngster, you're stepping on the wrong set of toes." Sticky wondered why Jewels had foolishly crossed him. "You don't have any idea of how this is going to escalate beyond a simple robbery. Do you know—"

"I don't give a fuck who either one of you bitches is." Trouble had a hard look on his face. "Punk ass, suck my dick. You the middle man. Open your mouth again, and I'll shove a barrel in it. Jewels told me that you'd throw around a few subtle threats."

Fats looked at Sticky. "Out of all people to set up, you pick me. You're right, these guys here don't know, but you...you know there's going to be repercussions." He switched his attention on Trouble. "Your partner over there is carrying a forty-caliber. That thing will sound like a nuke going off in here. The only way you'll leave this building is with a police escort, and I'll have you murdered before they set your bond. You have to shoot me, which you're not." He finished his rum and Coke. "I'm not giving you a motherfucking thing, young jitterbug."

Trouble laughed. "You have a valid point about busting a gun in this small room, but you're gonna give me what I came for regardless of security." With swiftness, he produced a butterfly knife and drove it through Fat's left shoulder.

$ $ $

"Please, Mr. Reynolds, please let him out. He's afraid of the dark." Secret kicked and scratched as Mr. Reynolds dragged her toward a coffin next to the one Junior was locked in. "Why do you hate us so much?" She could hear Junior's pounding. "Why, Mr. Reynolds? What have we done?"

He lifted the struggling young girl with ease and forced her into the coffin. "I hate all of you little bastards. If it wasn't for your good-for-nothing father, I wouldn't still be selling these damn things." He banged his meaty fist against the coffin. "If he hadn't stolen my money, I wouldn't still be babysitting a bunch of worthless kids, either. Damn you all to hell."

§ § §

The knife entered his shoulder with ease. Fats screamed out in pain as the enormous crowd roared in laughter.

"Shh!" Trouble held a finger to his lips, then stuffed a wad of napkins in Fats's pie hole. "No screaming, gangster."

"Bite down on that," Dirty said. "While you give them numbers up."

Nothing.

Sticky Fingers was still thinking about his next encounter with Jewels.

Trouble whispered in Fats's ear. "Are you really gonna make me stick you again?"

Fats spat out the napkins and leaned slightly to the left, favoring the injured shoulder. "My inside pocket...the right one." Sweat dripped from his temple.

Trouble examined the combination of the ten sets of numbers before putting the slip of paper in his pocket. "It's been a pleasure doing business with you ancient cats." He stood and snatched the knife out of Fats' shoulder.

Fats gritted his teeth in pain.

Trouble wiped the blade clean on Sticky's silk shirt. "Jewels told me to tell you thanks for the hook-up. Oh, yeah, and that cut you was trying to get now belongs to me."

§ § §

Secret looked up at Mr. Reynolds from the confines of her padded box. "Take it out on me. Please, Mr. Reynolds, just let my brother out. He's afraid of the dark."

"He'll get used to it. Your father did." He slammed the coffin's lid shut and locked it.

"My mother will be here in the morning. She'll—"

"She'll be lucky if I let her visit. Now shut your mouth and go to sleep."

Darkness.

Secret heard the dock's door close. "Junior, calm down and listen."

Nothing but crying and more pounding.

"Junior, you little punk. I know you hear me."

Silence.

"Answer me, Junior."

"Huh?" He turned on his side in the complete darkness.

"Stop working yourself up and chill. Remember when we used to play hide-and-seek?"

"Yeah." He sniffled as his chest rose and fell.

"You used to hide from me and Carinne in the clothes hamper for—"

Mr. Reynolds banged on both coffins. "Shut the hell up and go to sleep. Don't make me say it again."

Junior lost his cool again.

❸ ❸ ❸

Jewels was adjusting the medical bed when her first visitor entered her hospital room. "Who the hell swole your eye? Kitchie must have finally got tired of your ass."

GP touched the tender knot under his eye. "Don't worry about it. What happened?"

"Don't even trip." She pulled him close and whispered, "Sticky Fingers is a dead man walking. He had me set up."

"They get it all?" He perched himself on her bed.

"Yeah, but don't trip."

"Listen at what you're saying, Jewels. I'm worse off than when I started. How am I supposed to pay Squeeze?"

"What about Squeeze?" Kitchie entered the room with Ndia.

"Are you okay?" Ndia leaned over the bed's railing to kiss Jewels.

"My head is split pretty good, but I was bred for this shit. Comes with the territory."

Ndia saw the back of Jewels's head. "They shaved you bald."

"Fucked up my brush waves and replaced them with forty-seven stitches." She swung her feet to the floor. "I have to take a leak."

"You need some help." GP reached out for her arm. He wanted to get her alone so they could continue their conversation.

"Nah, I'm cool. I've been pissing for twenty-six years all by myself. I'm a big girl."

"I meant, did you need help to the bathroom."

"You wanna take a guess at how long I've been walking?" She headed for the restroom.

Kitchie folded her arms. "GP, what's going on, and what does Squeeze have to do with it?"

Jewels staggered on her way to the bathroom.

GP and Ndia rushed to her.

GP caught her before she hit the floor. "Slick mouth, you can't be the same person who just told me you've been walking for years."

A young doctor was entering the room. "Ms. Madison, you're not supposed to be out of bed. Your equilibrium isn't functioning properly."

"Goddamn, I needed to take a piss."

"I'll have the nurse bring you a bedpan."

"Don't worry about it, baby," Ndia said. "I'll take care of you when we get home."

The doctor wrote some notes on a chart. "I'm afraid that won't be for a few days. She took a nasty blow."

"GP, can I see you in the hall?" Kitchie walked out the door.

He followed, knowing he would have to come clean. "Let's discuss this later. I'll tell you everything when we get back to the apartment."

"Everything?"

"I don't want to hear your mouth, though."

"I'm not promising." She waited for an elderly woman to walk by. "GP."

"Huh?"

"I apologize. That was nothing between me and that Desmond guy. He didn't try to hit on me or anything. He was just really being nice." She gave him the money. "Now let's finish up with Jewels because I want to hear this."

Jewels watched GP and Kitchie hold hands as they came back into the room. "Because I ain't coming home tonight don't mean for y'all to be fucking in my bed."

Kitchie smirked. "I'm not making any promises. He loves to hear me yell Papi at the top of my lungs."

GP grinned like a Cheshire cat.

§ § §

"You're making excuses 'cause you're scared."

"I'm not arguing with you; call it what you want."

"You coming or not?"

The rest of the girls listened to Nise and her comrade exchange comments from their cots.

"Well?" Nise tied the laces of her sneakers.

"What you care about her for? She kicked your butt and now you wanna help her. What's up with that? If Mr. Reynolds catches you snooping…That off-limit sign is up there for a reason."

"I'll go with you." Samone peeled the covers back and stepped into her shoes. "I'll help you."

"Samone, don't get into that," another girl said. "You're looking for trouble."

"So be it."

Nise stuck her head in the hall and looked both ways. Once she was satisfied that the coast was clear, she flagged Samone with the wave of a hand. The two started their journey into the building's sinister darkness.

Samone stopped Nise at a flight of stairs. "We should go down the emergency exit and cut through the cafeteria."

"But this way is closer."

"The shortcut isn't always best. Trust me; the long way is better. Mr. Reynolds brings his fat ass up these steps all the time when he makes his rounds."

"Lead the way."

"What makes you think they're in there?" Samone pushed open a door with a red exit sign glowing above it.

"Think about it. They're not in the sleeping quarters with everybody else. Where else could they be? Besides, I got caught playing hide-and-go-get-it with this boy named Tim. Mr. Reynolds locked both of us in them scary caskets two nights straight."

"He caught y'all doing it?"

"Not actually. We were trying, but Tim couldn't get it in."

They made it to the bottom of the stairs.

"Nise, can I ask you something without you wanting to fight?" She held the cafeteria door open as Nise passed through it.

"Ain't nobody gonna mess with you."

"You're mean and hateful to everybody. Why, all of a sudden, would you risk breaking the rules to be nice to someone you don't even like?"

"Secret isn't a punk like everybody else. She's the only person who stood up to me since I came here. I like that. She even had the heart to run away. I won't even do that. I don't have nowhere to run to anyway."

"Who's there?" Mr. Reynolds turned toward the direction of the voice, leaving the walk-in refrigerator wide open. "Who's there, I said?" He stuffed the remainder of a slice of cheesecake in his mouth.

Nise and Samone ducked into a cabinet under a long stainless-steel countertop that stretched the length of the kitchen.

He used the light of the refrigerator to navigate through the room. "I know you're here; you stink."

§ § §

Kitchie hung her purse on the weight bench. "You did *what?* I can't believe you would consider doing something like that. That's crazy on you and Jewels's part. More so yours because you borrowed it."

"It was the only solution I had. I would've tried anything if the results meant getting the kids back."

"While you were concentrating on the results, did you work on a backup plan if something happened to the money?"

GP hadn't thought that far. He'd be damned if he would tell her that he hadn't.

❧ ❧ ❧

Mr. Reynolds knelt to scan the length of the kitchen from beneath a table while licking cream cheese from his pudgy fingers. Nothing.

Nise cupped a hand over Samone's mouth.

"It's going to be hell on earth if you make me find you." He snatched open a broom closet.

Samone's guess was that Mr. Reynolds was still on the far side of the kitchen. She peeled Nise's hand from her mouth and reached for the cabinet door.

Nise latched onto her shirt. "Chill before you get us busted. I knew I should've left you upstairs."

Mr. Reynolds yanked open a pantry door. "Aha!"

Still nothing.

"There's no sense in both of us getting caught," Samone spoke in hushed tones. "You help Secret and her little brother, and I'll handle Mr. Reynolds."

Nise flicked her cigarette lighter to see Samone's face. "You sure?"

"Yup. We're running out of time." Samone eased out and crawled away on the tiled floor.

Mr. Reynolds squatted to look into a set of cabinets on the opposite side of the ones Nise had found refuge in. When he found the cabinets to be empty on that side, he struggled with his weight to get back on his feet. And that's when he saw Samone standing in the center of the kitchen. "Damn you, child."

§ § §

GP paced in the small area between the coffee table and the couch. "You have every complaint in the book. How about being a part of the solution instead of the problem?"

"You should've confided in me first, GP. I should've been a factor in the decision made to borrow that type of money." She held up her hand to display her wedding ring. "I'm married to you, not Jewels. You and I laid in the back seat of that old Datsun and made Secret, not you and Jewels. Ain't no tellin' where Junior was conceived at."

"If you wasn't bitching and complaining all the time, then maybe you could've been a part of the conversation. Don't nobody want to talk to someone when they know they're only gonna meet force and resistance."

§ § §

Samone started toward the cafeteria tables with a smile on her face.

Mr. Reynolds sighed and went after her. "Samone Gates, you wake up this instant." He quickly closed the gap between them, slapped her in the face, then backhanded her. "Wake up!"

She blinked a few times as if she were gradually coming back from some distant place. "Mr. Reynolds." She surveyed her surroundings. "What are we doing here?"

He latched onto her ear and pulled her toward the doors. "This is the last warning. If you don't take your medicine, I'll start tying you to the bed again. I'd like to see your ugly self walk in your sleep then."

"I'm sorry, Mr. Reynolds."

"Tell me something I don't know." The door closed with a thud.

Nise hurried to reach the dock, which was where she remembered the coffins to be.

The door that led to the rear dock squealed as it opened. Nise had no idea where to begin. There were twenty coffins waiting to be picked up. The sight of the pine boxes brought back memories of two long nights that she never wanted to relive. She swallowed. "Secret! Secret...where you at?" She walked the aisles of boxes for the dead. "Secret."

Secret had fallen asleep hours ago to the sound of Junior's phobia.

"Secret, Tough Guy, somebody. I know you're here."

Secret stirred in her sleep; Junior's eyes popped open.

"Secret."

She thought she heard Nise's voice echoing through her tired mind.

"Secret, I didn't come down here for my health."

She raised her eyelids and listened for Junior.

"This is bullshit, Secret. Where the hell are you?"

Couldn't be. No way. I must be dead. Nise? She heard the soft voice again. "I'm over here." She kicked the coffin's lid.

Nise turned toward the sound of thumps.

"I'm here." Secret kicked.

Nise unfastened the latch and lifted the lid. "What are you doing, trying to get us busted?"

"Was I that loud?" Secret said, climbing out.

"No, I only asked because my health depends on it. Of course you were loud. Are you gonna thank me or am I gonna have to lock you back in here?" She helped Secret to the floor.

"Thank you."

"Where is—"

"Junior!" Secret hurried to open the coffin adjacent to the one she had been in.

He lay there with his small body pulled into a ball, shivering. His eyes were as wide as high beams.

"Come on, Junior. It's all right now." Secret reached out to him. No response.

"He's scared shitless." Nise came closer. "Help him out and let's get out of here."

Secret used her leverage to pull Junior out with Nise's assistance. "What's the catch? Why are you helping us?"

"If I don't, who else will?"

The door hinges squealed.

Secret and Nise looked in the direction of the door.

Junior stood there, unresponsive.

§ § §

"Granted, you've done some dumb stuff, but this…this is the epitome of retarded." Kitchie gave GP a pillow and a sheet, then pointed at the couch. "You'd been better off keeping that to yourself." She sang the words, "If you think you're lonely now, wait until tonight, boy."

"Don't play. You're the one who wanted to know." GP leaned on the doorframe of Jewels's bedroom.

"We already have more problems than we're capable of handling. You should've known better than to gamble with somebody else's money and somebody else's life. Jewels could've been killed, and Squeeze ain't playing with a full deck."

"It was a sure thing."

She giggled. "Sure? You're still screaming that. Well, let's see about that." She held up a thumb. "We're exactly where we started from—broke." A second finger. "We have another debt that we don't have a clue as to how it's going to get paid." Another finger. "My babies aren't any closer to home—they're further. Do you want me to go on? I still have some more fingers to count on." She started to close the door. "Excuse me, I need to get some sleep. I'm going to visit the kids in a few hours."

"Mami."

"I'm going to sleep. Good night, GP." She shut the door.

§ § §

"Well, well, well, what do we have here?" Mr. Reynolds flicked the light switch on lighting up the rear dock. "Denise, the cemetery is full of people who didn't know how to mind their business."

She shrugged her shoulders and turned to Secret. "Ain't no turning back now. It's his fat ass or us."

"Without a doubt, it's fat boy. What you wanna do?"

"He can't walk from one end of the hall to the other without losing his breath. He can't handle both of us. We have to kick his ass."

Junior's body was there, but he was definitely in someplace reserved for the traumatized.

Nise unscrewed the handles of two push brooms and gave Secret one. "Whatever you do, don't stop swinging."

"I can handle a stick. My aunt taught me." She twirled the broom handle, causing it to whip through the air, and rested it under her armpit. She assumed a fighting stance.

"Okay. You got to teach me that."

Mr. Reynolds laughed as he wobbled from one end of the dock to the girls. "I'm going to beat both of you bitches raw."

"Who you calling a bitch, bitch!" Nise struck him in the center of his forehead.

Secret followed suit with a vicious blow to the sternum, then a sharp hit to the meaty part of his neck.

He staggered. "You little Black—"

Nise struck again. "This is for old and new."

She remembered when he had used that line each time he had beat her.

He latched onto Nise's broom handle for dear life.

Secret delivered a blow that broke her handle in two.

He fell on his face as the air escaped his lungs.

Nise hit and cried and hit and cried. "Mean old man, die." And hit and cried.

Secret grabbed her around the waist and pulled her away. "That's enough, Nise. Let's go." She took Junior's hand and the three of them left, locking Mr. Reynolds on the dock. "Think he'll be all right?" She was worried but was really more concerned about Junior.

"Who gives a fuck?" Nise lit a cigarette.

CHAPTER 13

M r. Reynolds awoke on the concrete floor. His bones ached and he suffered from an enormous headache that had Secret Patterson and Denise Holcut written all over it. He caressed his temples and felt the dried blood that had matted his hair. *Secret and that despicable waste of a good nut, Denise, will wish they were never born when I'm finished with them.* He staggered to his swollen feet and checked his watch. 6:49 a.m.

Mrs. Patterson was scheduled to visit in less than an hour.

He rushed to the door only to find it locked. "Rotten bastards." The metal door rang out when he kicked it. He turned to the coffins and thought …

And thought some more.

He made his way to a phone mounted on the dock's wall. He poked in a number.

"What?" Tucker Reynolds put his cordless phone to his ear as his eyes focused on his one-room trailer home.

"Tucker, I need you."

He stretched in the thread-bare La–Z-Boy and wiped last night's crumbs off of his chest. "What do you want, Claude?"

"I need you to haul a load ASAP."

"Forget it." He swatted at two flies that were swarming around his lap. Then, he noticed the remainder of a pastrami on rye squished between himself and the chair. "Find somebody else. Brother or no brother, I'm through fooling with you."

"I'll pay you up front."

"You still owe me; pay that. Find Daddy's coin collection you claim was stolen, and pay the family what you owe us."

"Stop accusing me of stealing from my own family. I'll square you away on my debt and give you a thousand dollars for this load." He glanced at the coffins.

"You never have cash on hand, so you claim. Why the hell would I believe you have eighteen hundred today?"

"Tucker, you fuck, I only owe you two hundred."

"The other six is for waking me up to talk to your lard ass. It ain't like you don't have it. You've been spending the family's fortune for years now. That's my price, little brother. Take it or leave it."

"Be here in twenty minutes and you have a deal."

Mr. Reynolds went to the loading platform and pushed a red button. The mechanical garage door was electrically raised, inviting the early morning sunlight to the rear dock.

§ § §

Kitchie slammed on the brakes and pressed both palms against the horn. "Diablo!"

Tucker honked the horn on the big rig as he wheeled the semi out of the group home's lot with no regards for the stop sign.

Kitchie hummed along with an Avant and Lil' Wayne tune as she parked the Escalade near the front entrance. She saw her children and at least fourteen others sitting on the porch.

As she approached with a smile, she heard someone say, "Uh-oh, the shit is about to hit the fan now." Her smile went flat when she saw the distraught look on Junior's face.

Secret lifted her head, met her mother's questioning eyes, and burst into tears. "Mr. Reynolds done it, Ma."

Junior never acknowledged Kitchie's presence.

She set her purse on the pavement and knelt in front of the children. "He did what? What's wrong, Secret?"

The front door eased open. "Good morning, Mrs. Patterson. It's—"

The children screamed and dispersed.

Junior never moved.

Nise and Secret took cover behind Kitchie.

Nise's heart pounded hard. "Don't let him get me, Mrs. P. I was only helping Secret. I don't want no more black eyes."

Kitchie's heart sank when she looked at the dark rings around Nise's eyes. "He did that to you?"

"Yes, ma'am."

Mr. Reynolds stepped forward. "Don't pay that lying child any—"

"Ma, he locked me and Junior in caskets last night because we ran away."

"Sick cracker!" Kitchie went into her purse. "I swear I'm gonna kill you."

Mr. Reynolds backed into the group home and secured the door.

§ § §

"Vivian, I hope you didn't have to go too far out of your way coming down here this morning." GP stacked some Street Prophet shirts on the table of his booth.

"It's quite all right," the lawyer said. "I have a friend in the business, an injury lawyer, who has an office in Terminal Tower and a view of Public Square. I might drop in on her while I'm down here."

"So, what is it you wanted to talk to me about? I have a lot of work to do; haven't made a dime going on two weeks now."

"Do you mind?" She rested her briefcase on the table's bare spot.

"Not at all."

"The light company is willing to drop charges, provided you pay your previous bill in its entirety—including the charges for the damaged meter and the electricity you stole."

"Borrowed."

"It was stolen, Mr. Patterson."

"If I have to pay them back, it must've been a loan."

"Whatever floats your boat. Just pay them within the next ten working days or no deal. Also, you can't get electricity in your name for a year."

GP held on to his airbrush gun. "How much do they want?" He stared out at the busy street as motorists added to the noise pollution, rushing to begin their day.

Vivian flipped the briefcase open and handed him an itemized list.

GP scrolled the sheet until he saw the cuss word *Total.* "Thirty-nine hundred. Bullshit! Now who's doing the stealing? I didn't owe anything near this."

She pointed to the paper. "The fine imposed for tampering with the meter is what cost you. But that's the least of your worries."

"You need a drum roll? Don't stop now."

As the traffic congested, pedestrians filled the sidewalks.

"I can get Mrs. Patterson probation, but I'm afraid, because of your record, you're going to do a few years in prison."

"I'll be damned. Prison!" He took a deep drink of air. "Then tell me, Vivian, what the hell is my family supposed to do while I'm in the pen? I thought you said you and the DA were buddy-buddy."

"He's going to do everything he can for you. The child endangering charges—dropped. Public disturbance—dropped. He's fully aware of the whole situation. The fact of the matter is, whether Mr. Tharp deceived you or not, you and your wife assaulted the man with a deadly weapon. I assure you that Mr. Tharp has no intention of dropping the charges." She handed GP another document. "He's even pressing the DA so you can compensate him for the time he's been out of work."

"What's this?" GP wasn't in the mood for another bit of bad news that would anchor him deeper in debt.

"It's the criminal complaint that Mr. Tharp filed against Mrs. Patterson and yourself."

§ § §

Kitchie sat on the porch of the group home, surrounded by the other boys and girls, rocking Junior in her arms as Nancy Pittman and two squad cars entered the lot. "Help is here now, baby." Her tears fell to his face. "No one is gonna hurt you again." She exchanged looks with the other children. "Any of you."

"Mrs. P." Nise slid an arm around Kitchie and leaned on her shoulder, imitating what Secret was doing at that exact moment.

"Yes."

"I wish I had a mother like you; someone who cared about me."

Nancy slowed her pace when Kitchie's facial expression rattled her sense of well-being. "I hope there's meaning behind this."

"I told your stupid, spoon-fed ass not to separate me from my children. My husband even showed you proof that this Reynolds bitch was abusive. Now look at my baby. He won't talk."

An officer came forward. "Your language, ma'am, in front of the children. Calm down and tell us what the problem is."

Junior blinked occasionally but failed to focus on anyone in particular.

"He locked us in caskets 'cause we ran away." Secret held hands with Nise around Kitchie's back.

"The old faggot beats me 'cause…" The boy lowered his head and his voice. "'Cause I wet the bed."

"That ain't nothing," Samone said. "He ties me to the bed most nights."

"Uh-huh, sure does."

"That's awful. Why would he tie you to the bed?" Nancy felt her anger mounting as her cheeks turned red.

Jason stuck his tongue in Samone's direction. "'Cause she's a creepy sleepwalker."

"Shut up, pussy, I can speak for myself. At least I wasn't traded for crack."

Nise nestled against Kitchie. "I get punished with the nearest thing to me just for being me. Look what he did to me." She took the cheap sunglasses off.

Son of a bitch. An officer headed up the stairs. "Where is this Mr. Reynolds now?"

"He locked himself inside." Kitchie kissed Junior's forehead.

Nancy's eyes searched to find Secret's, to read them, as she took her hand. "I know you want to go home with your mother. Telling stories won't make it—"

"Where the fuck do you get off insinuating that my child is a liar?"

"That's not what I meant." Nancy looked at Secret, her probing eyes continuing their search for truth. "Are you telling me that Mr. Reynolds locked you inside a coffin, a dead person's coffin? That's just a little far-fetched."

Secret sucked her teeth. "Yeah, me and my brother. Why do you think he's acting that way?" She aimed a finger at Junior. "You know he's afraid of the dark. Go inside and see for yourself."

"You got a lot of nerve," Nise said. "Coming down here, accusing people of lying. You don't know any of us. You high-class white hoes is a trip, with your ugly outfits. I'm the one who let Secret and Junior out, but I guess I'm lying, too." She pulled out a Newport. "Somebody give me a light; this bitch shot my nerves."

Kitchie shook her head, communicating much more than no.

"Sorry, Mrs. P." She shoved the cigarette back in the pack, then placed them in the palm of Kitchie's open hand.

One officer went to the rear of the facility. Another began to interview the children one by one. Nancy and the remaining officer pounded on the heavy oak door.

The door eased open. "Thank God you're here. I want that woman arrested." Mr. Reynolds pointed to Kitchie.

§ § §

Grief overwhelmed Miles as he watched his mother strain her tired eyes, staring at a school picture of Jap. Miles set his skateboard down and closed the door behind him. "Are you okay, Ma?"

Ms. Silex lifted her saggy eyes. "I miss him." Her hands trembled. "I miss him; that's all. I can feel it; he's never coming home."

Miles walked around the glass coffee table, eased the photo from her grasp, and sat beside her. "There's something I should tell you."

She grabbed a hold of his wrist. "You got your cast off. Boy, you need to get this thing some sun. It's so pale. How does it feel?" She rubbed his arm.

"It's good."

"Now, if I can only keep you off that skateboard. You're too old to be breaking bones. Baby, you don't heal like you would if you were still a teenybopper."

"I didn't break my arm on the board…"

Her forehead wrinkled; her brows pointed inward. "You told me—"

"I know what I said, Ma." His voice softened. "That's what I came over to talk to you about."

"Why would you lie to me about a broken arm?"

He sighed. "Because...I didn't want you to worry."

"Well, I'm worried." She folded her arms.

"I owed these people some money. They broke my arm because I couldn't pay them on time."

She took her purse from behind a throw pillow. "I have about twenty dollars; my Social Security check will be here in a few days."

He stopped her from rambling through the purse. "Ma, I—"

"No, you take this money, you hear me?"

"It was ninety-thousand I owed."

The look in her eyes was disturbing. "How could..." She paused. An irritating silence hung heavy in the air. "How could you owe somebody that type of money, Miles? You fooling with them cracks?"

"I have a gambling problem. I'm getting help now, and I haven't gambled since Jap's been missing." His eyes fell on the photo. He whispered, "I'm sorry, Jap."

Her skin puckered with goose bumps. "What...Miles, what does Jap have to do with this?"

"I think they did something to him as a personal message to me." He blinked a tear loose.

Ms. Silex nibbled on her lip. Her heart began to pound irregularly in her chest. She staggered a bit as she attempted to stand.

Miles tried to assist her.

"Keep your filthy hands off me." She felt light-headed. "If you're the cause of something terrible happening to Jap, then I've lost two sons. I'll never forgive you for...for—" She went into cardiac arrest and crashed through the glass coffee table.

§ § §

"There has to be a thorough investigation done into the accusations made by these children." Nancy followed the group to the loading dock. "There will be someone here from Social Services around the clock. Whatever is going on here is going to stop today."

Secret stopped in front of a door marked with an *Off Limits* sign. "Right in there."

"Your fat ass is going to jail now." Nise rolled her eyes and put her hands on her narrow hips. "Betcha won't lock nobody else in a coffin."

The tallest officer tried the door. "Open it up, Mr. Reynolds."

"I always keep it locked. I don't want the kids playing back here and hurting themselves."

"Yeah, right." Kitchie held on to her mute son's hand.

Mr. Reynolds unlocked the door and pushed it open.

The loading dock was bare, with the exception of a broken broom handle.

"I told you that these children have outrageous imaginations." Mr. Reynolds shook his head at Secret. "I haven't stored coffins back here in over a year."

Secret turned to Nancy. "I swear they were here last night."

"Sure were." Nise tugged on an officer's sleeve. "On my grandma's grave."

A truck horn was blown just outside the mechanical garage door.

Mr. Reynolds went to the loading platform and pressed a pudgy finger on a red button. "The dairy delivery is due." The door was fully raised.

Tucker leaned out of the semi's window. "Claude, will you ever stop being an asshole?" He scratched his beard stubble. "The Smiths have no room for these caskets. You need to find a place for them, or you and these brats can get them off my truck."

"You're carrying coffins for Mr. Reynolds?" the smallest of the three officers said.

Mr. Reynolds frowned, a signal for his asinine brother to keep his rotten mouth closed.

"Yes, sir. Took the job this morning. Picked up twenty from right where you're standing."

An officer took a set of handcuffs from his waist. "Mr. Reynolds, you're under arrest for child abuse. You have the right to remain…"

The children clapped as the officer recited the Miranda warning.

§ § §

Jewels punched in the numbers on the phone's keypad. "May I speak with Congresswoman Cynthia Martin?" She rubbed her stitches; they were still sore.

"Speaking."

"My name is Jewels Madison, and I'm calling in support of Parole Bill H.R. 3072."

"What state are you in?"

"Ohio. Ms. Martin, get them brothers out of prison."

"We're trying, but it's going to take the people to force the government to act. Your call is the first step, and it will be logged in its proper order. Thanks for your support. Spread the word."

"You're welcome." She hung up and called GP.

§ § §

GP leaned against the pay phone while keeping a watchful eye on the booth. He wiped the receiver with his shirt, then placed it on his ear. "Ninth Street Artwork; GP speaking."

"One day you're gonna be able to answer the phone like that for real, in your own place of business."

"Let's face it, Jewels, this is a dead dream. How are you? Ready to come home?"

"Yeah, homeboy. I'm getting discharged now. I was thinking about Limbo, Tink, and Manny Cool. Man, GP, you don't know how things would be different if they were home."

"Tell me about it. When is the last time you heard from them? I wonder how they are."

"I haven't heard from them in a minute, but I called Congress today and played my part so they can bring parole back."

"That's what's up. Give me the number. I'll call, too. Kitchie will be here soon; then we'll be there."

Jewels zipped her jeans. "You sound fucked up. What's wrong now?"

"Ain't nothing."

"Motherfucker, please. I hear it in your voice."

"Looks like I'll be finding out how Manny Cool and them is doing for myself. I found out today that I'm going to prison. This white boy is really pressing charges, knowing he was in the wrong." GP glanced at the dark clouds circling overhead. He smelled rain. "You should see all the shit in this criminal complaint against me and Kitchie."

"You have the actual criminal complaint?"

"A certified copy of it." A spec of water hit his nose.

Jewels tied her shoe and was ready to leave. "There's an address on it, right?"

"Yeah. The lame lives in South Euclid."

"Don't stress the charges. I'll handle it."

"Jewels—"

"I ain't trying to hear it." She touched her stitches again. "People get hurt every day. You can't help me get my niece and nephew back, or help me pay Squeeze, if you're blowing my phone up with collect calls from the joint. I'll handle it."

"You are truly a jewel."

"And I'm still waiting on my diamond."

"Let me go; it's about to rain. We'll be there soon." He returned the receiver to its cradle.

The weather had changed for the worse over the course of the last twenty minutes. By the time the Escalade stopped at the curb, GP was soaked. The afternoon downpour showed no sign of slowing. He opened the rear door to load the merchandise and saw that Kitchie was crying. "What's wrong with you, Mami Chula?"

CHAPTER 14

It had been exactly two weeks and one day since Jewels was discharged from Metro Hospital. Now she stood inside Conrad Tharp's bedroom, disgusted. She could feel her stomach churn. The room had been converted into a porno set. There was high-tech equipment and high-velocity power cords all over. Pornographic pictures and film clips had been thumbtacked to a corkboard. Everything from leather restraints to sex toys to libido-stimulating drugs were in this room.

Jewels was not one to frown upon an individual's sexual practices or preference, but Conrad Tharp was a deviant. The stars of his homemade films were he and boys and girls who couldn't have been any older than Secret, Jewels speculated, while forcing herself to view the images on the corkboard. "Sick caveman." Jewels held her stomach, which now felt queasy, then threw-up. She wiped her mouth with a sleeve, then flipped a light switch.

A pulsating instrumental music began to play. She went to the stereo and lowered the volume. The electronic equipment lit up. Fluorescent tube lights lining the ceiling shined bright, and the video cameras zoomed in on the messy bed. Two computer screens showed the bed from different angles. Another screen boasted the video footage of some of the same shots that had been pinned on the corkboard.

She knocked a set of cue cards, with script lines on it, to the floor and began to ramble through the computer station's drawer until she found a CD. She sat down in front of the computer and burned Conrad Tharp's entire file onto the CD.

Thirty minutes later, Jewels yanked the CD out of the disc drive. She heard the door slam shut as someone hummed the same tune that she heard earlier.

§ § §

Crutchfield and his annoying sidekick, Thomas, made their way up a broken sidewalk, then rapped on a warped screen door.

"Go away."

"Miles, it's Detective Crutchfield. Can I have a word with you?"

"Come back when you die." His words were slow and slurred.

Thomas cupped his hands around his face and looked through the screen. "Sounds like he's been drinking pretty heavy."

"Miles, thanks for inviting me in." Crutchfield opened the door and led the way.

Thomas fanned the air. "You look like shit, Miles...and this place smells like a used pamper."

Miles was stretched across the couch. He was holding on to a bottle of brown liquor. He sat upright and paused until the room was no longer spinning. "What are you...Why are you here bothering me? I don't like you."

"Sorry to hear about your mother's passing," Crutchfield said.

Miles turned the bottle up to his face and let out a satisfying, "Aaah. Did you arrest Squeeze?" He stood and staggered in place. His shirt had been buttoned all wrong.

"I think you better sit back down." Thomas helped Miles to the couch.

"I need to take a look in Jap's room." Crutchfield pointed out a bag of marijuana to Thomas.

"Don't be scoping out my weed. Get your own; it ain't enough for all of us." He shoved it in his pocket. "Don't worry yourself about busting Squeeze." He beat on his chest. "'Cause can't nobody, nobody, you hear me? Nobody can make things right by my mother and Jap but me." He started laughing. The scent of alcohol poured from his breath.

"You're drunk; you don't know what you're saying."

"You're right; I am a little tipsy." He hit the bottle again. "But my tongue is sober. Look around. I don't have a fucking thing to lose. It's gone already."

"If I thought you really knew what you were saying," Thomas said as he touched Miles' shoulder, "I'd take you in. Instead, I'm gonna let you sleep your liquor off."

"You'd take a drunk man to jail…" Miles paused to remember what he wanted to say. "Just 'cause I had a few drinks, you'd threaten to arrest me, but you won't arrest Squeeze for…whatever he did to my brother. I'll arrest him since you two are chickens." He closed his eyes. "I'm gambled out. I have to make it right."

Crutchfield patted Miles's back. "Get some rest. I'm gonna take a look in Jap's room."

"Hurry up and get out. Jap ain't into people bothering his things."

§ § §

Blue Eyes closed the back door of his home with a dull thud. "I'm home, honey. I've been thinking of you all day." He adjusted a leather bag that he had thrown over his shoulder. He hummed an upbeat tune and danced his way to a downstairs closet. He pulled the door open and smiled. "Were you thinking of me like I've been thinking of you?"

An adolescent blow-up doll wearing a training bra and lace thong smiled back at him.

"You're trying to make me love you; tell the truth." He picked up the life-sized doll with care, pinched its synthetic nipples, and kissed its mouth. He turned around and caught a vicious blow from the butt of a nickel-plated .45.

"You nasty fucker." Jewels knelt down and latched on to his blond hair and looked into his blue eyes. "If I didn't need you alive, I'd kill you."

"Don't hurt me. There's plenty of money in the bag. Take it. Please don't hurt me."

Jewels glanced at the open leather bag beside him. "That's a bonus. Open your mouth."

"I didn't mean to—"

She backhanded him. "Open your mouth, pervert."

He complied.

"Wider."

She could now see his tonsils. She filled his mouth with the long barrel. "I'm only gonna say this once, so turn your ears on."

He nodded.

§ § §

"This guy was a true military fanatic." Thomas placed a model tank back on the dresser. "Might have served our country well."

Crutchfield backed away from a closet filled with camouflage clothing and various styles of army boots. "I always knew you were a little off, but to be slow *and* off brands you retarded."

"You're worse than my wife. What are you fussing about now?"

"It finally sank into your mentally-challenged head that Jap is dead."

Thomas examined a plastic model of a .50-millimeter machine gun. "I never said that."

"Not per se, but you implied it. What does *'might have* served our country well' mean? For some apparent reason you think he's not capable of serving our ass-backward country anymore."

"Uh…" Thomas opened a drawer. "You made me lose my train of thought."

"Impossible; you've never been trained to think. So what does 'might have' mean?"

❄ ❄ ❄

Conrad stretched his mouth as wide as he could.

Jewels pushed the barrel in. "I'm only gonna say this once, so turn your ears on."

He nodded.

"I know all about your extracurricular activities. I've saved everything in your computer files on my CD. All of it, including the pictures and the parents who rent you their kids." She tightened her grip on his stringy hair and pushed the gun deeper until he began to gag. "Sick, perverted bastard, you probably like it this way. You want to keep me quiet?"

He nodded as best as he could.

"You filed some bogus charges against my partner GP."

His brows furrowed.

"Greg Patterson and his wife."

His eyes widened.

"Now you remember. You have two days to drop the charges or I'll turn my CD of your child molesting ring over to the cops, if I don't decide to come back and rid the world of you myself. Did I make myself clear enough for you?"

"Hmm." He confirmed.

She released his hair to show him the CD. "Two days."

Another nod.

184 O A S I S

"Good." She delivered a blow to his head so hard, that when Conrad awoke from the realms of never-never land, he'd certainly have a splitting headache.

§ § §

"Well, make something up. You're due to tell me a good lie." Crutchfield waited on Thomas's answer.

"I'm leaning toward believing Jap is amongst the dead."

"Thought so." Crutchfield went to the door. "Let's get out of here. It's nothing here but stinking boot camp memories." He reached for the light switch and noticed a wastepaper basket positioned directly beneath it.

Thomas had a smirk on his face while Crutchfield sifted through the rubbish. "Looks like you're skilled in the sanitation department. How long have you been a professional garbage picker?"

"Ever since your grandmother showed me the ropes." He picked out an empty watch box, returned to the living room, and found Miles snoring, laid face down on the bare floor.

Crutchfield shook Miles.

"Forgive me, Momma. I'll make it right." Drool pooled between his scruffy face and the floor.

"Get up, Miles." More shaking.

He opened his eyes.

Crutchfield stuck the watch box in his face. "Was Jap wearing this watch when he disappeared?"

He shrugged. "I thought I told you to get out." He closed his eyes again.

Thomas entered the room.

Crutchfield tossed Thomas the watch box.

Thomas read the words displayed on the box. *Suunto's X 9 GPS Watch.*

§ § §

Kitchie sat on the building's stoop watching the neighborhood children playing stickball. She thought about all the ups and downs that had taken place in her life. She even recalled the time she had stormed out of her parents' house, holding GP's hand, after announcing that she was going to marry GP whether they gave her their blessing or not.

"Snap out of it. Come back down here with us." Desmond flashed his Academy Award-winning smile.

"Hey, Desmond. How are you?"

"I'm good. What about you? I saw the newspaper. That's fucked up how that Reynolds cat been abusing kids all these years. I hate that your kids got mixed up in that bullshit."

"Me, too. The state placed some of the kids with another organization until the courts decide Reynolds's fate. I'm officially a volunteer, which is a plus for me. I get to spend time with my children until my husband and I can bring them home."

Desmond watched her lips move as she spoke. "How's your little man? Is he…"

"No, he hasn't spoken a word since the incident. The doctors say he'll be fine. Something will trigger him to talk again."

Desmond started up the steps. "It won't rain forever. The sun will eventually shine on you. Take it easy, with your fine self."

"I'm glad you think so." GP poked his head through a hall window just above the stoop. "Mrs. Patterson, come upstairs." He shot Desmond a look of contempt.

When Kitchie rounded the corner, GP was leaning against the wall near Jewels's door. "Is there something you wanna tell me?"

"No. Is it something you want to hear me say?"

"You got this guy in your face, cracking on you and shit."

"He wasn't in my face, GP. And as far as the compliment, you don't have a problem with people admiring me when it comes to making sales for Street Prophet. What you should've done is sat back and watched how I handled the situation, instead of making your presence known. Then, we wouldn't be on the verge of an argument." She touched his face. "I never thought that I had to reassure you. I'm in love with you more than I was yesterday. It's been that way since the day we met." She held up her hand. "That's why this ring is on my finger. And you're kind of cute."

GP smiled. "I got some good news."

"Share it. I can use it."

"I rather you see it for yourself." He took her by the hand and led her into the apartment.

Her eyes widened. "Tell me the truth. Where did all that come from?" She was staring at five stacks of money, each containing five thousand dollars.

"You can't handle the truth, so we'll call it a…gift."

Jewels swiveled her chair around from her PC monitor. "Did y'all know that, as of May 16, the 2005 census states that there are over five hundred-thousand registered sex offenders, and the number of reported child abuse cases are in the motherfucking millions?"

GP picked up a stack of rubber-banded bills. "This is to get us a place."

Kitchie jumped in his arms and wrapped her legs around his waist. "We're bringing the kids home?" She kissed him with passion. "I love you, Papi. I can't wait to tell Secret and Junior."

"The other money is to buy me some more time with Squeeze."

"Fuck y'all, ignoring me like I wasn't talking." Jewels turned back to the computer and typed in meganslaw.com.

Kitchie's excitement vanished. "Squeeze is a fool. What are you going to tell him about the rest of his money?"

"Come over here and look at this." Jewels beckoned them with the wave of a hand. When they were gathered around, she poked the computer screen with a finger. "Look at that."

Conrad Tharp's name, date of birth, and current address were listed. He was a registered sex offender.

"Isn't that the guy who's pressing charges against us?" Kitchie looked at GP.

"Not if I can help it." Jewels shut the computer down.

"Deranged asshole," Kitchie said, spite dripping from her voice. "Here I am thinking he was hanging around our booth recklessly eyeballing me, but the puto was sizing up my baby. Talking about taking pictures for some damn online magazine." She rolled her eyes. "Now I'm really pissed. So what about the rest of Squeeze's money?" She rested a hand on a cocked hip.

"We're still working on that," GP said, thinking about Conrad Tharp's lusting over nine-year-old Secret. *That'll cause me to break my principle and be violent.* "Honestly, right now I don't have a clue as to how Squeeze is gonna get paid. I wish money grew on trees."

"That's why we're stalling him with this payment." Jewels had a few clues, though GP didn't approve of them.

He rubbed the small of Kitchie's back. "How about you call Secret and tell her that we're going to bring them home."

§ § §

"A man who pays his bills a day early. Now that's what I call a proactive businessman." Squeeze offered an oversized leather chair with a hand gesture. "Have a seat. Can I get you something? Matter of fact, Hector, bring GP a shot of Louis XIII."

"No, that's okay." GP held up a hand. "It's not...I don't have all your money. Not yet, anyway."

"Yeah, hold that order, Hector." Squeeze stood with his back to a spectacular view of the sunrise. "From the sounds of it, you're not gonna have my cash tomorrow, either."

GP was already nauseous, being up so high, sitting this close to a floor-to-ceiling window facing the horizon. But he became more nervous the instant Hector stood behind him, smacking on a piece of chewing gum. "From the looks of it, no," he said while watching Hector over his shoulder.

"I warned you not to mishandle my cash when you borrowed it. Now, let me recite the fine print: I have zero tolerance when it comes to getting what's mine. Get my cash up."

"Look, Squeeze, I'm gonna handle it." He jerked a thumb toward Hector. "Would you call Hubba Bubba off? He gives me the creeps." GP dropped four stacks of rubber-banded bills on the seat beside Squeeze. "It's twenty thousand right here."

"Twenty doesn't cover your interest rate."

GP kept an eye on Hector. "Technically, my payment isn't due until tomorrow. I brought you this money in good faith. Don't trip, Squeeze."

"You know what? You're right. Come tomorrow, I'm gonna expect my hundred-fifteen thousand. If I don't get it, I'm gonna tax you accordingly."

"I'm gonna need a few weeks to clear my tab."

"You know the rules." Squeeze dismissed GP with the wave of a hand, then turned back to his picturesque window view.

Hector crossed the spacious room with GP at his side.

"GP," Squeeze said, never looking away from the breathtaking horizon.

"Yeah."

"After tomorrow, the full court press is on."

§ § §

Crutchfield entered the forensics lab and knocked on the back of the technician's head. "Hey, packed shit, what do you make of this?"

Anderson Ford caressed his sandy-colored hair. "Why can't you ever use my name? Everyone else calls me Ford. I can go for that. Furthermore, I'd appreciate it."

"You're an ungrateful, confused sperm, you know, Ford. I was being nice. I could've chosen a few other choice names that are more befitting—fudge-packer, dookie dick, frustrated queer, penis pruner, pillow biter, cum—"

Ford threw up his hands in surrender. "Okay, okay, packed shit is fine."

"So, rectum fish, what can you tell me about this?"

Ford took the object from Crutchfield's hand, then adjusted his granny glasses on the middle of his pointy nose. "It's an empty watch box. I knew you possessed the awareness of a brick, but if you needed me to tell you what this is, I can no longer give you brick credit." He turned back to face a tray of bullet fragments.

Crutchfield thumped Ford's head.

"Ow." Ford rubbed.

"Nut breath, I know what type of box it is. I wanna know about the watch that was in the box."

"You should have said that." He glanced at the box once more. "The watch that was in here is the best GPS watch on the market. It's big amongst ROTC students. It's capable of storing up to fifty routes of over a hundred miles apiece, or the routes can be combined for more distance." He slid the watch box across the table to where Crutchfield was now standing. "If a person were wearing that watch and somehow managed to get lost, they could hit the *Mark Home* button and the watch will guide them to the location they started from. Crutchfield, this is a good watch if you're into GPS gadgets. You can even trace your children's hourly whereabouts from a computer with this thing."

"So what you're telling me is if someone had that watch on, I could find them anytime I wanted to."

"Duh, didn't you just hear me say that? But not anybody can find someone wearing one of these."

"Why not?"

"Because the seeker has to have the code to this particular watch. Do you have any idea of how many of these things are out there? Literally millions. Why does this watch concern you?"

"I have reason to believe that Jap Silex—"

"The missing high school kid? ROTC honoree?"

Crutchfield sat on the edge of the table. "Bingo. I think he's wearing the watch that came out of this box. Can you track down the code?"

"Can I squeeze your Charmin?" Ford made his brows jump.

Crutchfield's stomach flipped as his anger swelled. "Don't make me put on a pair of gloves and pound you until my unborn daughter graduates from college."

"I'll have to get around some red tape but it's possible that I can get the code. I'll start with Jap's service provider."

"How long will it take?"

"Few days, few weeks…"

"I want it in a week." Crutchfield went for the door.

Ford made an ugly face and stuck out his tongue.

"I see everything," Crutchfield said without looking back.

CHAPTER 15

Destiny's Child was on the radio crooning a love ballad about catering to their men. Kitchie increased the volume a notch. "Papi, if I could blow, I'd sing this song in your ear all night long."

"You can pretend. That'll be cool with me."

She blushed.

Wendy's parking lot was nearly filled. GP filled in an available space. "I hope you really like the apartment. It's not much, but it'll do for the time being."

She ran a hand over her ponytail. "Liking it isn't a concern of mine. All that matters to me is that it's ours. I can't wait to furnish it and have Social Services inspect it. I'm too ready to bring the kids home."

He traced the length of her arm with a fingertip. "I apologize for all that I haven't been. I never meant for any of this to happen. What I should've done was taken that job. Kitchie, I swear, if I could go back and change it all, I would."

"Papi, things happen. It's the way of this screwed-up world. I haven't been…I could do a much better job at controlling how I say things when I'm angry. I be tripping, I know. You accept my apology?" She closed her eyes and puckered up.

GP forgave her with a passionate French kiss, reminiscent of their first.

She licked her top lip. "Let's somehow get Squeeze's money, move in our apartment, and store this entire ordeal in the past. You, me, and the kids will start brand new."

GP opened the door.

"Hey, wait a minute. You didn't ask me what I wanted."

"We can't afford to eat out. I have to handle something; that's all."

She watched him bop his way into the restaurant. "I love that man with every heart beat."

Jewels's car phone rang.

Kitchie put the radio on mute. "Hello."

❄ ❄ ❄

GP bypassed the line, excusing himself as he made it to the counter. "Can I see the manager, please?"

The cashier looked him up and down, then crinkled her lips. *Another fucking complainer.* She picked up a phone and told the manager that he was being summoned.

GP found contentment as he observed a young couple interacting with their infant child. It reminded him so much of Kitchie and himself when Secret was just a little bigger than a football. Proud parents.

"Is there something I can help you with, sir?"

He turned to face a clean-shaven, buzz-cut wearing, middle-aged black man who reminded him more of a drill sergeant than a Wendy's manager. GP looked into his murky irises and braced himself for the worst. "You don't know me, but you more than likely remember the incident. I was in your drive-thru about a month ago. I ordered about fifty dollars' worth of food that I took off with without paying for."

"I remember quite well. You caused—"

"Please don't tell me; just let me explain."

The line of patrons hushed and zoomed in on GP's conversation. He could feel that he was under observation. "All I wanted to do was break up the monotony at home. Sit down with my wife and kids to share a decent meal together. It's no excuse, but it doesn't happen often in my household. I'm fully aware that what I done was wrong, and I apologize for any harm I may have caused." He placed a hundred dollar bill on the counter. "If I could have paid it back sooner, I would have. The extra is for your troubles."

Even the staff was now gathered around the manager, listening to GP's confession.

"Why?" The manager removed the money. "Why did you make it a point to come back here under these circumstances? I don't understand; you'd gotten away with it. People who are faced with hard times would've kept going and never looked back."

"Because I want my family to always be proud to have me as a husband and a father."

He offered GP a hand. "Thank you. Things will work out for you. Honorable things happen to virtuous people. You're proof that there is still some good in the world. If there's ever anything I can help you with, don't hesitate to ask."

"How about a job? I could really use one."

"Come see me the day after tomorrow, and we'll talk about it."

One person clapped, which urged the staff and patrons alike to follow suit.

A mahogany-colored woman wearing a straw hat and a sundress nodded in approval. "That was all right. Now that's something you don't see every day," she said to no one particular.

GP turned to leave, feeling good about himself, and saw Kitchie standing there.

"Papi, I don't think a day will ever come that I won't be proud that you're my husband. They don't make them like you anymore." She took his hand. "Come on; Jewels is on the phone. She said it's important."

§ § §

GP put the phone to his ear while backing out of the parking space. "What you know good, Jewels?"

"It took you long enough to come to this motherfucking phone, punk. Attorney Green is on the three-way."

"Good afternoon, Mr. Patterson." Vivian chewed on a pen cap, a nasty habit she had while talking on the phone.

"I'm putting the phone down," Jewels cut in. "Y'all hang up when you're finished. I got a move to make."

He tapped the turn signal and eased into the left lane. "What's up, Vivian? I had planned on calling you today."

"I have some good news and some bad news. How do you want it first, the pain or the pleasure?"

"By definition, all news is bad news. So how about you give me the version of what you think is good."

"Conrad Tharp dropped the charges against you and Mrs. Patterson yesterday."

"Shit, I'm on the verge of believing the definition of news is wrong."

"The District Attorney refiled. The state is going to prosecute you and your wife because of the severity of the charges."

"Fuck! I can't stumble on a break."

§ § §

Caribbean Cutty pushed four bundles of money across the hood of a Porsche as he looked at Squeeze. "At what point did you convince yourself that it was cool to test my intelligence?" He used the nub of his missing finger to emphasize his words. "Don't you ever come around my way, trying to pass this bogus bullshit."

A vein throbbed at Squeeze's temple. "Cutty, I don't know what you're talking about, but make that your last time you ever come at me sideways, tropical sucker."

Hector eased his narrow suit lapel back, revealing a gun stuffed below his protruding belly. "You heard the man."

A man in greasy coveralls came from beneath a hydraulic car lift carrying a torque wrench. He let out a piercing whistle, alerting others in the garage. Within seconds, six men were standing behind Cutty. Three other men appeared on a tier above the lopsided standoff with automatic weapons.

The torque wrench carrier positioned himself beside Cutty. "I see you got your chest all poked out, Squeeze. Need some help letting that hot air out?"

"Self-checked coward, I don't see you. Shut the fuck up." Squeeze shot Cutty a warning look. "Let me get this straight. I've spent hundreds of thousands of dollars with you, and all of a sudden my cash ain't good no more?"

"Nah, it ain't. I don't accept counterfeit money. There's a small-time crew on the rise over on Hayden; go beat them out of their rides."

Counterfeit? Squeeze's brows knitted. He focused on the Porsche's hood and pointed at the money. "You saying this ain't legit cash?"

"That's exactly what I'm saying. Now gather your confetti and find the door before shit gets ugly."

§ § §

Squeeze and Hector didn't like being made out to be fools. Squeeze steadied his hands on the roof of his car while staring at the front door of Cutty's chop shop. "If it's one thing that will cause me to hurt a bunch of people, it's a chump playing on my intelligence."

"Yeah, Boss. It makes me want to be violent, too." He stretched and yawned, then looked at Squeeze from the other side of the Mercedes.

"GP played me like I rode the little yellow school bus. You know what I want you to do?"

"What's that, boss?"

§ § §

Two days later, GP was stretched out across the couch, his head resting on Kitchie's lap, staring at the ceiling. "Are you sure, Mami Chula?"

"Yeah." She caressed his face. "I don't care. I don't have to have the car. You and Jewels do what you have to do. I'll get myself together in a little while, then get on the bus. Besides, it'll work out anyway. The Goodwill is only a block away from the group home. When I leave the kids today, I'll walk over, pay for the furniture, then ride with the delivery men to the new apartment."

He was transfixed by the movement of her lips. "By that time, I'll be done and will be waiting at the apartment for you and the furniture to get there. I hope like hell that Ms. Pittman approves of the place."

Kitchie could hear Desmond walking across the floor in the apartment above them. "Ms. Pittman said that the only thing she's concerned with is that we have our own place. After she does her walk-through in the morning, she promised me that Secret and Junior will be home by lunchtime."

"One thing is for certain; this is the last day we'll be away from the kids until they go off to college."

Jewels came out of the bathroom, keys in one hand, cell phone in the other. "Come on, GP, you slacker. Let's bounce. Kitchie, we'll holler at you later."

"Alright."

GP sat up and shared an intimate kiss with Kitchie. "I love you so much, girl. See you later on."

"I love you, too." Kitchie heard Desmond's footsteps fall again, thought for a moment, and then a smile stretched across her face.

§ § §

GP wanted to shout into his new neighbor's phone, but he didn't want her to think that he was rude. He kept it respectful. "What do you mean, she never showed up?"

"Aren't we talking English? No one came in and paid for that order, and the last delivery has gone out for the day."

GP hung up and called the group home.

"Eastside Group Home, attendant Felicia speaking. How can I help you?"

"Felicia, this is Greg Patterson, Secret and Junior's father."

"Yes, Mr. Patterson; your wife has told me so much about you. When I find time, I'm going to come purchase some Street Prophet gear."

"May I speak with my wife, please?"

"She was scheduled to volunteer today, but she never showed up. She was talking about getting the place together for the children; maybe she's there."

"I'm here now. Uh…Felicia, if you hear from her, have her get in touch with me. And, Felicia?"

"Yes."

"Tell the children that I love them."

"Not a problem, Mr. Patterson."

GP stared at the phone for a few moments after he returned it to its base.

His neighbor looked up from the daily paper. "Use it again if you need to."

"No, I'm done. Thank you. I'm gonna go back next door. Thanks again, Mrs. Fletcher."

"Make sure you pull the door up tight." She turned her attention back to an article about a bill that would bring back parole to the federal system. *I want my son home*, she thought. "They need to let them folks out. All that damn time they passing out don't make sense."

When GP left the neighbor's apartment, Jewels was coming up the stairs. "Is Kitchie with you?" He was trying to remain calm.

"Nah, I just came from getting a piece of pussy. She's supposed to be with you. That was the plan, right?"

"Something's wrong." GP headed down the steps. "Let's go to your house."

"What's up, homeboy?"

"That's what I'm trying to find out."

§ § §

It wasn't twenty minutes later when Jewels stuck a key in her apartment door.

GP brushed past her. "Kitchie!" He went into the bedroom only to find it empty.

And that's when he heard it.

The headboard in the apartment above Jewels's was banging violently against the wall. All he could hear was, "Take this dick. Take this dick. His fuck game ain't like this, is it? You love this long dick, don't you?"

Bang. Bang. Bang.

"Ooh, Papi!" she screamed at the top of her lungs. "Give it to me."

Jewels's mouth dropped. She looked at the ceiling with eyes likened to headlights.

GP's lips tightened. He tossed the queen-sized mattress aside. Out of the six weapons resting on the box spring, GP chose the biggest—a .357.

"GP, fool, what the hell are you about to do?"

"Get the fuck out of my way! I knew something was up with them two."

Jewels was witnessing a side of him she had never seen. This side revealed a raving lunatic on the verge of a mental hiccup. She stepped to his left.

GP ran to the fourth floor and blew the entire lock off of Desmond's door. He kicked the door in to find Desmond running in the nude across the living room for his gun.

GP took aim and fired.

Desmond changed directions, knowing he couldn't make it to the gun.

GP fired again.

Desmond never broke his stride. Curtains fell and the window shattered when he dove through it.

GP rushed into the bedroom to find a stunning Puerto Rican. She was a fascinating sight to see, but not as captivating to his eyes as Kitchie.

With no regards for her nudity, she threw her hands up. "Don't kill me. I don't know shit about his business other than he's a hustler. I saw him stash money and coke right there." She aimed a finger at the closet.

GP stood at the edge of the window and looked out. Desmond was on the ground, in a fetal position, exposing his naked ass to the whole neighborhood.

§ § §

Kitchie awoke in a comfortable bed stacked with large pillows. The spin of the ceiling fan was slow, hypnotizing even. *I don't have a ceiling*—she sat upright. Her wrists were bound together as well as her ankles. She tugged at the plastic flexicuffs with her teeth.

"You have a better chance at chewing your hand off than you have with that cuff," came from a dark corner of the room. "I thought you were going to sleep through the night. I could've watched you all night."

Kitchie withdrew from the center of the bed. She settled her back on the headboard and screamed as loud as she could.

"You can be easy. I'm not gonna hurt you. Screaming is useless; there isn't a neighbor for eleven miles in either direction. While you're here, you'll stay locked in this room, and try not to damage the bars on the window."

She could see that the speaker's legs were crossed, but the top of his body wasn't visible, due to the way the main light was being eclipsed by a curtain. "What do you want with me?"

"Nothing more than to make a point." He emerged from the shadow, sucking on a Tootsie Roll Pop.

Kitchie couldn't believe her eyes.

"If I didn't know any better, I'd think you are really surprised to see me." Squeeze sat at the edge of the bed. "Is there something I can get you?" He pointed. "That's your private bathroom. There's clean towels and a change of clothes in your size on the counter."

"Untie me. What in the hell has gotten into you?"

"That's a question you should ask GP. Not that you could at this point. I'm curious to know, though. Why did he put you in jeopardy by fucking with my cash?" He took the lollipop out of his mouth. "I expected more from the man who claims to love you."

"Untie me, Goddammit!" She kicked him off the bed.

Squeeze let out a hair-raising chuckle as he picked himself up from the floor. He put his face up to hers.

She could smell the candy.

The door burst open. Hector came in with a gun leading the way. "I heard something go bump."

Squeeze reared back and smacked her across the face, reddening and stinging it. "Don't make me murder you sooner than I plan to."

§ § §

"Is he gonna die?"

Jewels sat down on the sidewalk beside GP. "He's busted up pretty bad, but he'll live. Have you heard from Kitchie? I checked everywhere."

GP looked at the pay phone. "No, I'm worried about her. I'm angry. I feel defeated. Everything came down on me at once. I can't even keep my own kids. I just exploded. I...shouldn't have shot him."

"You missed." She looked at the booth from which GP had tried for years to make a living.

GP lifted his head as if he had experienced instant relief.

"For a motherfucker who doesn't want anybody to get hurt, you did a good job your first time out."

He examined the palms of his hands as though dirt covered them. "So the police looking for me?"

"Desmond ain't telling the cops shit. Street dudes like Des hold court in the streets. The broad was gone before the paramedics hit the scene."

A squad car stopped curbside and shined its searchlight, illuminating the immediate area and the showcase window of the costume shop. The lone officer poked an elbow out. "No loitering. There's a shelter two blocks down, if you need a place to sleep for the night. They stop accepting at nine."

Jewels and GP stood.

GP squinted to avoid the brilliant light. "This is my art booth." He gestured toward the bare tables. "I've rented it for years now. We're just waiting for a phone call. I've been personally using this phone quite awhile, too."

The officer leaned his head out some. "You do the Street Prophet comics?"

"Airbrushing, T-shirts, sweats, comic books."

"When does the next issue come out? My son loves the Prophet."

"I'm working on it now; it'll be ready come the first of the year."

"I'll be looking forward to it."

"Excuse me," Jewels said, approaching the car.

"Yes, what can I do for you, sir?" He shifted the car into Park.

She removed a CD from her vest pocket. "I was going to drop this off at the police station, but you saved me the hassle. Police stations ain't my type of hype; might fuck around and jinx myself. Feel me?"

He took the CD. "What's this?"

"Put it this way, it's enough evidence there to put a ring of molesters behind bars and get you a pay raise in the process."

She watched the squad car's taillights fade into the night. "You couldn't think of nothing else other than you're waiting on a phone call?"

"I am," GP said. "You did the right thing."

Jewels began to walk away. "No, what I should've done was broke his ass off with this steel dildo I got. Show him how that shit really feels, then blow his fucking head off like I'm gonna do Sticky Fingers when he comes out of hiding. People like Conrad Tharp don't stay in jail. Let's bounce, fool."

"No, I'm staying. Kitchie knows to show up here or call if she's in trouble, no matter what time it is."

She turned to face him. "Then we wait a little longer. In the meantime, you can tell me why your punk ass turned down that motherfucking job and what you plan to do about Desmond. Keeping it real, fuck Squeeze. He can charge it to the game. If he gets to tripping, I'll cancel his chicken dinner."

"I'm not worried about Squeeze or Desmond right now. Dude jumped out a window; he's twisted, right?"

"That he is."

"Then he's not a threat right now. I got too much shit on my mind as it is." He stared at the pay phone. *Please let her be safe.*

CHAPTER 16

Crutchfield stepped off the elevator in a busy precinct.

"Good morning." A beautiful uniformed officer stood at the automatic coffeemaker. "Ford has been calling you since my shift began. You two got a thing going on?"

He couldn't keep eye-to-eye contact with this woman because her silicone boobs were magnets. "Did you know that your left tit is bigger than the right?" He strolled off to his desk, leaving her looking from one breast to the other.

He kicked his feet up on a dented metal desk and placed the phone to his ear. "What do you want, pillow-biter?"

Ford sat atop a lab stool with his legs crossed. "Hey, you asked for my assistance. I haven't been calling you to chitchat."

"Hell, it's only been two days. I didn't expect to hear from you for a week."

"Well, I'm good at what I do. Literally. I cracked the code to your mystery watch."

"Give me what you got."

"Oh no, this is much too good to talk about over the phone. You should come visit me."

"I'll be there in five minutes." He hung up and dashed to the elevator.

§ § §

"I see you took the liberty of cleaning yourself up." Squeeze came in with a breakfast tray. "The outfit fits you well."

Kitchie turned away from the window. "You've never liked GP from the time we were all in job corps. Why would you even give your money to someone you don't care for?"

"I always cared for you, though." He set the tray at the foot of the bed. "Come have a seat." He patted a spot on the bed next to himself.

Kitchie was hesitant but figured she should comply in case there was any chance of her walking away from this with her life.

He admired her beauty as he always had. "I'll tell you what: If you answer just one of my questions honestly, I'll answer one of yours."

"You first." She avoided his probing gaze.

He took a large gulp of air and let it out slowly. "I was the popular one. Me, nobody else. It was me who had all the girls. I'm the one who sent you expensive gifts. You couldn't even pronounce half the shit I bought for you. GP was a nobody; ain't much changed." He fell into thought. "I let him borrow money for bus fare to take you to a free movie. Why did you choose him over me? What did I do wrong?"

"It's not that you did anything wrong. You're just not GP. He's the apple of my eye. From the time that I was a little girl, I fantasized about the man I'd spend my life with. The moment I saw GP, I knew it was him." She looked him square in the eyes for the first time. "When you get your money, you're still going to kill me, aren't you?"

"You don't kidnap people and give them back. That script only happens in books and movies." He reached out to touch her but she withdrew. "Didn't you just hear me say I care about you? I can't hurt you…Hector's gonna do it."

"All because I chose GP?"

"At this stage of the game, that isn't a factor. This falls under the categories of business and my favorite—self-preservation."

He placed the tray of food between them. "You should eat something." He lifted the lid to each dish as he called it out. "An omelet with cheese...buttermilk biscuits...turkey bacon—bet you didn't think I would remember that. And for the main dish." He lifted the stainless-steel lid to reveal a cell phone. "Call GP. I want my fucking cash or you won't be the only Patterson to die."

$$ \text{❆ ❆ ❆} $$

"Homeboy, fuck this shit." Jewels yawned. "We've been out here all night, like we were hustling crack on the block. Motherfuckers are on their way to work. Let's go check out the new apartment, the group home, and my crib again. If she still hasn't shown her face, then it's time you file a missing person report."

The pay phone rang.

GP was overwhelmed with an instant sickness. He let the phone ring twice before bracing himself and easing the receiver to his ear. "Hello."

"Missing something?"

His heart dropped. He began to shake as if he had Parkinson's disease. "Squeeze, where is Kitchie?" His words were slow and deliberate.

"She's in real good hands." Squeeze looked at Kitchie, who had Hector's huge hand clamped around her mouth. "Where the fuck is my cash?"

"Let me speak to my wife."

"Business first; play later."

Jewels was pacing, driving a fist into the palm of a hand.

"I just gave you twenty grand. I—"

"You thought I wouldn't find out it was counterfeit? You tried to play me; I did you a fucking favor. Your games is gonna cost you more than you're willing to lose." He winked at Kitchie.

"I don't know anything about counterfeit money." GP's nerves were blowing fuses by the dozens.

"Too bad you don't. This phone will ring again tomorrow evening at six. Have two hundred thousand cash or you'll never see this pretty bitch again."

"I'll have it. Please just let me hear her voice."

Squeeze put the phone to her ear and Hector removed his hand.

"He's gonna kill me, GP." Her voice had been stripped of its fire and strength.

"That's enough." Squeeze disconnected the call.

"Kitchie!" The phone went dead. GP tapped it against his palm, then stuck it to his ear again. "Kitchie!" This time there was a dial tone.

Jewels watched a single tear roll down his face. "Well, what's going on?"

"That money you got from Conrad was fake. Squeeze wants two hundred grand by six tomorrow evening or he's gonna kill Kitchie."

She sighed as grief overcame her. "He kidnapped her; he's gonna kill her whether he gets the money or not. There's no doubt about it."

"I'm not gonna risk not trying. There's always that chance."

"I say we kill him first."

"We'll have to find him, which we don't have the time to risk. Six o'clock tomorrow will be here in seconds."

"I know a couple of home invasions we can do, but I don't know if we'll come off with that type of money. Homeboy, it's your call. What you wanna do?"

"If something is wrong, Jewels, and I have the ability to take action, then I will. I gotta do what I gotta do," GP said with conviction. "When push comes to shove, I steal. I know where we can get all the money in one shot." He strolled a few feet away and held the door of the costume shop open. "I got an idea. You down?"

§ § §

Squeeze turned the phone's power off. "Hector, give us some privacy."

Within seconds Hector was gone.

Squeeze shoved Kitchie on the bed and pounced on top of her, pinning her beneath his weight.

"Get the hell off me! Fucker!" She struggled beneath him. "What is wrong with you?"

"Should've gave me this pussy a long time ago." He freed her supple breasts from her blouse with one tug. He fumbled with the fastening of her hip-hugger jeans.

"Squeeze...you...bastard." She bit his chest and drove her tiny fists into his solid back.

He yanked her jeans and thong past her hips. "I wouldn't like it if you didn't make it rough, challenging."

She kicked but to no avail. "Fuck you, you foul bastard." She clawed at his face, then spit. "Take it, then. Take the AIDS that comes with it."

He laughed. "You're lying. You don't sound convincing. Long as I've been trying to get in your panties, I wouldn't stop anyway."

She struggled.

He used his foot to push her jeans and thong down to her ankles. "This is all the fight you got in you. Fight me, dammit. Resist me!" He clamped a hand around her neck while undoing his own pants. "I finally get to see if it's as tight as I thought."

"Please get off of me."

Her punches were equivalent to mosquito bites.

"Don't do this to me."

His laugh is sickening, she thought.

"That's it, Kitchie. Fight me harder. Make me come back for seconds." He pried her legs open with his.

Tears ran into her ears. She was becoming exhausted.

"Don't give up so easy." He held his penis and pointed it at home base. "Make it fun for me."

She twisted and turned beneath him, exerting the remainder of her energy. Bile formed in her throat when she felt his penis push into her vulva halves. "No! Please, God, don't let this happen to me."

§ § §

The forensic lab was a little colder than normal. Crutchfield walked up to Ford at a computer workstation. "You got me here; this had better be good."

"Take a look." He turned the screen in Crutchfield's direction.

Crutchfield leaned in to study the screen. "It's a bunch of lines on a layout of the city."

"The lines you see are of the route the watch traveled on April third."

"The day Jap Silex was last seen."

"Correct." Ford poked his ink pen at the screen. "This is the starting point from which the watch began recording its course."

"Can you narrow the starting point down to an address?"

"GPS narrows things down to inches." Ford pointed to a pocket folder. "I already took it upon myself to do so." He traced the lines on the computer. "It started here, stopped here, and this is where the watch is now. Whether there's an arm attached to it is something you'll have to figure out."

Crutchfield opened the folder. The starting point address corresponded with the high-rise Squeeze lived in. The second address was situated in a rural area just outside of the city limits. The watch was signaling from the same general area that they had unearthed Hector's goldfish, Pablo.

§ § §

"I swear, if I didn't know that you were under all that plastic and makeup, I wouldn't recognize you." GP looked at Jewels's reflection in a seven-foot mirror.

"I'm not with all this dress-up bullshit, homeboy. Let's just rob the place and get it over with."

"No guns. I mean it. We don't want this to come back and haunt us. The disguises stay." He spun around with his arms out. "How do I look?"

"Old. Like you're about to die any minute."

"Good. We'll use these hookups to get the money." He pulled out a ski mask and two automatic-styled water guns from a paper bag. "We'll use this stuff to pull off the first part of the plan. Where's the camera?"

"Right there." She pointed to a nylon case that sat on the shelf of her closet.

"Take it down. Make sure it works."

"GP, this shit better work or we won't have no other choice but to murder this motherfucker, Squeeze."

"It'll work. I'll prove it to you first thing in the morning."

The camera flashed and the instant film eased out of the front. "You satisfied? Can I take this shit off my face now, old man?"

§ § §

Crime scene investigators hoisted Jap's remains from a shallow grave. Crutchfield and Detective Thomas watched as a technician placed a piece of gum in an evidence bag.

Thomas thumped the butt of his Marlboro. "Whose DNA you think we'll find on the gum?"

"Hector's. Put out an APB on him and Squeeze." Crutchfield ducked under the yellow crime-scene tape. "If Johnnie Cochran were alive, not even he could beat this case." He moved toward his car.

Thomas was still standing on the opposite side of the tape. "Hey, Crutchfield, where are you going? We have a lot of work to do yet."

"To break the news to Miles. This is the part of the job that separates the men from the little girls."

After a thoughtful sigh, Thomas ducked under the tape. "Wait up."

§ § §

The last week of school had finally arrived. The children were waiting at the bus stop, at 6:45 a.m., ready to be hauled away for the day. Tameka and Kesha Stevens did what they do best—brag and hurt feelings.

"I hope you don't come back to school...Put it this way," Kesha said, "when school starts over, your wardrobe does, too."

"Everybody ain't got it like y'all," a girl wearing last year's jeans said, with her shoulders hunched and head hung low.

"I know that's right." Tameka slapped hands with her sister.

"That's right, bow down to the divas that's much greater than you."

Everybody laughed, some because they found humor in the sisters, others because they didn't want to be on display next.

GP and Jewels rounded the corner.

"Excuse me." GP interrupted the laughter and walked toward the children, his hands in the pockets of his jeans, carrying a leather book bag. "We're A & R's for Ghet-O-Vision, and I'm looking for two volunteers who wants to make twenty dollars apiece."

Tameka sucked her teeth. "Twenty dollars ain't money in my book."

"We just want to take one picture." Jewels paused as she exchanged glances with seven children. "Y'all know who Ray Cash is, right?"

"*'Cause I'm a pimp in my own mind*," Kesha sang out and did some sort of dance. "You better know we know who he is."

"The picture is for him." GP blinked. "If he likes it, there's a good possibility he'll choose you to play a part in his new video."

Kesha put hands on what she thought were hips. "Twenty dollars is cheap for me and my sister. We've been in a video before. You're paying for experience."

Another little girl pulled on Kesha. "They're strangers. You shouldn't be talking to them."

"Shut up, Carinne!" Tameka and Kesha said in unison.

"Tell you what." Jewels started counting out money. "Since you have some experience, we'll give you and your sister thirty apiece. Or we'll just pick someone else."

"Look at it this way, even if Ray Cash don't pick us, you're getting your money's worth." Tameka held her hand out.

You damn right, GP thought as Jewels handed over the money.

"We're not going anywhere." Kesha rolled her eyes.

"Nah, that's cool. We're gonna take it right here." Jewels retrieved the camera from GP's bag. "Don't trip and start running, I'm about to pull out two water guns."

"Shoot, I thought she was about to say a snake or some crazy shit like that." Kesha bit her bottom lip.

All the children watched as Jewels squirted GP in the face, which gained all of their trust—except Carinne's.

"This isn't right." Carinne shook her head.

GP cut his eyes at her while wiping the water away with the ski mask. "Let's take the photo next to the building." He walked off and waved Kesha and Tameka over.

Jewels gave him the water guns before he put the ski mask on.

"Y'all ready?" He put his arms around both girls' shoulders, resting the guns across their chests. "Now, y'all have to look real scared."

"That'll cost you a little something extra." Tameka looked at the masked man. "Like I said, it'll be worth it."

Jewels snapped the picture when the sisters made facial expressions of panic. GP and Jewels strolled away as Jewels pinched the instant film between two gloved fingers.

§ § §

Matthew pushed his employer into National City Bank. The wheelchair stopped inches away from a brass name plaque that displayed the words: *Aubrey Stevens, President*.

"Thank you, Matthew." The old man confined to the wheelchair had a violent coughing attack.

Mathew inserted an inhaler into the old man's mouth and pumped twice.

Mr. Stevens turned his PDA off and placed it near the phone. "Is he going to be all right?"

"He'll be fine." Matthew put the inhaler away. "He suffers from black lung; made his fortune in the mines."

The old man caught his breath. "They're beautiful. They yours?" His shaky finger pointed to a picture on the desk.

Mr. Stevens found himself lost in the images staring out from the picture frame. "Yes, these are my girls. My pride and joy. Wouldn't trade their bad behinds for the world."

"Good, good."

Mr. Stevens threaded his fingers and straightened his back. "What can I do for you, Mr. ..."

"I'm Mr. Wagoner." He coughed in his hand and waved Matthew off when he approached with the inhaler. "I would like to make a large withdrawal."

"I'm not familiar with the name." Mr. Stevens pulled his keyboard to himself. "I'm going to need your first name and account number."

"I'm afraid you won't find any of that in there."

"Run that by me again." Mr. Stevens lifted a brow and dropped his hands into his lap.

"Put your goddamn hands back on the desktop. Now." Matthew revealed a gun in a holster beneath his blazer.

"Thank you for being cooperative. Matthew tends to become quite nasty when he's upset." Mr. Wagoner gave Mr. Stevens an envelope. "You'll find my account number and balance inside. Open the envelope; take out the withdrawal slip; then pass me the envelope back."

Mr. Stevens shriveled in the chair and clamped his eyes shut with every intention of forcing the image out. His efforts were fruitless; he could still see the mental version of his terrified daughters in the picture with a gunman.

"The envelope." Mr. Wagoner's hand trembled as he held it out.

"I beg you not to hurt my children, Mister."

"At this moment, Mr. Stevens, the only person who can bring harm to your pride and joy is you."

Matthew pulled a leather bag from the pocket on the back of the wheelchair. "If you ever want to see them alive again, you'll listen to me with careful ears."

Mr. Stevens nodded. "Anything."

Matthew continued: "Fill the bag with large bills. No dye packs and no electronic tracking. If we're not at our destination in the next twenty minutes, our friend in the picture will stop Tameka's and Kesha's clocks. Are you with me?"

"Yes." He nodded. "Yes, I'm with you."

Matthew threw the bag at his chest. "Do you know what will happen if you slip us a tracking device?"

"I won't do anything stupid. I'll do what's necessary to have my girls returned unharmed."

"Good, good." Mr. Wagoner looked at his watch. "Sixteen minutes left. You don't have much time to sit here with us."

With the bag in tow, Mr. Stevens left his office.

Jewels looked at GP. "I apologize, homeboy."

"For what?" He spun the wheelchair around to face her.

"I switched the water gun for a real pass out of here if shit don't go right." She touched the gun handle and glanced out the door every now and then.

"Dammit, Jewels, I meant no guns. He's not gonna buck."

"Shut up, old man. If he does, there's a nine taped to the bottom of your chair for you. No matter what, I'm coming out of this bank."

"Jewels, if there is one thing that I know something about for sure, it's a parent's love."

Mr. Stevens entered the office two minutes and some seconds later.

Jewels took the bag, gave the money the once-over, and hung it on the back of the wheelchair.

"Now what?" Mr. Stevens loosened his necktie.

"Go back to what you were doing." GP rested on the wheelchair's arms. "It's going to be hard, but try to relax. You'll be contacted when we're safely away with clean money."

Jewels wheeled GP out of the bank as easy as they had come.

CHAPTER 17

Two hours of self-inflicted torture was all that Mr. Stevens was capable of enduring. He hit the bank's silent alarm, then phoned his daughters' school.

"Euclid Central."

"Uh…this is Aubrey Stevens, Tameka and Kesha Stevens's father."

"Good afternoon, Mr. Stevens. What can I do for you today?"

"Who am I speaking with?" He stared at the two contrasting photos before him, one where his girls were smiling and full of life; the other, well to him, his girls were scared as hell. So was he.

"Missy Hinton, Vice Principal. Mr. Stevens, you sound upset. Is there something wrong that I should concern myself with?"

"I'm just notifying you that I'm going to need the names of all children who get picked up at the same bus stop as my daughters in order for the authorities to question them."

"Why would the police need to speak with these children?" Missy walked from around her desk to shut her office door.

"Either it happened when Tameka and Kesha left the house this morning on their way to the bus stop or the incident took place at the stop." He could hear sirens in the vicinity.

"When what happened, Mr. Stevens?" She held the phone between her ear and shoulder while removing a pen cap to take notes.

His voice trembled. "My daughters were kidnapped by…by bank robbers."

She dropped the pen onto the desk. She was taken aback by the information given. "Mr. Stevens, there is an assembly taking place as we speak in the auditorium. I just left there; I personally saw Kesha and Tameka with my own eyes."

Mr. Stevens looked up when three police officers rushed into his office, followed by the bank's manager.

The slender officer stepped forward. "What type of situation are we faced with?"

$$\mathcal{S} \; \mathcal{S} \; \mathcal{S}$$

GP paced in front of the pay phone. "What time is it?"

"Don't ask me that bullshit again. It hasn't been two mother-fucking minutes from the last time you asked." Jewels hopped onto the bare table of GP's booth. "I would've never thought that close to seven-hundred grand would fit into that bag."

GP grabbed her wrist to see the watch himself. 5:58 p.m. "Only thing I want out of it is the money to get Kitchie back and buy a cheap house for the kids. You keep the rest."

"Hold up, punk. When you rob something, you don't give it back. That's against the rules. People rob so they can keep the shit, fool."

"I promised the kids that I wouldn't steal anymore. Keeping my word to them means more to me than the money." He turned around to find an older man dropping coins into the pay phone. "Hey!"

The man paused.

GP put his finger on the connection lever and held it down. "I'm waiting for an important call."

"You're still waiting until I'm done."

"Look, old man, I'm not trying to disrespect you, but you're gonna get off this phone." He yanked the receiver from him. "I apologize. It's another phone down the street."

He pump-faked at GP. "I know you're a punk. The eyes never lie. Never lie." He aimed two fingers at his own eyes.

Jewels doubled over with laughter.

"I'm thinking about losing my religion and fucking you up, but this arthritis in my hip saved your ass, youngster." He pumped at GP again, then went away.

"You was about to get whipped by a senior citizen, homeboy." She laughed tears in her eyes. She went into a dead silence when the phone started ringing. GP armed himself with the Lord's Prayer and picked up. "Hello."

$$\text{\$ \$ \$}$$

Hector scrolled the cable channels, pausing a few moments at a time, viewing anything that caught his attention.

"You're hell with a remote. Give me that thing." Squeeze motioned for him to toss it. Once the remote was in his hands, he positioned the channel on a network broadcasting the local news. He increased the volume.

"...that brings us to our special segment on children's rapidly growing issues," the newscaster said. "Authorities have crippled Ohio's largest child-pornography and White-Slavery rings. Thirty-six suspects, including two city officials, are in the hands of justice this evening, held on multiple child abuse, molestation, and pornography charges. There are talks that Mayor Brandon Chambers is planning to award the officer, and perhaps the unknown tipster responsible for the arrests in this case, with a medal of honor." The newscaster folded her hands. "In other child-related news..."

Footage of Mr. Reynolds leaving the Justice Center appeared in the corner of the screen.

"Claude Reynolds," she continued, "of the Reynolds Eastside Group Home has been officially brought up on charges. The children who were once under his care are in the process of being moved to other facilities per a judge's orders. Mr. Reynolds maintains his innocence. This is new footage of him being released today after posting a hundred-thousand-dollar property bond."

Mr. Reynolds looked into the TV camera as he wobbled down the courthouse steps. "I would never do anything to bring harm to a child. I love all children."

Hector's watch alarm went off. Six o'clock p.m.

Squeeze turned down the TV's volume a few notches and picked up the phone at the same time Kitchie began to bang on the bedroom door. "Go see what she wants." He punched in a telephone number.

"Hello." GP glanced at Jewels, who was now standing inches away from him.

"You got my cash?"

"Yeah. Put Kitchie on."

"You'll talk to her after you cash in. If you slide me some bogus paper this time, I'll send my friend to the group home to pay your crumb-snatchers a visit."

"It's real."

"It better be. If you ever want to see Kitchie alive again, keep the cops out of my business."

"The cops don't know shit. Now let's do this."

"Good, here's what I want you to do…"

§ § §

Squeeze placed the phone on its cradle. He tilted his head toward the bedroom. "What did she want?"

"Woman products. It's that time."

"Fuck her. That ain't the only hole she's gonna bleed from."

Hector stuck his tongue through the gum and blew a bubble until it popped. "I knew GP wouldn't come up with the money."

"He has it, but this is how we'll play it." Squeeze started toward the door with Hector close behind. "We'll meet GP with the money, show him where to find his wife, then kill them both at their reunion."

"You're gonna have to stop loaning folks money. The results are messy more times than not."

As they secured the front door, the newscaster came back from a commercial break. "Local authorities have brought their search for missing ROTC student, Jap Silex, to an end. His body was…"

§ § §

A minivan was parked catty-corner to the Lakewood high-rise's entrance. Crutchfield and Thomas eased into the back and closed the double doors behind them.

"It's about damn time." A brunette sipped coffee from a Styrofoam cup. "We were supposed to be relieved over an hour ago. This is why I hate stakeouts: nobody respects nobody's time."

"Don't start shooting off your fat speaker box, Darlene. Some of us actually have something to do with our time." Crutchfield took off his blazer and loosened his tie.

"Yeah," Thomas said, "I'm not in the mood to hear your mouth, either." He shifted his focus to the man behind the steering wheel. "Max, how do you put up with this snapping turtle?"

"I learned to keep my fingers and opinions out her face." Max

passed Crutchfield a pair of binoculars. "I can't remember his name."
He pointed toward the high-rise. "The dead guy's brother."

"Jesus, Miles! What's on his mind?" Crutchfield took the binoculars away from his face and passed them to Thomas.

Darlene clapped her hands, then held one in front of Max. "Pay
up. I told you his name was Miles. We've been partners for six
years and you still don't respect my memory? Hell, I remember
things for you."

Max dug into his pocket. "He rode up on a skateboard a few
minutes after one this afternoon and hasn't left. How long before
the media goes public with the discovery of Jap's body?"

"We managed to hold them off until the eleven o'clock news."
Crutchfield looked at Max. "They understand that they could
give the suspects a heads-up and send them into hiding. I have a
good rapport with Tracy Morgan down at the paper and the head
honchos at the news stations. They'll keep quiet." He tossed
Darlene his car keys. "Bring it back with a full tank."

She opened her door. "Hope you slackers have a long, miserable
shift. I'm going to find something to waste Max's hard-earned
money on."

Crutchfield and Thomas climbed into the front seats.

Thomas watched Darlene and Max drive away in Crutchfield's
Caprice. "Max has to be feeding her the worm. I'd like to bang
her one good time. I just need three minutes with her. Anybody
with that much attitude…I know it's a good roll in the sack."

"Miles is gonna get himself hurt, trying to tangle with Squeeze."
Crutchfield gazed at Miles through the binoculars.

"He's not here to do the Harlem Shake. He's here with intentions
of killing the man." Thomas shifted in the seat. "Them threats he
made that day he was drunk, I suppose you thought he was making
a funny."

"Radio in and have a black-and-white arrest him. I'm sure we can get him with a concealed weapon's charge."

A large Voices Books truck carrying bundles of trade paperbacks stalled, blocking Crutchfield and Thomas's view, steam rising fast from its overheated engine.

§ § §

Miles was disheveled. His clothes hadn't been changed in days, and his unkempt cornrows were in desperate need of grooming. He'd lost the will and the desire to keep himself orderly after he'd watched his mother die. He leaned against a wrought-iron fence just outside of the high-rise's main entrance, caressing the handle of a .380 inside of his windbreaker. Tupac's "I Came To Bring The Pain" thumped in his ears from the Walkman. The song had been replayed over and over. As Tupac's hypnotic voice mesmerized him, Miles convinced himself that he was the administrator of pain. A box truck gusting smoke from its engine stole his attention for a moment. It conked out yards away, but that was of no interest to him once Squeeze's flashy Chrysler drove through the front entrance. He stepped on his skateboard and pushed off. "I came to bring the pain."

§ § §

Crutchfield displayed his badge as he fanned the smoke away from his face. "You have to move this thing immediately. You're obstructing official police business."

"I suppose you want all hundred-ten pounds of me to push this two-ton truck." The driver wiped sweat away from his forehead with a sleeve, then put his Voices Books cap back on.

"I don't care what you do or how you do it; just move it."
Crutchfield smacked the truck's body.

"I'm already having one hell of a day. I don't need racial
profiling, harassment, or any of that other stuff cops do to hard-
working black folks to add to it." He turned the ignition; the
truck fired.

"Back it up." Crutchfield waved a hand.

The truck rolled back just enough for Crutchfield to see that
Miles was gone; then its engine gave out again. Crutchfield looked
in both directions.

Nothing.

§ § §

Within minutes the wind picked up and the sun tucked itself
behind a dark congregation of clouds. Miles discarded his skateboard and scurried under an electronic garage door, right before
it lowered itself to the pavement. Inside the private parking
structure, situated under the high-rise, Miles crept up to the
Chrysler—only to find it empty.

Ding!

Across the parking structure, Squeeze and Hector stepped inside
an elevator. Miles opted for the stairs.

§ § §

"Calm down, GP," he said to himself as the locking mechanism
to Squeeze's lobby buzzed, giving Jewels and himself access to the
building.

"Hold that elevator." Jewels pointed at an Asian couple. She
and GP hurried across the lobby.

"Thanks." GP pressed the button that promised to take them to the penthouse, to his Kitchie.

§ § §

"Where else could he have gone?" Crutchfield threw his hands up. "Think. If he would have went this way—" He pointed down the avenue. "—or that way, we would have seen him. There's no possible way we couldn't have. He has to be—"

"If it'll stop you from crying, let's go check it out."

"I was gonna do that anyway, without your consent."

"I'm willing to bet that Miles just got tired of waiting there and found himself somewhere else to post up."

Crutchfield started the minivan and shifted it to Drive.

§ § §

"Would you stop smacking on that goddamn gum?" Squeeze swallowed his second shot of brandy. "You sound like a pregnant cow."

"How do you think GP came up with the money so fast? He couldn't come up with a hundred stacks one day but has two the next. What's wrong with that picture?" Hector stood in the entrance of the penthouse, watching the floor-indicator light of the climbing elevator.

"I don't care if he robbed a bank. I want paid. Then, I want paid for making me look like a fool. Don't nobody assassinate my street credibility."

The indicator light finally held its position.

"The moment of truth." Hector went into the hall to greet GP.

The elevator doors eased open effortlessly.

Jewels and Hector locked gazes.

"You were instructed to come alone." Hector addressed GP but never took his eyes off Jewels.

"As far as I'm concerned, this is alone." GP passed a hand between himself and Jewels. "It won't make a difference as long as we all get what we want."

Hector grunted. He waved them out of the elevator. "Turn around and put your hands on the wall. You know how this works."

"Ain't no need; I'm strapped." Jewels showed him a .44 tucked in the front waistband of her jeans.

Hector's face tightened. The gum chewing stopped. "Hand it over."

"Y'all ain't gonna be the only ones up here with guns." Jewels moved forward, but Hector blocked her path.

GP brushed by Hector and pushed the front door open. "Kitchie!" He tossed the bag of money onto the sofa.

Squeeze turned away from the stunning view offered by the floor-to-ceiling window. "Slow down, Tiger."

"There's your money. Now where's my wife? Kitchie! Where is she, Squeeze?"

There was a ruckus outside of the suite, followed by thumps and bumps. Squeeze and GP stared at the front door.

Jewels entered the penthouse pointing Hector's gun. "Where's Kitchie, homeboy?"

Squeeze took a step but hesitated at the sound of Jewels's voice.

"Bitch, I'm dying to see if you can digest lead."

"Where is Kitchie, Squeeze?"

Jewels cocked the hammer back. "That was the last time either of us is asking. You've been warned."

§ § §

"Something smells like shit." Thomas knelt down beside the abandoned skateboard.

The wind whipped about. Crutchfield shielded his eyes with a hand as he stared at the 100-story building. He dashed for the lobby when he saw a body falling from the sky.

CHAPTER 18

Miles stepped over an unconscious Hector. He pulled the .380 from his pocket. His hand trembled as the point of the gun led him through the door of the penthouse.

Squeeze's eyes widened with alarm.

"Jap didn't have anything to do with it." Miles clamped his eyes shut and pulled the trigger in one motion.

The floor-to-ceiling window shattered. An angry wind swept through the suite. Various pieces of mail were blown from the bar and were tumbled out into the public. Jewels flinched at the sound of the gun blast and turned her weapon on Miles; GP ducked.

Squeeze took two quick steps but stopped in his tracks as more bullets whizzed by him. He threw his hands up.

Miles looked at the dark hole at the tip of Jewels's gun and laughed. Then, he started toward Squeeze. "You dragged my brother and mother into this. Why? What did they do?"

"Miles, relax, man. I don't know nothing about your people." Squeeze took a step backward as Miles came forward.

Jewels began wiping her fingerprints from her gun as well as Hector's.

"Liar!" Miles clamped his eyes closed, then opened them. "Liar. They found Jap's body and traced it to you." He poked the gun in Squeeze's direction and pulled the trigger.

Squeeze took another step back, bracing himself for a shot that was likely to hit him this time. His footing reached the window's ledge. He whirled his arms to catch his balance and bring himself forward. The wind proved to make that quite difficult.

Miles tugged on the trigger again and again, delivering nothing more than a clicking sound. "Bring the pain…I came to bring you pain."

Squeeze reached a hand out as he fell backward. "Fuck you!" Death awaited him at the end of his skydive.

Miles looked into the open sky. "I told you that I'd make it right, Ma. I'm almost done… Then, everything will be right."

"This Motherfucker is off the hinges." Jewels tapped GP. "We got to get the fuck out of here. You check the rooms while I get rid of these burners."

$$\text{\$ \$ \$}$$

When Crutchfield reached the penthouse floor, he checked Hector for a pulse, slapped a pair of cuffs on him, then nodded at Thomas. They put their backs against the hall wall, moving closer to the door with their Glocks in hand.

"She's not here." GP returned from checking the bedrooms.

"We don't need to be here, either."

Miles held his arms out to either side. The breeze caressed his face. "It's all better now, Ma. I promise."

"Yeah, Jewels, let's bounce. This cat is tripping on something."

"Miles!" Crutchfield stuffed his gun in a holster. "Miles, don't do it. It's not worth it; talk to me about this."

"This isn't the answer to your problems, Miles," Thomas said, taking small steps.

What the fuck have I gotten into? Jewels thought.

Miles glanced at Crutchfield. "I have to make it right." He turned back to the sky and jumped.

"Miles!" Crutchfield went as close to the ledge as safety would allow.

GP closed his eyes and prayed that Kitchie was safe.

§ § §

Night had fallen on the city. Kitchie stared from the barred window at the stars. She was thinking about all the things that she and her family hadn't done, the things that they would never get to do. Red and blue strobe lights all of a sudden began to bounce off the trees in her immediate view. Her pulse quickened. Then, she heard a two-way radio coming from somewhere inside the house. She banged and kicked the door. "Somebody, help me." She backed away from the door when the knob spun in both directions. She had no idea of what to expect.

"Mrs. Kitchie Patterson."

She thanked God in her mind. "Yes."

"This is the police. Step away from the door. We're going to break it down. Are you okay in there?"

"Yes, I'm fine." She noticed an officer outside the window, beaming a flashlight into the room.

The door buckled and the doorframe split from the applied pressure. It opened and there GP was standing behind the police.

§ § §

One week later, Jewels looked at the information written on the paper, then looked up at the obese man. "I must have the wrong address. Please forgive me."

Mr. Reynolds opened the door wider. "What is it that you're looking for?"

"I was told that there was a coffin and headstone supplier in this area." She switched a large purse from one shoulder to the other.

"This is the place. Well, actually, my store is next door. Come in." He stepped aside to let Jewels pass. "I don't have any coffins in stock at the moment, but you can take a look at my catalog." He locked the door of the defunct group home. "If you see something you like, I can have it delivered to any funeral home in the city within forty-eight hours."

"That may just work out." She followed him into the visiting room while putting on a pair of tight leather gloves. "This is a beautiful place, and it's quiet." She studied the hand-carved wood trimmings that outlined the room.

"Trust me, it wasn't always like this." He picked up a three-ring binder. "It's been a long time, but I enjoy being here by myself. Today is the first time I've had this place to myself in over twenty years."

"What a shame."

"No, really. I don't want a houseful of people...especially kids."

"I meant it's a shame you let me catch you slipping. I've been wanting to fuck you up so bad, I was having nightmares about it." Jewels rushed toward him.

§ § §

"Do I have to?"

"Secret, it's either study or go to summer school. It's not too late to sign you up." GP removed a new set of dishes from a box and began to arrange them in a cabinet above the sink.

She sighed and plopped down in her seat.

"Don't look at me; you heard your father." Kitchie removed the dishes that GP had placed on the shelves.

"What are you doing, woman?"

"Just because they're new doesn't mean they don't need to be washed first."

GP stared at Junior, who was in the next room watching *The Parkers*. "I'm worried about him."

"He'll come around." Kitchie touched GP's hand. "Just do what the doctor advised."

"How can I? Keep it real. How am I supposed to pretend that everything is normal when it's not?"

Kitchie cast her brown eyes on Secret. "Get your nose out of grown folk's business and put it in that math book."

Secret looked at the equation. *They act like my ears don't work.*

"Papi, he'll talk when he's ready. He's been through a lot."

"I hope you're right."

"Me too, Daddy. I miss him getting smart with me."

"What counts right now," Kitchie said, "is that we're all together."

For now, GP thought. "I hope Vivian can postpone our next court date for a few more weeks. I'm trying to stretch this out for as long as possible."

Kitchie put a Wendy's cap on GP's head, then rose up on her toes to kiss him on the mouth. "I'll take care of the dishes. You better go before you're late for work."

GP kissed Secret's forehead and pointed at the second problem. "That's the wrong answer. Slow down and take your time. I'll check it tonight and go over it with you tomorrow."

"Daddy, when we get the apartment together, can Nise and Samone come spend the night? I miss them."

"I don't see why not."

"That will be nice." Kitchie pushed a box that was marked *Pictures* into the corner.

GP went into the living room. "Junior, I'll see you later." He held out a solid fist. "Hit that rock."

Junior banged his fist against GP's, then turned back to the sitcom.

GP held Kitchie's hand and led her into the hall outside of their apartment. "I get off at midnight."

"When you get in, just tap me. I'll roll over. I don't know if I'm ready for sex again, though."

"Marques Houston's 'Naked' might help you to come around." He smiled. "If it doesn't, I'm willing to wait as long as it takes."

"Thank you for being so understanding, Papi."

"You know, I always figured that the Street Prophet would grow into something bigger than the boundaries of the booth, but closing it down completely didn't have a scene in my dreams." He looked down at the Wendy's uniform. Mr. Reynolds invaded his thoughts. *You're worthless. Your mother doesn't even want you. You will never amount to anything.*

"Papi, everything doesn't always work out as planned. I fuss at you, but I commend you for having a dream and striving for it in a respectable way. It takes a man to endure what you have in the name of honesty. The average brother would've turned to the streets a long time ago. You stuck it out; whether it worked out or not." She was quiet for a moment. "I wish it had worked out, the whole notoriety and wealth you want for our family, but I'm happy with what we have. It's not much, but it's ours and we're together."

GP leaned against the wall. "Dan hired me full-time."

She frowned. "How are you gonna pull that off? I have—"

"That's why I'm closing the booth down sooner than I had planned. This is the last week. I'll draw at home in my spare time."

"But...I never wanted you to quit doing what you love."

"It makes more sense. I have to start thinking responsibly. I'll make more steady money working at Wendy's full-time than I can make on average working the booth in the day and flipping Double Classics at night. We're not going to lose anything again."

§ § §

While in the attic of the group home, Jewels pulled a chain that she'd thrown over an overhead beam.

Now she was lifting Mr. Reynolds. She hooked the chain to a stationary two-by-four post in the attic.

Blood dripped from Mr. Reynolds's nose. His left eye was swollen shut. "No more, please."

"Never thought you'd be a product of your own torture, did you? You got off stringing up defenseless kids to this ceiling. I'm about to get off, too. Let you get a taste of your own medicine and then some." She took all the items from her leather bag, all except one—the *main* one. She set upright three mayonnaise jars filled with gasoline, then peeled away the thin plastic film on a box of double-edged razors. She tore off a piece of gray tape.

She stood up and slammed a gloved fist into his naked body. "Now you know how this shit feels." She delivered a kidney blow that caused urine to leak down his legs.

He could no longer voice the extent of his discomfort. All he could do was grunt, "Please."

"What?" She positioned her ear near Mr. Reynolds's mouth. "Pussy, speak up. I can't hear you beg."

"P—please. I quit."

She clenched a fist of his hair, then shoved six double-edged razors into his mouth and taped it closed. She punched the center of his face until she felt his nose bone crunch under her punch.

"You want to quit now." She circled him.

"Did…" Punch. "You…" Jumping knee thrust to the ribs.

Mr. Reynolds bit down on a razor.

"…Stop…" Elbow to the groin.

He let out a painful grunt.

"…When…" Front snap-kick to the lower abdomen. "Them…" Spinning back fist to the cheek.

Blood filled his mouth.

"…Kids…" Palm-heel strike to his solar plexus.

His blubber shook.

"…Asked…" Knife-hand strike to the throat.

He struggled to catch a breath.

"…You…" A thumb gouge to the eye. "To…" A reverse punch to the mouth.

A razor sliced his tongue.

"…Stop?"

The blood backed up in his mouth and found an escape route through his nose.

Jewels lifted his wrinkled eyelid with a thumb. "I ain't done yet. I'm gonna show you how it feels to be taken advantage of, to be fucked around."

He was still swallowing blood.

Jewels stripped until she was nude—with the exception of her boots and leather gloves. She went to her bag and took her special treat out—a steel strap-on. She slapped Mr. Reynolds in the face with all thirteen inches of it. "Open your eyes, bitch. I said, I ain't done yet."

He found his last-resort strength and tugged at the chain suspending him from the ceiling.

"You must have never seen one this big. Wait until you feel it." She circled his body and stopped behind him. "When I'm done, you're gonna know what it feels like to be really abused; what it feels like to have an asshole with stretch marks." She rubbed the cold steel head along his crack.

He clenched his cheeks—tight.

She hit him with a combination of punches that started on the left side of his fat body and ended on the right. Then, she began the stretching process, wearing out his sphincter.

His face contorted and his eyes bulged with each violent thrust. He prayed to die. She pulled his head back so hard that he was forced to swallow a razor, which sliced his windpipe. The suffocation began.

"If you had never put your hands on my loved ones, I'd never have been thinking of ways to torture you." She detached herself from the strap-on, leaving it wedged inside of him. "That looks painful."

Blood started to fill his lungs. His face was discolored, livid. Veins protruded around his strained eyes and temples. Jewels answered his prayer. He was dying, but in the worst way.

She stood inches away, looking into his eyes as life escaped him. "Die."

The strap-on fell to the floor just when death consumed him. Jewels dressed herself, then began to soak the attic with two of the three mayonnaise jars of gasoline. She poured the last jar over his head.

Jewels jumped from the loading dock and eased into the shadows of the night as the hellish inferno consumed the group home.

S S S

"I don't feel sorry for him at all. I might change my opinion in some other life, but right now, that's what he gets." Kitchie stuffed a stack of Street Prophet jeans into a duffle bag. "I'm glad there were no children in there."

"God don't like ugly." GP packed the last of their merchandise into the back of Jewels's Escalade.

"God has to like ugly; He made it. The Big Guy and I would've had serious issues if He'd waited until Judgment Day to let old man Reynolds feel the fire." Jewels stroked the top of Junior's head and helped him into the car.

Secret climbed from the backseat and pointed to a crowd of suits and ties on the other side of Euclid Avenue.

"Girl, get your butt back in the car so we can leave." Kitchie cocked a hip, resting a hand on it.

"That's him," Secret said, still pointing a finger.

"That's who?" GP gazed in the direction her finger was aimed.

"That's Brandon, Daddy."

Everybody looked.

"Get in the car, Secret," Kitchie said. "We know who the mayor is."

"No, that's Brandon. The man who found Junior and me in his car. The one who...you know."

"Are you sure?" GP closed the Escalade's hatch while watching Mayor Brandon Chambers and his colleagues. "Do you know what you're saying?"

Kitchie witnessed the way Junior's eyes lit up as he saw the mayor.

"Fool, don't act like you can't hear." Jewels went to the driver's door. "She said that our mayor is a crackhead who has extramarital affairs with crack hoes. The boss of our city is a motherfucking addict. They need to let me boss this shit."

Jewels and GP sat on her bumper, in front of his building, passing a joint back and forth.

She pushed the thick marijuana smoke through her nose. "Sticky Fingers fell off the face of the earth. Heard he crossed some official headhunters on the rob tip, too. I swear, when I find him, I'm gonna do some Chinese torture shit to him for hours before I split his watermelon."

"Let it go. He'll get what he has coming. Everybody does sooner or later." He plucked the marijuana roach.

"Punk, I could've hit that again."

"What you could've done was blistered your lips." Five seconds passed. "Hold Kitchie and the kids down for me. I go to court next week. Vivian worked out a sweet plea bargain. I'm gonna take it."

"I can't take a plea. They gotta spend their money fucking with me. I'm picking twelve of my peers every time. You see what they did to Manny Cool and Limbo. I understand you gotta do what's best for you, though."

"When I come home, I'm gonna break down and buy you that diamond ring."

Jewels looked at her finger. "Punk, stop faking. You've been selling me that dream for years. How much time are they talking?"

"Eighteen months. It's official; tomorrow is my last day at the booth."

"It's fucked up. The mayor is an undercover crackhead. He be making decisions for the city with a glass dick in his mouth."

GP sighed. "I'm not surprised by nothing anymore. You had something to do with Mr. Reynolds's death, didn't you?"

Her brows furrowed. The marijuana made her feel good. "What makes you say that?"

"You saying that you didn't?"

Silence.

"I knew it." He looked at the light shining from his apartment.

"Somebody had to get it. I couldn't find Sticky Fingers while I was in the mood."

"Thank you." He closed his eyes. "I rehearsed it in my head a million times. I just couldn't bring myself to act it out. I ain't got that type of heart."

"I can't tell; you tried to let Desmond have it."

"It's a difference when you do something in the heat of the moment instead of doing it in chill mode."

Our mayor is a crackhead. Jewels stood up. "I got a plan."

"I got the munchies. A plan for what?" He wondered what Kitchie was fixing for dinner.

"To keep your punk ass out of the pen."

"Nah, I'm good. All your plans include dead people." She climbed behind the steering wheel. "Get off the front of my car before you become Cadillac's new hood ornament." She turned the key and the engine began to purr. "When I drop y'all off in the morning, I'm taking Secret and Junior with me."

"What are you up to?"

"You need to be getting yourself together so you can go flip burgers. I'm gonna need to get that diamond out of you." She stepped on the gas and sped away.

CHAPTER 19

Morning had arrived much too soon for GP. Between working the booth during the day and his Wendy's gig at night, he was exhausted. The fact that Jewels was leaning on the horn seemed to fatigue him more.

When Kitchie opened the car door, Peabo Bryson's "I'm So Into You" poured into the quiet street.

"It's too early for your bullshit, Jewels." GP slid in next to Secret and Junior, then slammed the door. "Turn it down; everybody don't want to hear that."

"Fuck you! You know how I get down. If you don't like it, beat feet; get on the motherfucking bus. I ain't begging you to roll with me." She pulled the gear shift into Drive. "Excuse him, y'all. Good morning."

"Hey," Kitchie said as she settled against the headrest.

"What's up, Aunty," Secret said. "Daddy said we get to hang out with you today."

"Would you have it any other way?" Jewels looked back at Junior and winked.

§ § §

He pulled his leg back inside the Honda when a family of four came out of a building and piled inside of Jewels's Escalade. "Son of a bitch!" His patience was wearing thin, waiting for the right moment to exact his punishment. He sat a silenced .9mm on the seat beside him, gripped the steering wheel, and continued to follow Jewels.

❃ ❃ ❃

Jewels pulled next to the booth's curb and switched the hazard lights on.

GP put a duffle bag on the sidewalk, then leaned inside the car and kissed his children's foreheads. "Drive her crazy. You have my permission."

Jewels peered at him through the rearview. "Nobody can out-do you."

"Be good." Kitchie waved at Jewels and the children.

Jewels hit the horn two quick times as she pulled into down-town's growing traffic.

GP began to unpack. "This is it, Mami Chula. When we walk away today, the fat lady will be singing."

"Papi, there's still time to reconsider this. You don't have to do this. As long as you're working and using this as a secondary income, we'll be fine. Ms. Pittman said that if I pass the test next week, I'll get the opening with Social Services. Volunteering worked in my favor. I'll ace the test, so we'll have even more income. Baby, we'll be straight." She laid T-shirts on the table. "You can still do this, and I'll still help."

"Good morning, GP, Kitchie," the book vendor said and set a box of doughnuts on their table. "I brought you guys a little something-something for your bellies." He rubbed his gut in a circular motion.

"Thanks, Smitty. What you know good?" GP said.

"Not a damn thing."

"You're a sweetheart, Smitty." Kitchie plucked a glazed doughnut from the box. "How's business?"

"For the first time in a long time, I must admit that it's good. I have this book, *The Key To Life*; I can't keep enough of them. They want it like it's crack. I have a line of books from 4Shadow Publishing that are flying off the shelves, too. Come by and get you a copy. See you guys later."

Kitchie leaned against the table. "GP, I want to ask you something."

"What's wrong with your asker?" He lined the booth with comic books.

"You don't really trust me, do you? You *say* you do, but on the inside, you don't."

He stopped what he was doing. "Where'd that come from?"

"You. You had the audacity to think that I was in another man's bed. You disrespected me, and for you to even have a stupid thought like that is not to trust me."

"Ahh, Kitchie." GP shook his head. "Don't do this. I don't want to talk about this right now. Why you always want to show your ass in public?"

She rolled her eyes. "I want to talk about it. You tried to kill a man. If I were in there, would you have shot me, too?"

"Mami, no! You sound crazy."

"When did you start not trusting me?"

"This conversation is a wrap. If you were going to stress me, you could've got your ass in the car and went with Jewels and the kids."

"You're bobbing and weaving real good. Answer me, GP."

"The pieces just fit, Kitchie. You satisfied now? It made sense for it to be you."

§ § §

He trailed Jewels as she circled the congested block for the second time. She wheeled the Escalade into an alley and parked.

He picked the .9mm up from the seat. "Time to pay the piper." He parked and his Nikes hit the pavement.

§ § §

Jewels walked through the door of the Mayor's office as though she had been given permission.

"You can't go in there." His secretary went after her.

Mayor Brandon Chambers spun his chair around to face the door. He took the phone away from his ear. "Who the hell are you?"

"Like you give a fuck." She tossed a piece of crack cocaine on his desk.

He covered the rock when his secretary crossed the threshold.

"I tried to stop her," the secretary said.

"Don't worry about it, Karen. It's okay. Close the door behind you and hold my calls." He hung up on his caller.

Jewels spoke again once Karen was gone. "I know all about you and how you get down."

"You don't know a damn thing about me."

"Motherfucker, watch your tone. I don't let crackheads get away with one fucking thing. Now, if you don't want me to let the public know you suck glass dicks, I need you to yank a few judicial strings for me." She took a bag of Starbursts from his desk and began eating them. "Your wife know about Shea?"

"That bitch." He watched her throw candy wrappers on his floor. "So what is this, blackmail?"

"Call it a favor that only the boss of this city can do."

"Whatever it is, forget about it." He poked a finger at Jewels. "Fuck you. Fuck Shea. You can't prove a damn thing. If it's one thing I know how to do, it's how to cover my ass. Neither one of you are credible enough to make accusations against me." He leaned forward with confidence. "I'm the mayor, the head niggah in charge. Now get the hell out of my office before I have your ghetto ass arrested."

She got up to leave and placed a crack pipe and lighter on the desk. "I didn't know if you had one stashed here or not." She went to the door and pulled it open. "Y'all come here for a minute."

Secret and Junior came in.

The head niggah in charge seemed as though he was struggling to get air into his lungs.

"You better breathe, Mayor." Jewels smiled. "The public won't have any problem believing them."

"Hi, Brandon," Secret said. "I didn't know you were our mayor. I would've let you drop us off at our front door."

He sighed and looked at Jewels. "What is it you want me to do?"

"How tight are you with the district attorney?"

"I'm having lunch with him today."

"That's a damn good answer."

§ § §

"Stop the car!" Mr. Lee ordered his chauffeur.

"But, sir—"

"Stop the car this instant, Hartford." Before the limo came to a complete stop, Mr. Lee had the door open. He dodged coming-and-going traffic to get to one of the several street vendors.

Kitchie slapped GP with all the strength she could muster. "That's such bullshit, GP, and you know it. I can't believe you'd disrespect me by thinking so low of me. Explain to me what the hell 'it just fit' is exactly supposed to mean."

"Goddamn, girl, I trust you!" He watched her closely, expecting her to swing again. "Keep your hands to yourself. That's your warning." He lowered his voice an octave and rubbed the warm side of his face. "It didn't have anything to do with you. It was a combination of things dealing with me on a personal level. It was my own insecurities—not you. I was looking for a way to validate my insecurity. I was upset. I had no idea where you was, and when I heard that girl yell out—"

"Pardon me, I don't mean to interrupt." He stuck his hand out. "I'm Stan, Mr. Stan Lee, owner of Marvel Comics."

"Get the hell out of here. You expect me to believe that?" GP took in the European suit on this distinguished-looking white man as he shook his hand.

"I remember you." Kitchie moved closer to GP. "You spent over a hundred dollars about a month and a half ago."

"That is correct, young lady. I've been looking for you ever since. Honestly, I had given up. This place wasn't occupied for weeks."

"Well, you found us." GP straightened a stack of Street Prophet comic books. "What can we do for you? Good thing; today is our last day in business."

Stan picked a book from the table. "I read every one of these—twice. I know raw talent when I see it. What you have here is a talent that is highly marketable."

Kitchie hung on to Stan's words while GP acted as if he had heard it all before.

Stan put both hands in the air, touching the tip of his thumbs together, and gazed through the opening. "I see the Street Prophet on the Cartoon Network, action figures, animated films, lines of comic books distributed nationally. I love the urban essence this guy brings to comics."

"Yeah, and I bet you want all the rights and complete creative control." He put his arm around Kitchie. "We're fine. I won't sell out like that."

"You'll receive a fifteen-percent royalty on all rights. I'm an artist myself; I wouldn't dream of taking away your creativity. That's what I'm impressed with. I'm interested in the Street Prophet."

GP devoted his full attention to Stan for the first time. He threaded his fingers with Kitchie's. "How interested?"

"Say, a signing bonus of…" He took his checkbook from his inside pocket and neatly printed a large figure. "This is just a bonus."

§ § §

"Thank you, Keith. You're saving my ass with this one." The mayor gave Jewels a thumbs-up as he spoke into the phone. "Yes, of course lunch is still on…See you then." He placed the receiver on its base.

"How soon?" Jewels thumped a candy wrapper in the mayor's direction.

"The charges against Mr. and Mrs. Patterson are being dropped as we speak."

"Good looking out, Mayor." Jewels stepped to the desk, blocking the children's view. "Here's a little something extra for your troubles." She gave him a few more pieces of cocaine and a cell phone number. "Your secret is safe with me. Hit me up when you want to get right."

"What you go by?"

"Jewels."

When they left the office, the mayor secured his door and stuffed a rock inside the crack pipe.

Outside of the mayor's office, Junior followed behind Jewels and Secret as they talked.

"That's cool; my daddy ain't going to jail."

"Secret, you gotta get this shit right. You can't be sounding like a square when you're kicking it with me. If you say 'that's cool,' you have to put *as hell* with it. That's automatic. Now let me hear you say it the right way this time."

They rounded the corner where Jewels's Escalade was parked in an alley behind the mayor's office.

"Mommy told me not to. She said there's a lot of intelligent words to use in the place of cuss words, and she said if I really want to use bad words, that I'll have plenty of time to when I'm grown."

Jewels typed in a code on the car door and paused. "*Hell* ain't a bad word."

"Why not?"

"Do you think God uses bad words?"

"No. God is good. He wouldn't do that."

"Hell nah, His good ass wouldn't. But He says it a thousand times in the Bible."

Junior's eyes bulged with fright as he watched a dark man running toward them with a gun pointed at Jewels. "Aunty!"

Jewels and Secret turned to face him.

Jewels was astonished. "Junior, that's what the—"

"He's got a gun." Junior pointed.

She turned in the opposite direction, just in time to…

§ § §

"Three hundred grand?" GP stared at the fresh ink on the check.

"All you have to do is tell me who to make it out to. It's all yours as soon as you can go over the contract and sign it."

Kitchie began to tremble.

"I need a Street Prophet clothing line."

"That shouldn't be a problem. Our subsidiary rights department will take care of those things."

Kitchie began jumping and shouting.

Smitty, the book vendor, rushed over. "What's going on?"

Stan stuck his hands in his pocket. "That's usually the reaction when you're about to become a well-known artist in a matter of days."

GP held on to Kitchie while she emotionally unraveled.

"I forgot to tell you, GP," Smitty said, pointing at Stan. "This guy has been around here looking for you awhile now. It slipped my mind."

§ § §

Sticky Fingers pointed a Glock 9 at Jewels. "You think you could rob me and live to enjoy the proceeds? Spend this, bitch." He pulled the trigger five consecutive times.

The silencer muffled the shots. The first bullet slammed Jewels into the Escalade, leaving a hole in her chest. The next shot entered through her eye and exited her head, shattering the driver's side window.

Secret screamed while Junior repeatedly called out to Jewels.

The third, fourth, and fifth slugs were for general purposes. Secret grabbed Junior and they ran in the opposite direction of Sticky Fingers.

§ § §

The hospital lobby was quiet. It had been two weeks since GP had decided on a tribute to the memory of Jewels. Now that the day had arrived, he was hesitant about relinquishing the urn.

"Everything will be fine, Mr. Patterson." Markell Rawles, Family Gewels's representative, peeled GP's fingers from the urn's handle. "You'll never regret your decision. It's all about keeping a connection to the deceased."

"Papi." Kitchie put an arm around his waist. "Jewels wanted this. I know that this is hard for you, but don't forget that we need to get upstairs. Visiting hours are almost over."

GP pulled in a deep breath and released it slow. "You'll have her back to us in two weeks, right?" He fingered the briefcase on his lap.

"No more than, but maybe less, if our technicians can get her ashes under a million pounds of pressure in the next twenty-four hours."

Kitchie reached out a hand. "Thanks for going out of your way to meet us here."

"I'm not too fond of hospitals, but it wasn't a problem. I'll be in touch very soon. If there are any questions or if you just want to check on the status, please feel free to call me at the lab or log onto FamilyGewels.com to check the status." Markell carried Jewels out of the hospital.

Kitchie and GP rode the elevator to the rehabilitation wing in silence.

§ § §

After a gentle nudge from Kitchie, GP entered Desmond's room. GP couldn't understand how a person could have a cast on one side of their entire body. Knowing that he himself was the sole reason behind the painful sight, GP wished that he could take it all back. He stared at Desmond, who was suspended from something resembling a bed minus a mattress.

Desmond was face down with a limited view of two floor tiles. He was held in perfect stillness by wires and suspension straps. He smelled an expensive perfume consume the room. "Who that?"

Kitchie's eyes began to water. She couldn't stand to look at Desmond any longer. She went back into the hall as GP moved closer to the therapeutic gurney.

"Who that?" Desmond moved his toes.

"I...I came to apologize."

Desmond remained quiet as his anger raised his blood pressure.

The silence unnerved GP. It was irritating. "Say something." He set the briefcase down.

"What, you want me to give you a blow-by-blow account of how I'm gonna fuck you up? You apologized. Now roll out." He began counting the speckles in the tile once again.

"Just hear me out. I was wrong—dead wrong for disrespecting you and your company. There's no excuse for my actions, but I was going through a lot of things."

Twenty-four, twenty-five, twenty— "What does that bullshit mean to me, dawg?"

"My wife was missing. Come to find out, she'd been kidnapped. At the time I didn't know that, and when I heard you getting busy with that Spanish mami, I jumped to conclusions. I thought it was you and Kitchie getting down." GP paced the length of the gurney.

"So that's supposed to make everything cool? Justify why you was shooting at me? Now you're up in here trying to cop a plea. You should have made sure I was dead. We going to trial in the streets."

"However you want to carry this situation, I respect your call. But know that I apologize for this mess." GP passed a hand over Desmond.

"Apologize? Motherfucker, you screaming apology and these folks are screaming that if I walk again, I'm still gonna be a fucking cripple. You can't apologize for that. Nah, not with words."

"My accountant is taking care of your hospital bill."

"Broke-ass people don't have accountants."

"I used to be broke."

"Even if you did, do you think I give a fuck about a hospital bill? I wouldn't pay it anyway. And the next time I get hurt they gonna fix me anyway. Fuck out of here."

GP flipped the lid of the briefcase open, then pushed it under the gurney with his ostrich-skin shoe, giving Desmond a view other than speckled floor tiles. "A hundred thousand for the trouble I've caused. I'm asking you to accept my apology and let this go."

"How is my big brother?" Sahara came in and set her purse in a chair near Desmond. "They said they're going to turn you over today."

"I'm all right." Desmond studied the dead presidents' faces. "I'm glad you're here. Take the briefcase under me home with you when you leave."

She looked through the wires and straps at the money. "You just won't get enough, will you, Des? I pray every night that the person who did this to you would die by suffocation or worse. And you're laid up in here on this...on this *thing*, still making drug deals." She finally acknowledged GP. "Couldn't you have at least waited until he got out of the hospital?"

"Sahara."

"Nah, the hell with that, Des." She glared at GP. "See what happened to him because of the things y'all are involved in. You black men make me sick."

"I apologize for the intrusion, sister." GP turned to leave.

Desmond could hear GP's hard bottoms click against the floor. "Tell your girl, Jewels—"

"She was murdered two weeks ago."

Sahara watched the door close. "Who was that?"

Desmond thought while staring at the money. "Nobody."

CHAPTER 20

"And this is the indoor pool." Suzette pushed the glass sliding doors open. "Consistent with the rest of the house, the floors are heated around the deck. And as you can see, the pool area offers a spectacular view of the backyard."

"Looks more like a park." Kitchie pictured GP and Junior tossing a football around.

"This house sits on two-and-a-half acres of land."

"I love it," Kitchie said. "Suzette, I want to thank you again for everything you did for us. You're an angel."

"I'm glad everything worked out for your family. Sometimes you have to go through hell before you can experience heaven."

"Uh, that's deep." Kitchie looked at her reflection in the pool. "So what happened with you and…"

"Todd."

Kitchie nodded.

"He and I, we're getting divorced. We had our season. I would've liked for us to have made it through all the seasons, but life doesn't give you what you want, only what you need." She paused to think. "It took me some time and a lot of bruised feelings to learn that we couldn't make a relationship work for the sake of our children. Fire and gunpowder don't sleep together. We're working on communicating the best message to our children now. In my opinion, that's what's important."

"I'm sorry it didn't work out."

"Don't be. Only God's perfection is active in my life."

"Mommy." Junior came running. "Guess what?"

"Stop running," Kitchie said as Secret came behind him. "What is it?"

"This house is so big I can hear my echo."

"Now this is tight." Secret admired the pool. "We can have my friends over for pool parties and everything."

"Where is your father?" Kitchie ran a hand over Junior's head.

"He's in that one room, looking at the paintings."

"The entrance hall," Suzette said. "If you all would follow me, I'll show you to Mr. Patterson."

When they made it to the entrance hall, GP was staring at a painting in deep thought. The painting was of a nun cradling her deformed infant.

Suzette stood beside him. "This piece is called *Sister Francine's Baby*. All of these paintings came from the Parousia collection. *Sister Francine's Baby* is estimated to be worth eighty-thousand, as well as these." She gestured toward the remaining paintings.

GP looked at Kitchie. "Do you like it?"

"The painting or the house?"

"Both."

"I've always been a fan of T. Clary's artwork, but I'm in love with this house."

He turned to Suzette. "We'll take it."

"Nine thousand square feet is a lot of house. What do you plan on doing with it?"

"This is where my family and I are gonna enjoy life."

Later that afternoon, GP met with Nancy Pittman in her downtown office. "Thanks for seeing me on such short notice." He sat in a comfortable leather chair facing her desk.

"What brings you here?"

"I'm in a position now where I can help someone else out."

"Congratulations. I've been following your story in the paper."

"Thank you. Samone and Denise. I want them to come and live with us."

"I'm afraid that won't be possible. Samone Jefferson is no longer in the care of the state. Her sister turned eighteen and came for her. Denise Holcut is another story. She's a troubled kid who's more than likely going to move from group home to jail. I hate to say it, but I've seen it before. I'm not sure you want to invite the problem she's bound to bring into your home."

"So you're willing to throw her away and let jail be her fate? You're not even willing to offer her a more constructive alternative?"

"All I'm saying is that she's been around. Denise has the body of a little girl, but she was forced to grow up a long time ago. If I were you, I wouldn't want her around my children. You're asking for trouble."

He fixed her with a stern look. "I know Denise's kind better than your files, statistics, and reports. I used to be her and look how I turned out. I don't deserve a Nobel Prize or no shit like that, but I'm a decent man. I have values and I'm integrity-driven. All Denise needs is someone who is willing to direct her energy in a positive direction. She just needs someone who will love her. My family and I are willing to do that. Will you deny us that?"

"If you insist on planting a weed in your garden, I'll do the paperwork. I think it's a bad idea, though."

"She isn't a weed. Her flower is just taking a little longer to blossom than others."

"Have it your way, Mr. Patterson."

§ § §

Aubrey Stevens shut his computer off and was preparing to leave the bank for the day.

A stout man who worked in the mailroom poked his head inside the office. "Looks like I caught you in the nick of time. I have a package here for you." He sat the box on the desk and left.

Aubrey searched the package for a return address. There wasn't one. He laid his suit jacket over the arm of his chair and began to tear the packaging tape from the box. He opened the box and saw a typed letter sitting on top of bundles of money. He took the letter, sank in his chair, and began to read.

Mr. Stevens:

I made a very large withdrawal from your fine bank some time ago. Once again, I'd like to thank you. Without your assistance, it would not have been possible for me to repair my life.

Enclosed you will find the entire $670,000 withdrawal, plus the current interest. Please forgive me for the scare I caused you. Unfortunately, sometimes push comes to shove.

Mr. Wagoner

§ § §

It had been a month since the Pattersons' lives had taken a turn for the best. Kitchie stood in her stainless steel and marble kitchen, gazing through the window at Junior zipping through the backyard. She went out on the patio and waved him over.

The minibike rushed toward Kitchie. Its engine became louder as it approached the house. Junior mashed the rear brake, sending the minibike into a three-foot skid. He took the helmet off. "Huh, Ma?"

"Do you have to ride that thing like that? You don't have to go so fast, boy."

"Wait until I learn how to pop a wheelie."

"And that's exactly when I'm gonna make you ride a regular bike. So my advice to you is keep both tires on the ground."

"Okay."

"Turn it off and come inside. Your father just came in with Secret's present, and the show will be on in twenty minutes."

"Okay, Ma, one more spin."

"Park it and come inside now."

Junior put the kickstand down and turned the engine off.

§ § §

GP carried a large box with a blue ribbon attached to it down a corridor on the house's left wing. The corridor led to a state-of-the-art theater room with the seating capacity of forty-eight. He set the box down and poked his head into the theater and overheard Secret and Nise talking.

Nise lounged in a theater chair next to Secret. "Would you feel some type of way if I called GP and Mrs. P. Mom and Dad?"

Secret stared for a moment. "We all agreed to invite you into our family. I didn't want to tell you because I didn't want you to think I was a punk and being all mushy. But that day you helped Junior and me, you became my sister for life. I told all my friends you're my sister. You're family, so if you're comfortable with *Mom* and *Dad*, I don't mind."

Nise reached over and hugged her. "That means a lot to me. Thanks. I never had a mom or dad or a little sister or brother."

"Yeah, it's weird. I've always been Junior's big sister; now I have a big sister. None of that bullying stuff, though."

"Shit…I mean shoot. I learned my lesson a long time ago. I got a tough little sister. So what are we gonna do for the weekend when Samone comes to visit?"

Secret crossed her legs. "Ma said we can have an all-girl's day. Go shopping at the mall and get our hair done."

"What are you going to wear? I'm thinking about rocking my new Claiborne outfit with those Nine West shoes your mother picked out."

"Our mother."

Nise smiled.

"That'll be tight, though," Secret said. "I might wear Burberry from head to toe. I don't know yet; I might decide to wear something else from my wardrobe."

Kitchie tapped GP on the shoulder. "Eavesdropping on the girls?"

GP shut the door. "No. Well, kind of." He looked at Junior. "What's wrong with you?"

"He's mad because I made him get off of his motorcycle."

"Straighten your face, little man. You can ride later." GP picked up the box and addressed Kitchie. "You bring it?"

She tapped her pocket. "She's right here."

"Good." He pushed the door open and led them into the theater. "Special delivery for a Ms. Secret Patterson."

Secret's eyes lit up as she marveled over the big pretty box in her father's hand. "What is it?"

Kitchie lifted her shoulders. "Your father and I found it at the front gate with your name on it."

GP pinched her cheek. "Open it."

Nise nudged her. "Girl, hurry up."

Secret dropped to her knees and unraveled the bow. She lifted the lid and a puppy poked its head out. "He's mine?" She picked it up. "It's so cute."

"What kind is it?" Nise asked, looking at the brown and white dog. "I've never seen one like that."

"Me either." Junior took a closer look.

"It's a Basenji." Kitchie removed the nicotine patch from Nise's arm and replaced it with another.

"Thanks, Mommy."

Everybody looked at Nise. She blushed and Kitchie hugged her.

Secret turned to her father while rubbing the tiny puppy. "What's a Basenji dog?"

"It's the only dog in the world that doesn't bark."

"I knew it," Junior said. "That ain't no dog. It's a cat. Any dog that doesn't bark is a punk."

"You're a punk."

"Not like you and your cat-dog, sissy."

"That's enough." GP scowled at Junior. "Now, there's something else I want everybody to see. Well…I should have said *somebody* else. Where is she, Mami?"

Kitchie removed a ring box from her pocket and flipped it open. The 3.12-carat diamond was brilliant. It caught the overhead dome lights and glowed with life.

Everyone stared with astonishment at the yellow diamond.

"It's so pretty, Daddy." There was a twinkle dancing about Secret's eyes.

"But I thought you wanted us to see somebody." Nise looked at GP, then Kitchie.

"Yeah, that is a ring." Junior touched the puppy's wet nose.

"This is your Aunty Jewels," GP said.

Secret's eyes filled with tears.

Junior's brows furrowed. "It's Aunty?"

"This is a little too weird for me." Nise took the puppy from Secret's arms and sat down.

Kitchie draped an arm over each one of her children. "It's going to be hard for you to understand now, but your aunty wanted this.

You know how some people are turned into ashes when they pass, like Aunty Jewels?"

Secret blinked a tear loose. "Yeah."

"Now it's a way to turn people's ashes into real diamonds." GP wiped away Secret's tears. "Now Aunty Jewels is with us forever."

"I'm not sure I understand, Daddy." Junior looked at the ring once more.

"You will one day."

Kitchie glanced at her watch, then dimmed the lights. "Come on, we're about to miss the movie." She pointed a remote control at the control center.

A 120-inch screen came to life. It turned navy blue, then bright yellow as a drug-prevention commercial came to an end.

GP smiled at Jewels when the *Street Prophet: A World Premiere* stood out in bold letters across the screen. It took months for the project to come together, and for GP, it was definitely a dream come true.

"You did it, Papi."

ABOUT THE AUTHOR

Oasis is the award-winning author of *Duplicity*. He is the CEO of Docuversion, a full-service editing firm, and an expert creative writing instructor. He is a native of Cleveland, Ohio, and a proud father. For more information on Oasis, visit www.oasisnovels.com

DISCUSSION QUESTIONS

1. As a child, GP was abused by Mr. Reynolds. Why was it that, as an adult, GP still allowed Mr. Reynolds to torment him in the recesses of his mind? Is this a form of self-defeating behavior?

2. GP was offered a job with the *Plain Dealer* newspaper. Was it a selfish act to turn down the job when he had the responsibilities of father and husband? Should priorities always precede integrity?

3. Was Kitchie's mother, Mrs. Garcia, right or wrong in her position of not taking Secret and Junior in during their time of need, predicated on her disapproval of GP and Kitchie's relationship? Explain.

4. It's obvious, due to Jewels's mentality, that she had a different idea of how children should be raised. How did her influence affect Secret and Junior? How did that influence affect her relationship with Kitchie?

5. Should Kitchie have taken it upon herself to use force with Conrad Tharp over the money he'd duped her out of? Should she have handled the situation differently? How?

6. Share your insight on the statement Secret made when she said, "Once you know something, you're held accountable for what you know."

7. Should children have homosexual role models? With Jewels as a role model, was Secret at risk of becoming curious about same-sex relationships? Explain your position.

8. Should Kitchie have accepted money from Desmond? Why? What was the best way for her to handle this situation? Why?

9. There will obviously be times when adults will have to discipline children, as in Mr. Reynolds's case. What are the acceptable guidelines when administering discipline? When does discipline become abuse?

10. GP responded irrationally when he heard a couple having sex in the apartment above Jewels's, having assumed that one of the participants was his wife. How should he have responded to this situation?

11. If Mayor Brandon Chambers was so concerned about Secret and Junior, as he portrayed to be, do you believe that he should have taken more initiative in making sure to drop them off in the care of an adult? Why? Was his decision based on self-preservation?

12. Did Jewels go too far when stepping outside the boundaries of the law when she sentenced Mr. Reynolds? Why?

13. In Miles' situation, would you have told your mother if you had been indirectly responsible for your sibling's disappearance? Explain.

14. GP once took the position that his stealing was justified when there was no other solution. Is there ever a right time to do the wrong thing? Explain.

15. What are the pros and cons of GP and Kitchie welcoming Denise into their home?

16. In your opinion, will Desmond take the money and leave things be, or do you think we'll be hearing more from him? Explain.

17. Is it vain to have a loved one's cremated remains turned into a diamond?

AUTHOR'S EXIT

The apple of my eye, JaVenna. You are my ideas, hopes, desires, moral obligations personified. You are more woman than I would even dare pray for. You have enriched my existence, added new color and meaning to my world, and supported and believed in me effortlessly. Girl, to you I humbly extend my eternal gratitude for blessing little ole me with your presence this lifetime. Your love is awe-inspiring. (Okay, right now I'm down on my knee, gazing into your eyes.) Baby, I love you with all my heart. I want to spend the rest of my life with you, showing you. Caring for you and protecting you. Will you make my dreams come true and continue this journey with me as my wife?

I am very thankful for everyone who contributed their talents and skills in order to make *Push Comes To Shove* a reality. Specifically, Brenda Hampton, Zane and Docuversion.

Of equal measure, I thank my family (Williams, Myrieckes, Smith and the Harris boys), knowing I have people like you in my corner is all the encouragement I need to write just one more page.

And to my amazing readers, I swear none of this would be possible without you. Thanks for holding me down.

Oasis
Fort Dix, New Jersey
July, 2010
Oasisreader@oasisnovels.com

Duplicity

BY OASIS

AVAILABLE FROM STREBOR BOOKS INTERNATIONAL

Chapter 1

Parrish Clovis awoke naked on his neighbor's lawn. He was stretched out beside a mountain of Rottweiler shit. He absolutely had no idea of how he'd managed to be spooning with dog crap. He scrunched up his stubbled face at the tangy smell. He distinctly remembered climbing into bed last night and screwing his wife into a frenzy. This change of location, he couldn't explain. In fact, a lot of absurd and peculiar things had occurred lately that he couldn't explain.

He glanced at his bandaged hand. He still hadn't figured out how he'd fractured three fingers, either. One thing, though: he was grateful that daybreak was just approaching, and that his ass hadn't been busted. The thought of explaining this bout of bizarre behavior to anyone embarrassed him.

Parrish turned up his nose at the rotten stench again, pulled himself to his feet, and trudged to the fence that divided the yards, his hands covering his sacred parts. When he hurdled the fence, his wife swung open the back door of their home.

Hana looked at him with disdain. "This is absolutely ridiculous." Her Hungarian accent was intense, matching her glare.

"Don't start, Hana. I'm really, really not in the mood. I smell like dog poop." He stalked by her. "I hate that dog."

"The enforcements are coming."

"You called the cops?" He sighed. "Shouldn't have done that, Han."

"My anxiety has been agitated all night." She followed him through the house. "Last time you showed up—"

"I don't need reminding."

"You swore everything was under control." She looked at the pieces of grass that clung to his brown ass. "You're nude. That's miles away from control."

He froze in his tracks and turned his head to a painting that decorated the wall of their staircase. A line creased between his brows. "Where did this come from?"

"You brought it home two days prior. Monday." Tears streaked her beautiful face. "Don't you remember?"

✪✪✪

A stolen UPS truck plowed toward its destination. Ace, the driver, was a colossus man. Six-foot-eight with a stony, pale face and hands the size of baseball mitts. He had a balding crown that peeled because of a constant thrashing from the sun. He smashed his size 16s against the gas pedal and put an eye on his passenger. "You are right about me; I am not a good man," the giant spoke, slow and without contractions. "It is true; I only joined the Rangers so I could kill people for free."

The passenger chuckled. "You didn't need the military. Y'all white folks been getting away with murder for centuries."

"The military was my gymnasium to practice in." Ace thumped a finger against the steering wheel. "Pop, and the enemy goes down. You are still sore that you did not beat me; could not beat me."

"I didn't kick your big ass because this trick knee gave out on me." The passenger rubbed his knee and thought back to the day Ace had taken advantage of the injury and pinned him to a mat in front of his platoon. "You don't feel good about the way you won the trophy."

"We are fifteen years away from the Rangers…Sergeant Lindsay, but it is never too late for a rematch. Fighting makes my dick hard." Ace parked curbside at an expensive home. He placed a toupee on his chapped, bald spot and patted it.

"Ace, I will fuck you up," the retired sergeant said, handing Ace a package. "Now, do what the fuck I'm paying you to do."

✪✪✪

"Two wrongs don't make it even, justify it, or make it right." Parrish shut CNN off, disgusted. "They're going to execute that brother no matter what. So what, they found him guilty? The conviction is iffy. People don't have the permission to decide who should live and who should die." He gazed through the window at his neighbor's yard and wondered about last night.

"Tookie Williams deserves the death penalty," Hana said, refilling her husband's favorite Garfield mug with coffee. "He actually did horrible things, Parrish."

"How do you really know that?" He gestured at the TV. "This thing is brainwashing you. You're becoming more and more Americanized." He said *Americanized* as if he were speaking of devil worshiping. "Trust me, Han; I know what it's like to want to be different. Before my mother died, I used to pretend I was someone else. You're Hungarian. You look Hungarian, so why do you want to feel American? Be yourself and think for yourself. Don't let the media dictate your thoughts and opinions. No human deserves to die at the hands of another human."

"I'm entitled to my opinion, of course."

"When it's yours."

"You did a great job of changing the subject. Americans are experts at deviating when they don't want to address an issue. I haven't adopted that practice."

Smart ass. He sighed. "I haven't had any symptoms since high school; I haven't taken any medicine since then, either."

"Um…things change with time. At least see a physician before something absolutely terrible happens. I'm worried."

The doorbell rang.

She shook her head. "Have a ball explaining why you slept on the neighbor's lawn."

"You shouldn't have called the cops." He adjusted his house-coat and went to the door.

Parrish was amazed at the UPS man's size. He stood eight inches over Parrish, maybe nine. His blond hair balanced on his head as if it were a foreign object. His fingers reminded Parrish of jumbo Oscar Mayer franks; his knuckles of lug nuts.

"Good morning," Parrish said as a police car parked in the driveway.

"I'm looking for Parrish Clovis. I have a package for him."

Two uniformed officers stepped out of the car.

"How can I help you?"

Ace thrust the package into Parrish's arms. "You must sign for it."

The uniforms started up the driveway.

"What is it?" Parrish eyed the package. The cops lurching up the walk were in his peripherals, and he was rehearsing the lie he would tell.

"I do not know. I only deliver." Ace gave him an electronic pen and a digital Toshiba tablet.

A Hispanic officer nodded at Ace in passing and then faced Parrish. "We got a call about a missing person."

Ace headed for the truck and emailed Parrish's signature to his personal computer.

Parrish tore the package open. It was empty.

Chapter 2

Murder. I had gotten away with it once; tonight was the perfect time to try my luck again.

The sky was dark and quarrelsome, reflective of my mood. Lightning split the night in two. The heavens cried a steady down-pour of tears. The heavens' choice of pain purging was tears. Mine? Double homicide.

The sway of my windshield blades was hypnotizing, sedative even. They seemed to wipe the blur away from my vision. They seemed to wipe her ugliness away from my thoughts. The SUV's idling engine was smooth. Meditative. Healing.

Only a moment slipped by before *her* ugliness tormented me again.

My palms were slick with evidence of my nervousness. I gripped the steering wheel, thinking. I forced a fidgety foot to keep pressure on the brake. My worn-out brown eyes were fix-ated on the Italianate structure eleven yards ahead of me, a place that I was once proud to call home. Neighbors, passersby, and associates from our inner circle of influence considered this type of home a symbol of status, success. I, on the other hand, know that it represented four wasted years, failure, regret.

Everything beyond the handcrafted doors facing me, taunting me, was what I once loved. A love that was patient, kind. Neither was it envious nor boastful—just love. I stored no records of wrong, not until she had taken her mask off and showed me her ugly face.

Now, everything beyond the threshold of those doors, beyond the security system, is everything I hate worse than my mother.

Lightning parted the night again; thunder barked behind it. Call me crazy, but it seemed as if the thunder were cussing me like I were a little boy in need of scolding.

My BlackBerry glowed; its ring tone crooned a neo-soul tune by Vivian somebody. The sultry lyrics reminded me of what I must do: *Gotta go, gotta leave.* I wished I could blend with the rain and trickle down the sewer. I pressed SEND but didn't bother to say anything. I wasn't in a talkative mood. I gave the caller nothing more than a deep breath.

"Parrish, is you…everything okay?" Sade said.

Stupid question. What can be said about any man wanting to kill his wife and her lover? "I'm fine."

"Twenty minutes is left before you hafta cross the Holland Tunnel and come to the airstrip. Then, we home free."

Her raggedy cadence set fire to my loins' erogenous zones. It's strange how humans desire sex in the presence of death. Even sitting here staring at those doors I could smell Sade. Her pussy perfumed my mustache.

She said, "You there?"

"Wish I were there with you."

"Is you sure you okay? Boy, you don't sound like it."

I put my eyes on the glove compartment. "I will be after tonight." My palms were still sweaty. My foot was still on the brake. The doors of that home were still taunting me. The rain was still pelting the windshield.

"Where are you?" She sounded irritated. "We gotta schedule to keep."

"Outside of my house…thinking."

"You done, then, ain't you?"

"No."

"No?"

"*No!*"

"Damn, boy, you 'bout to blow everything. You trippin'." Her voice was two octaves too damn high. "Hana deserves this. We done come this far; now ain't the time to be fuckin' thinking." She sighed in my ear, much louder than necessary—her ridiculous signature.

I hate it when she does that. I've hit myself upside the head several times for becoming involved with someone so...ghetto. I'd like to know what the hell I was thinking.

"You was s'posed to be done and on your way back to me. This plane gots to be in the sky before our cover is blown."

"Don't press me. I'm not in the mood. We'll make it."

"You scared. It ain't even difficult. Fuck that bitch."

I stared at the doors, thinking of all that I had been through.

She said, "Stay right there. I'm on my way. I ain't scared. I'll do it my damn self."

"I said, I'll take care of it."

A car horn was blown.

I studied the rearview; it studied me back, reflecting the pain trapped behind my eyes. There was a BMW with a missing head-light behind me. Behind it, from my Hoboken, New Jersey avenue, I could see the whore of America—the Statue of Liberty. Her crown and torch punctuated the night. I eased my fidgety foot from the brake.

Hoboken was a Hudson River city whose community was a cultural melting pot. The city had been long seasoned with writers, artists, singers, actors, professional athletes, and others. Most of us had chosen Hoboken because it was situated directly across the river from Manhattan. The commute to New York was swift and convenient.

The swift part would come in handy tonight.

It had never dawned on me that I was blocking the avenue this entire time.

I shut my headlights off and parked behind Hana's Mercedes. "Listen to me, Sade."

"Ain't I here?"

"I never want to feel this type of pain again. Every woman who's been in my life has hurt me. Promise me that it ends with you. I don't want to hurt anymore. I love—" My confession was interrupted by the roar of thunder.

"Boy, ain't I already done made that promise? How many times you wanna hear it? Keepin' it real, if I wasn't serious 'bout us, I wouldn't be mixed up in this bullshit with you. I woulda never aborted my baby for you." There was a pause that felt empty. "Love is a verb. Now is a damn good time to show me." She hung up.

Those ugly, ugly days rushed back. They poked their devious fingers at me. My eyes narrowed to slits. I opened the glove compartment and saw a Sig Sauer .9mm smiling at me.